A Lucy Novel

Lucy Doesn't Wear Pink

Other books in the growing Faithgirlz!™ Library

The Faithgirlz! Bible

Nonfiction-

Dear Nancy, The Skin You're In, Body Talk, Girl Politics, and
Everybody Tells Me to Be Myself but I Don't Know Who I Am

The Sophie Series

Sophie's World (Book One)
Sophie's Secret (Book Two)
Sophie Under Pressure (Book Three)
Sophie's Steps Up (Book Four)
Sophie's First Dance (Book Five)
Sophie's Stormy Summer (Book Six)
Sophie Friendship Fiasco (Book Seven)
Sophie and the New Girl (Book Eight)
Sophie Flakes Out (Book Nine)
Sophie Loves Jimmy (Book Ten)
Sophie's Drama (Book Eleven)
Sophie Gets Real- (Book Twelve)

The Lily Series

Here's Lily! (Book One)
Lily Robbins, M.D. (Book Two)
Lily and the Creep (Book Three)
Lily's Ultimate Party (Book Four)
Ask Lily (Book Five)
Lily the Rebel (Book Six)
Lights, Action, Lily! (Book Seven)
Lily Rules! (Book Eight)
Rough & Rugged Lily (Book Nine)
Lily Speaks! (Book Ten)
Horse Crazy Lily (Book Eleven)
Lily's Church Camp Adventure (Book Twelve)
Lily's in London?! (Book Thirteen)
Lily's Passport to Paris (Book Fourteen)

Check out www.faithgirlz.com

2 corinthians 4:18

A Lucy Novel

Lucy Doesn't Wear Pink

Nancy Rue

ZONDERVAN.com/
AUTHORTRACKER
follow your favorite authors

ZONDERKIDZ

Lucy Doesn't Wear Pink
Copyright © 2008 by Nancy Rue

Requests for information should be addressed to:
Zondervan, *Grand Rapids, Michigan* 49530

ISBN 978-0-310-71450-7

Published in association with the literary agency of Alive Communications, Inc., 7680 Goddard Street Suite #200, Colorado Springs, CO 80920. www.alivecommunications.com

Zonderkidz is a trademark of Zondervan.

Art direction and cover design: Sarah Molegraaf
Cover illustration: Mark Elliot
Interior design: Carlos Eluterio Estrada

Printed in the United States of America

11 12 13 14 15 16 17 /DCI/ 22 21 20 19 18 17 16 15 14 13 12 11 10 9 8 7

So we fix our eyes not on what is seen, but on what is unseen. For what is seen is temporary, but what is unseen is eternal.

— 2 Corinthians 4:18

1

Lucy wrote, "Reasons Why I Hate Aunt Karen," then she stopped and rolled the pen up and down between her palms. Dad always said "hate" wasn't a people-verb. It was a thing-verb. It was okay to hate jalapeno peppers in your scrambled eggs, which she did, and rock music that sounded like soda cans tumbling in a clothes dryer, which Dad did. It wasn't okay to hate human beings. Even Osama bin Laden. Or Aunt Karen.

Lucy drew a squiggly line through her words and wrote below them,

Reasons Why I Wish Aunt Karen Would Move to Australia:

Dad would say that was fine. Not that she was going to read it to him. Or anybody else. This was extreme-private stuff.

Lucy scowled at the page. The scribble messed it up, and she wanted to be so careful writing in this book. Anything to do with Aunt Karen made her mess up worse than usual. She would have to put that on the list of reasons. But she started with,

— Because Australia is as far away from me and Dad and Los Suenos, New Mexico, as she can get.

— Because she probably wishes our cats would move there.

The very round, coal-colored kitty on Lucy's pillow raised her head and oozed out a fat meow.

"Don't worry, Lollipop," Lucy said. "You're not going anywhere."

The cat gave Lucy a long, doubtful look before she winked her eyes shut, but she continued her nap with her head still up, as if she wanted to be ready to leap into the blue-and-yellow toy chest that Lucy kept propped open with a wooden spoon—for just such occasions—should the cat carrier, or Aunt Karen, appear.

Lucy leaned against her giant stuffed soccer ball, propped her feet on the blue-tile windowsill above Lollipop, and went back to the list of reasons.

— Because she wants me to learn to give myself a manicure.

She looked down at her gnawed-to-the-quick fingernails and snorted out loud.

— Because she says a ponytail isn't a real hairstyle.

Lucy flipped hers so it play-slapped at the sides of her face. She could see its blondeness out of the corners of her eyes. Yellow and thick and straight like her mom's had been. Not all weird and chopped-off and sticking out the way Aunt Karen's did. That was supposed to be a "style."

Lollipop's legs startled straight, and her claws sunk into Lucy's faded blue-and-yellow plaid pillowcase. She sprang to the window-sill—in the slow-motion way her chunky body insisted on—and pressed whisker-close to the glass. Lucy crawled to the headboard and leaned on it to peer out.

Granada Street was Saturday-afternoon-in-January quiet. Even J.J.'s house across the road looked as if it were trying to nap behind the stacks of firewood and tangle of rusted lawn mowers and pieces of cars piled around it. Dad asked Lucy just the other day if the Clucks still had everything but the kitchen sink in their yard. She reported that now there actually *was* a kitchen sink out there.

But there were no doors banging or Cluck family members yelling, which was what usually made Lollipop switch her tail like she was doing now. Unless the kitty saw something in the spider shadows of the cottonwood trees on the road, there was nothing going on out there.

At least it wasn't Aunt Karen already.

Lucy sank back onto the bed on her stomach, legs in a thoughtful kick. She pulled the top of her sweatshirt over her nose and mouth and wrote,

— Because she says clean jeans and a shirt with no writing on it don't count as Sunday clothes.

Aunt Karen said on the phone she was bringing Christmas presents.

"It won't be soccer cleats or a new seat for my dirt bike, I can guarantee you that," Lucy said to Lollipop. "You wait—it'll be some flowered dress." Whatever it was, it would make her feel like she was wearing sandpaper.

Lollipop rolled off the sill and burrowed herself between Lucy's pillows. Lucy didn't blame her. Aunt Karen hadn't even arrived yet and she was ready to hide under the pillows too. She set the book carefully on the bedspread and grabbed her soccer ball—the real one—between her feet and stretched her denim-clad legs in the air.

What was wrong with jeans and sweatshirts and tennis shoes in winter, and shorts and T-shirts and bare feet in summer? Nobody but Aunt Karen seemed to care what Lucy wore, but she couldn't come from El Paso without bringing skirts and bracelets and hair bows.

Lucy lowered the ball to the pillow beside Lollipop, sat straight up, and wrote one more thing—

— I wish Aunt Karen would move to Australia because she is nothing like my mother. Nothing.

She let the book sigh shut and smoothed her hands over its cover. Pale green with gold leaves she could feel under her fingertips. And gold letters too, which said, A WOMAN'S BOOK OF LISTS—not curly and girly, but clear and strong.

Lucy pulled the book to her nose and breathed in. In spite of how long it must have been in the box in the storage shed, it still smelled like Kit Kat bars and lavender soap, and it made Lucy sure her mom could be right outside her door, wanting to know if Lucy was finished with the book for now because she wanted to write in it too.

Lollipop's head came up again. She tumbled from the bed to the floor and skidded on the buttercream ceramic tiles as she scrambled for the chest. The wooden spoon went out as Lollipop went in, and the lid came down with a resounding slam.

That could mean only one of two things. Either Aunt Karen was pulling into the driveway—which couldn't be because she was never, ever early—or ...

Lucy crawled to the window again and slid it open this time, letting in a blast of cold air that dried out her nostrils in one sniff. With it came what anyone else would have thought was the beyond-annoying sound of a Chihuahua begging for food.

"Pizza delivery," the voice said.

Lucy settled her elbows on the windowsill. "What kind of toppings?"

"Um ... applesauce?"

"What?" Lucy said.

A dark ponytail surfaced to the window like a periscope on a submarine.

"Whatever," the Chihuahua voice yelped. "I've been out here for ten hours."

"No, you haven't, Januarie." Lucy watched as a round face came into view, chapped-red and puffing air. "Probably more like ten seconds."

Januarie stood up to her full short-for-an-eight-year-old height and clamped her hands, plump as muffins, on the outside stucco sill. "I have to come in," she said. "I have a you-know-what pizza."

"A message from J.J.?" Lucy said.

"Shhh!" Januarie sprayed the sill, her hands, and the front of Lucy's sweatshirt. "We're supposed to talk in code!"

" 'You-know-what' is not 'code,' " Lucy said.

"I forgot what it's supposed to be. Artichoke?"

"You might as well just say it."

"I *will* if you let me in."

Januarie inched her knee up the cream-colored adobe wall, but Lucy shook her head. "Not that way—use the back door."

The moon face plumped into a pout. "I feel more like a spy when I climb in the window."

Lucy didn't have the heart to tell her it had been several pounds since Januarie had been able to squeeze through there. J.J. and Januarie's mom had made a lot of her funnel cakes for Christmas, and Lucy suspected Januarie had scarfed down more than her share.

"Back door," Lucy said as she slid the window toward Januarie's turning-blue fingers. "My dad will want to say hi."

And she hoped he'd take his time with it. As soon as Januarie disappeared, whining, from the glass, Lucy scanned her room for a place to hide the Book of Lists. Since she'd discovered it yesterday in the storage shed, there hadn't been any need to conceal it, but Januarie had what J.J. called "a serious nose problem," especially when it came to anything that belonged to Lucy.

Lucy dove for the toy chest, but the tiny, pitiful mews coming from that direction changed her mind. Januarie always squeezed Lollipop like she was trying to get toothpaste from a tube. As soon as she heard the kitty, Januarie would go right for her.

"Hey, Januarie-February-June-or-July," she heard her dad say from the kitchen.

"How do you always know it's me?" Januarie said—so loud she might as well have been right outside Lucy's door. Lucy hated it when people did that with her father.

"Nobody walks like you do," Dad said.

"Really?" Januarie said.

Good. They were going to have a conversation. Lucy could always count on Januarie for that. She stuck the book under her sweatshirt and looked around again. She could put it in the corner behind the oversize rocking horse, but every time Aunt Karen came, she talked about how it was time to get rid of the "baby toys." The fact that Lucy's own mom had painted him didn't seem to make any difference to her.

She could put it in the fireplace, since Dad wouldn't let her have a fire in there anyway—but that was where she'd just stashed her stuffed animals when she was doing her Aunt Karen tidying. Their bear heads and bunny tails and lamb noses poked indignantly in all directions. If she put one more thing in there, they might stage a mutiny. Maybe she'd just conceal it on the bookshelf with the books she never read—No, too obvious.

"I gotta go talk to Lucy," Januarie half-shouted.

"I'm sure she knows you're here," Dad half-shouted back. Lucy heard him chuckle, and she heard Januarie's baby-elephant footfalls coming down the wide hallway. No wonder Dad knew her walk.

As the clumping neared her door, Lucy yanked open the underwear drawer in her dresser and thrust the book inside. It wasn't the place of honor she wanted, but it would have to do for now. She was just slamming it shut when the door was flung open and Januarie barged right on in, black eyes already gleaming toward the chest of drawers.

"Januarie," Lucy said, leaning against it, "when are you going to get it that my dad is blind, not deaf?"

"Huh?" Januarie said.

Lucy moved toward the rocking chair—as far away from the underwear drawer as she could get—and scooped up the school binder she hadn't touched since she'd flung it there on December 15th. "You don't have to yell when you talk to him. He can hear just fine." She chucked the binder under the bed.

Januarie blinked.

"Never mind." Lucy held out her hand. "Give it."

"What?"

"The message from J.J."

"Shhhhh!" Januarie shoved the door closed and leaned on it as if she and Lucy were about to be attacked by a pack of coyotes. "I remembered the code."

Lucy forced herself not to roll her eyes. It had to be hard to be eight, wanting to be like the eleven-year-olds. Besides, Januarie had been annoying at least since she was three, when Lucy first met her. J.J. said she was born that way.

"Okay," Lucy said. "What is it?"

"The pizza has anchovies."

That meant Januarie brought a message from J.J. Du-uh! Lucy sighed and held out her hand. Januarie dug into the pockets of her denim overalls, no easy feat since they fit her like another skin, and pulled out a rolled-up piece of a take-out pizza menu.

"He taped it closed," she said, a sure indication that she had been thwarted in her attempt to read it before she gave it to Lucy. She held it as if she were considering adding something more to the ritual of handing it over. Lucy took the opportunity to snatch it from her and shove it into the front pocket of her sweatshirt.

"Aren't you going to read it?" Januarie's voice curled into a puppy-whine.

"Later," Lucy said.

"J.J. said it's urgent!"

"You want a candy cane?"

Januarie looked torn. Lucy thought she shouldn't consider being a spy when she grew up. She could always be persuaded with food.

"Hey, Luce?" Dad called. "We need to go over a few things before Aunt Karen gets here."

Januarie's face lit up like a luminary. "Your Aunt Karen's coming?"

"Yeah," Lucy said, and for the moment, she was thankful. "You might want to go home and put on a hair bow or something."

"I want to show her my new coat! Did you know I got a new coat for Christmas?"

"I've seen it twelve times," Lucy said. "You've worn it every day since."

Januarie lowered her voice, spy-like. "I couldn't wear it today. It's too obvious."

"Yeah, it's hard to be inconspicuous in that color green," Lucy said as she ushered Januarie by the elbow to the door.

"Incon ... what?"

"Grab a candy cane on your way out. They're in the—"

"—basket by the front door. I know."

Of course she did.

When Januarie was gone, Lucy used her pen to slit the tape and unrolled the paper. Several letters and words were highlighted with a yellow marker, which at the moment annoyed Lucy almost as much as Januarie herself. She didn't have that much time.

"You coming, Luce?" Dad called.

"Be right there, Dad."

Lucy took the paper with her as she left her room and padded down the bright Navajo rug that led to the kitchen like the Yellow Brick Road. *Pepperoni and Sausage*—that meant "Meet me"—she got that much. *Extra Cheese*—"bikes"—she put that together.

She looked for the key word—and there it was. *Jalapeno.* That stood for "escape." J.J. and his codes.

Lucy stuffed the paper back into her pocket and bounced between the always-wide-open wood doors to the kitchen in a whole new mood. Dad sat at the tile-topped table by the window, holding the mug with the howling coyote on it. There was just enough sun to make a silhouette of his sharp triangle nose and his squared-off chin. He tilted his salt-and-pepper-crew-cut head in her direction and smiled—like nobody else in the world did. Lucy wondered sometimes if God smiled that way, because it made a room seem filled with sunlight. It happened a lot, like maybe Dad was trying to brighten the dark space where he always had to be.

"You're happy today," Dad said. He slanted in the chair, creaking the wood, and moved the coyote cup to his lips. "Did you get a pizza delivery?"

Lucy snorted. "You heard her."

"So did everyone in Tularosa County. What's on the menu today?"

"Bike riding with J.J.?" Lucy said.

"Let's go through the checklist first. How are we doing on the dishes?"

Lucy went to the sink and picked up the upside-down bean pot. She wiped off a small blob with her sleeve and said, "You did good. I'll finish putting them away." She used her foot to push aside one of the curtains with the big red checks that acted as cabinet doors and slid the pot onto its shelf.

"Check," Dad said. "Did I get all the laundry folded?"

"Yes, and I put it away."

"Thank you. I took the trash out and emptied Marmalade's litter box."

"I don't get why he can't go potty outside like the other cats." Lucy wrinkled her nose. "He stinks up the place. Even my backpack smells like him."

Dad put his coffee-free hand to his lap where an orange ball of a cat slept. That was what Marmalade did most of the time. Except when he was eating, which was the other most of the time.

"Is that everything?" Dad said.

Lucy consulted the chart hanging on the side of the refrigerator. Across the top were the chores, written in Lucy letters and also punched out in little braille bubbles so Dad could feel them with his fingers. Along the side were the dates, also in words and braille. Each of the squares they formed was outlined in braid Lucy had glued on. Dad had put fuzzy snowflake stickers in his squares, because it was January, and Lucy now applied her snowmen ones.

"All the boxes are filled," she said. "I'll just finish up the dishes."

As she crossed to the sink, her father lowered his cup carefully to the table. "Do I dare ask how your room looks?"

"That's not on the chart." Lucy picked up a handful of silverware from the drainer and let it clatter into its slots in the drawer. Her good mood was flattening.

"I know it's not on the chart," he said. "I usually leave that up to you."

There was a "but" in the air.

"Luce," Dad said.

He centered his eyes somewhere along the line of happy tiles that bordered the ceiling.

Lucy passed a fake-mouse cat toy across the floor with her toe so he wouldn't trip over it. "My room looks better than it usually does."

One side of Dad's mouth went up. "What's Aunt Karen going to say?"

"She's going to say it needs to be more girly."

He chuckled. "Okay. Go have fun on your bike ride, but be back by three thirty so we can make our famous MexiBurgers for Aunt K. Put your watch on."

"Man," Lucy said.

There was another chuckle as Lucy rode the rug to her room and straightened it with her foot when she got there. Her dad had been blind for four years, and she still hadn't figured out how he knew stuff like that. It would be so easy to be late and say she didn't know what time it was—as if she couldn't tell by the shadows on the mountains anyway.

"It seems like you'd get away with so much, having a blind dad," J.J. said whenever Lucy got in trouble.

"Ha," she always said to him.

"Zip your coat," Dad said as she returned with her watch and grabbed her fuzzy-lined jean jacket off the peg by the back door.

She poked her arms into the sleeves and said, "Okay."

"I don't hear it."

"I'm zipping!"

"Love you," Dad said.

Lucy gave him a wet kiss on the forehead. "Love you more."

"Loved you first," he said.

She knew he knew she was grinning as she bounded toward the back door.

"Take care of what I love, champ," he said.

"Always," she said.

With the back door shut behind her, Lucy went for her dirt bike, which leaned against the Mexican elder tree in the middle of the backyard.

"Took you long enough," a low voice said. It pierced upward at the end of the sentence like its owner didn't know where it might end up. That happened about once every paragraph with J.J.

He poked his head and shoulders up over the fence that surrounded the house like a row of straight gray teeth, and Lucy could tell he was kneeling on the seat of his bike. His thick, almost-blue-black hair was wet and slicked back from his face, which was as much like a rectangle as his sister's was like a circle. He must have just taken a shower, or some grown-up at the Cluck's house had stuck his head under a faucet — either of which had probably involved a fight.

He slanted his blue eyes downward. They and his lanky skinniness were the only things on him that hinted he had a white father. The rest sprang straight up from his mama's Apache roots.

"This cat's looking at me like he wants to eat my face," J.J. said.

Lucy laughed as she wheeled her bike through the gate and onto the sidewalk on Second Street. "Mudge won't eat you if you leave him alone."

She looked down at her brown tabby — who was actually gray striped, so she could never figure out why he was called a brown tabby — crouched behind a century plant whose thin, sharp leaves were like tongues, lashing up at nothing. Like the plant, Mudge actually did look as if he could eat a person. He glared at J.J. with eyes perfectly marked as if he were wearing eyeliner.

"So what took you so long?" J.J. said as Lucy got astride her bike seat.

"We're on Aunt Karen alert."

J.J. made a sound like a car alarm.

"Let's get out of here before she shows up," Lucy said. "You want to go up by the high school? I could bring my soccer ball, and we could practice — "

J.J. jerked his head back. "Not far enough."

"Gotcha."

J.J. pulled up the gray hood of his sweatshirt and pedaled into the street, gravel popping from his tires.

That was what she liked about her and J.J. They didn't ask each other nine thousand questions. He was way more interested in escaping — and right now, that was what she wanted too.

2

Lucy liked it that the main town of Los Suenos was mostly bunched up on Granada Street, a few blocks down from Lucy and J.J.'s houses. That meant it was easy to head in the opposite direction from the town hall and the church and the market and the cantina and Pasco's Café and not be seen by anybody.

"What are we escaping from today?" she yelled to J.J. as she followed the gray hood down the gravel road between the high school and the middle school.

"Januarie," he called back over his shoulder. "She's driving me nuts."

His bike bounced on a rock, and his bottom rose almost to his handlebars. Lucy laughed and steered around it to catch up to him.

"How did you get away from her?" she said.

"You don't want to know."

Lucy sat tall on her seat and felt the cracked plastic scrape at her jeans. "Did you lock her in the garage again?"

"I said you don't want to know."

"J.J.!"

"She'll get out. Then she'll tell my dad, and I'll get in trouble." J.J. shrugged his bony shoulders.

He was escaping from more than just Januarie, but Lucy didn't ask what. That, she knew, was one of the reasons J.J. liked her too.

They left the schools behind, which helped Lucy forget that Christmas vacation was over in two more days and they'd be returning to sixth-grade world. That was almost as depressing as Aunt Karen coming. As the playground and the sneaker smell and the metal clang of the empty chains against the flagpole fell away, Lucy stood up on her pedals and lowered her head.

"Race ya," she said.

J.J. shook his head. "You don't wanna do that."

"Yes, I do."

"You'll lose."

"Will not."

"I'll run you right into the ground."

"Will not."

"Okay—but don't come cryin' to me when I totally leave you in the dust."

Lucy sank back onto her seat and looked glumly at her handlebars.

"You're giving up that easy?" J.J. said.

"No!" Lucy said—and rising like a cobra, she was off down the trail that led across the desert.

"Dude!" J.J. yelled, but Lucy could hear the laugh in his voice as she pumped toward the mountains that watched her like old grandpas and uncles, as if Dad had told them to look after what he loved. She dodged a tumbleweed that had stopped tumbling. Behind her, she heard J.J. run over it, spraying pebbles with his tires.

"Wimp!" he called to her.

"Whatever," she called back.

Okay, so maybe she could show him who was a wimp just a *little* bit. The mountains wouldn't tell Dad. Pumping harder on the pedals, Lucy sped ahead, spewing winter-dry dust from both sides and squinting to keep it out of her eyes. She didn't actually have to see where she was going anyway. This desert and the Sacramento Mountains that guarded it were as familiar as her own house, where Dad always said if the furniture stayed right where it was, he could get around just fine. As long as nobody moved the cactus trees, Lucy could have woven in and out and around them if she'd had no eyes at all.

She left the trail and tore straight for a tall socorro cactus, the kind that looked as if it had a head and two arms stretched up like a school crossing guard.

"Look out!" she heard J.J. cry, his voice veering off into the stratosphere at the end.

Lucy waited until she could almost feel the spikes on the cactus before she whipped the wheel to the left and slid sideways. With one foot on the ground, she kept from going over and hopped back onto her seat.

"That's nothin'." J.J. flew past her while she was still getting her bearings and went for a whole scattering of socorros. Lucy expected them to come to life and give him hand signals as he stitched his way in and out among them.

"Piece of pizza," she told him, and went into a figure eight that fanned dust across his back.

She wasn't surprised that didn't stop him. He hunkered down over his handlebars and came at her, grinning with grit between his teeth. Lucy rode back at him, and her heart leaped the way jackrabbits run. Just as his front tire grazed hers, she pulled up and did a wheelie that matched his. Their bikes were like two horses, raring up and hoofing the air.

When they came down, Lucy put both feet on the ground and spit to the side. She looked at J.J., who pulled down his hood and shook dust out of his hair like ashes from rags. He wasn't smiling.

"What's wrong?" Lucy said.

"Bored."

Lucy watched him. "Bored" for J.J. was usually followed by something Dad would call "outside the box," which usually meant somebody could get grounded for weeks. Years, even.

But there was always the chance that it could be worth it, as long as no one got bruised up. Dad did hate that.

"What are you thinking?" Lucy said. "You want to try jumping over a barrel cactus?"

"Done that."

"True." Lucy had several puncture wounds in her backside to prove it. She didn't mention that to Dad. He couldn't see that she made a face every time she sat down—for a week—and the "worth it" factor was way up there. She and her bike had clearly jumped higher than J.J. and his bike.

J.J. turned toward the mountains and shaded his eyes with his hand, not that he needed to. The sky had turned to a gray slab of clouds, with only a small hole for the sun to trickle some weak light through. Lucy pulled up the collar of her jacket and stuck her hands in her pockets to warm them up. New Mexico winter air bit worse than Mudge when anybody but Lucy tried to pick him up.

"We gotta keep moving," she said.

J.J. punched his feet hard on his pedals, then shoved back on them so his tires burned into the sand.

"What?" Lucy said.

"Little Sierra Blanca," he said.

Lucy's mouth went dry immediately. "Aw, man, J.J. — no. There's too many ATVs."

"It's *all* ATVs."

"We can't race them." She didn't bother to remind him that all-terrain vehicles had big fat wheels and motors, and the kids who drove them were junior maniacs. Dad said nobody without a driver's license and clearance from a psychiatrist should be allowed behind the wheel of one.

"Who said we were going to race them?" J.J. said. He was already making a donut in the dirt.

"Then what *are* we going to do with them?"

J.J. clamped his teeth down so hard Lucy could hear them. "Whatever we want," he said, and he took off toward the hill where Lucy could already see clouds of dust billowing up from the other side.

She should go home. Tell Dad J.J. was headed for definite decapitation. Bring out Sheriff Navarra.

But there was hurt in J.J. today. She saw it in his teeth. Heard it in his tight voice. Felt it in those daredevil words, "Whatever we want."

The only thing to do was pretend to go along, and then do everything she could to stop him.

He was way ahead of her by the time she got going. He was good on the sprints, but he'd get tired and she'd catch up again. As she pumped until her calves complained, she just hoped it would happen before he reached the hill.

It wasn't really known as Little Sierra Blanca. It probably didn't actually have a name. J.J. and Lucy called it that because it looked like a miniature of Sierra Blanca, the most powerful mountain of any of them. Ski Apache, the ski resort, was there, but Lucy just thought of it as a giant mound of the very best vanilla ice cream. She could always see faces in it. Of course, she could see faces in everything in New Mexico — the clouds, the moutainsides, the gnarly desert ironwood trees. But the only face that mattered right now was J.J.'s. It had so much pain in it, he was likely to do just about anything.

As she'd predicted, he was slowing down some, and his back tire wobbled over a clump of sagebrush. Lucy was almost on him, and they were both almost to Little Sierra Blanca when she heard the first snarl of an engine.

"Sweet!" J.J. said.

"It is SO not," Lucy said.

She spun the bike out in front of him and stopped. He jammed on his brakes and hit her in the kickstand.

"Dude — you made me run into you."

"I know. J.J., this is insane."

J.J.'s blue eyes slitted down. "Don't call me crazy."

"I didn't say *you* were nuts, I said *this* is — whatever you're thinking we're gonna do."

The engine whined closer, and Lucy knew it was climbing the hill on the other side.

"We're just gonna make it fun for whoever's driving," J.J. said. "He's probably bored too."

The motor screamed, and another cloud of dust-smoke billowed above them.

"He doesn't sound bored." Lucy put her hand on J.J.'s handlebar. "Come on — I'll lie down over there and let you jump over me with your bike."

"Great idea," J.J. said. But he didn't move to where Lucy was pointing, away from the approaching growl of the ATV. "We'll both get down at the bottom of the hill, and when he comes over the top, he'll either have to go over the side or jump over us."

Lucy shook her ponytail, hard.

"Either way, it'll be cool. Come on," J.J. said.

"What if he misses?"

"No way—he'll totally see us."

Lucy didn't like the hard thing that came into J.J.'s eyes, like a lid slamming down on something. He was going to do this, no matter what. And Lucy wasn't.

She could hear the ATV making its final snarling-growling-whining push to the top of Little Sierra. She jerked her wheel to the left and shoved off with her foot.

Even as she got her other foot to the pedal, she heard the ATV scream in the air behind her. Someone yelled in a voice that rose into the air with it. When J.J.'s cry joined it, Lucy turned around. She was just in time to see the thick wheels of the ATV land and bounce and head straight for her.

"Get down!" J.J. screamed.

Lucy let go of her bike and dropped to the ground. Her spokes flattened her arm, pushing it down hard. Pain shot all the way up to her neck. Tiny things hit her face and stung and bit and then were gone with the machine that roared past, just inches from the top of her head.

Dust rained on her, but Lucy didn't care. All she could do was shake.

J.J. said above her, "You're okay, right?"

"I don't know." Lucy tried to sit up, but her right arm was pinned under what used to be her bike wheel. Now, it looked like it belonged on the pile of junk in J.J.'s yard.

Her clothes didn't look much better. Rips flapped open in both her jacket and her sweatshirt as if they were eager to show off the gash in her arm.

"Dude, you're bleeding," J.J. said.

"Of course I'm bleeding, genius. The spokes cut me. Could you get the bike off?"

J.J. crouched beside her, hands shivering. He managed to use them to pull the twisted wheel from her arm.

"How bad is it?" Lucy asked.

"You got, like, a major cut."

"No—my bike. How bad is it?"

J.J. got on his knees. "I can totally fix it. We probably got a hundred wheels at my house."

Before Lucy could tell him he probably had that many in the front yard alone, engine noise ripped the air.

"He *better* come back," J.J. said, scrambling to his feet.

Lucy cradled her arm against the front of her jacket. "Why? So he can run over me again?"

"Hey!" J.J. waved his arms above his head and jumped, puffing dirt into Lucy's face.

"Would you knock it off?" But Lucy could barely hear herself as the ATV roared toward them. She curled up and rolled away, but it stopped, and the motor noise dropped to a mumble, unlike Lucy's heart, which slammed against the walls of her chest.

"What was up with that?" the driver said. His "that" disappeared up into that range where only dogs can hear, the way J.J.'s often did, and Lucy uncurled herself to look at him. He had to be their age, but his face was so plastered with dirt she couldn't tell who he was.

"What are you asking me for?" J.J.'s words seemed to want to slide back down his throat. He crossed his arms and hid his hands in his armpits. His "You're the one who almost ran over somebody" came out only half sure.

Lucy stifled a groan. J.J. was backing down. That could only mean this guy was—

"I was trying to keep from hitting *you*," the kid said.

His "you" came out as "jew." Yep. It was Gabe Navarra, the biggest kid in sixth grade, Hispanic through and through, like most people in Los Suenos. He used "hate" as a people-verb when it came to J.J.—or anybody else who didn't speak English as a second language. Until now, he had never so much as spit in Lucy's direction. Now he narrowed his eyes at her in a way that would have made Mudge run for cover.

"If I killed you, it woulda been your fault," he said to her.

"So what?" Lucy said.

Gabe blinked. The whites of his eyes were bright against his ruddy skin.

"If I was dead," she said, "why would I care whose fault it was?"

He blinked again. The he hissed between his teeth and turned to J.J., who was starting to grin.

"What are you laughin' at?" Gabe said.

"Nothin'," J.J. said. The grin evaporated.

"You were laughin' at me." Gabe came off the seat of the ATV, and J.J. pulled his hands from his armpits, stiff, but at the ready.

"Hello!" Lucy said. "I could be bleeding to death here."

Gabe tilted his chin up. "You wouldn't be sitting there talking if you were bleeding to death. Right?"

Lucy kept her arm hugged to her jacket and managed to stand up. Her face burned. The tear in her jacket was turning red. And if she didn't get J.J. out of there, he was going to look worse than she did.

She glanced at her watch. 3:10. Barely enough time to get home and destroy the evidence before Aunt Karen pulled up.

"I want to go home," she said. "I might need stitches."

"It was your fault," Gabe said again, and spun his wheels to make an exit.

"Do you really need stitches?" J.J. said when he was gone.

"No, brain child," Lucy said. "I was just trying to get rid of him."

J.J. pulled his dark eyebrows nearly down to his nose. "I coulda done that."

"Before or after he tore you into little pieces? Come on, I gotta get home."

"Take my bike," J.J. said. "I'll fix yours before your dad even knows about it."

Lucy didn't go there in her mind. Dad would somehow sense with the eyes he seemed to have inside his brain that she'd gotten into trouble.

But he wasn't the one she was worried about. She looked at her watch again. She still had time to bury her jacket and sweatshirt in the bottom of the dirty clothes basket, put a couple of bandages on her arm—okay, maybe five—and get into a long-sleeved shirt before Aunt Karen—

But that plan slid down her brain pipe when Lucy rounded the corner from Second Street. The silver Toyota Celica with the Texas license plate was already parked in front of the house. Lucy peeled off her jacket and dropped it behind the century plant. Maybe if she slipped in the back door—

"Lucy Elizabeth Rooney," said a voice-like-a-supervisor. "What have you done to yourself now?"

3

The meow that rose from behind the century plant didn't sound as disgusted as Aunt Karen's voice, even though Mudge emerged with Lucy's jacket draped across him and only his disgruntled head sticking out.

"Thank you, Mudge," Lucy whispered to him as she snatched him up, jacket and all. "There's a can of tuna for you later if you'll hang with me now."

She snuggled him against her, careful to keep most of his coat-clad bulk over her arm, and whirled to face Aunt Karen. Her aunt had rounded the corner by then and stood by the fence, black-sweatered arms folded, hazel eyes squinting. Lucy hated it when she did that. She reminded herself to add it to the list of reasons Aunt Karen should move to Australia.

"Hi," Lucy said.

"Don't 'hi' me. What happened to your face?"

Lucy held back a groan. As bad as it was stinging, it must look like someone had thrown a handful of rocks at her. Actually, someone kind of had.

"I fell," Lucy said. "It's not as bad as it looks."

"You're not the one looking at it." Aunt Karen shook her head, sending one chin-length panel of dark hair against her cheek and another across her forehead. She jerked it out of her eyes. "What did you fall on, a box of tacks?"

"Luce? You okay?"

Lucy did groan then. Dad stood in the front doorway, looking frustrated because he couldn't see what was going on. Everything would have been fine if Aunt Karen had been late like she usually was. And if she didn't stick her stumpy little nose into other people's business.

"What's going on?" Dad said.

"She hurt herself." Aunt Karen sounded as if she were announcing that Lucy had just robbed a bank. "I don't know if she's going to need stitches or not."

"Stitches?"

Dad's voice sharpened to a point. Lucy gritted her teeth.

"I'm fine, Dad," she said between them.

"She is not 'fine'." Aunt Karen came to Lucy and hooked her arm around her back, already pushing her toward the front door. "Her face looks like somebody shot her twelve times with a B.B. gun—"

"It does not!"

"Have you looked in a mirror?"

"Lucy, what happened?" Dad said.

Lucy wrenched herself away from Aunt Karen and took the front walk in two long steps to get to Dad.

"I just fell off my bike, okay?" she said. "I'm fine—it doesn't even hurt."

She tried to edge around her father, but he stopped her with his arm and pulled her to stand in front of him. Before he could get his hands to her face, Aunt Karen charged up to them, voice still in supervisor mode.

"First of all, she doesn't even have a coat on," she said, "so I suggest we go inside before we add pneumonia to the mix."

Aunt Karen turned Dad around with one hand and pushed Lucy inside with the other. Lucy kept going, straight through the entryway toward the hall, until Dad said, "Lucy"—in that way that stopped time, forward motion, and Lucy's heart.

She froze.

"What happened to your jacket? I know you put it on before you left."

"How would you know?" Aunt Karen said. She clicked the door shut behind her. "I bet you don't know half the stuff she gets away with."

At the same instant that Lucy added yet another item to the move-to-Australia list, she remembered something else.

"My jacket is right here," she said. She crossed the entryway toward her aunt. "I'm carrying it—see?" she said, and she thrust it, Mudge and all, straight into Aunt Karen's arms.

A gray-striped head popped from the denim folds and pointed its toothy side at Aunt Karen's face. Mudge let out a yowl that sounded exactly like, "I hate you!" and Lucy vowed to make that *two* cans of tuna.

Aunt Karen matched him with a yowl of her own. Flinging her arms out in at least two directions, she stepped back, collided with the table by the door, and set a basket sailing. Candy fanned across the floor, which sent Mudge into a frenzy. He turned in frantic circles, sliding on plastic-wrapped canes and finally leaping between Aunt Karen's legs. She didn't stop screaming or flapping Lucy's jacket until Mudge was behind the totem pole in the corner. Lucy made a dash through the hallway and dove into the bathroom.

But she didn't quite get the door closed before Aunt Karen was leaning on it.

"No, you don't," she said. "Let me in, Lucy."

Only because Dad echoed with, "Let her look at you, Luce," did Lucy back away from the door and allow Aunt Karen to fall into the bathroom. She tripped over the basket of towels and stumbled against the sink—and Lucy plastered a hand against her mouth to keep from laughing out loud. When she drew it back, it was speckled in blood that sobered her up like a splash of cold water.

"Yeah," Aunt Karen said. "Look."

She took Lucy by the shoulders and turned her to face the tile-framed mirror. Lucy had to admit she did look like she'd fallen on a box of tacks—very large tacks.

"I don't even want to know what happened," Aunt Karen said.

"I do," Dad said from outside the door.

Lucy sighed at the bedraggled picture of herself in the mirror.

"I fell on my bike trying to get away from an ATV." She shrugged for Aunt Karen's benefit. "When it went past me, it sprayed stuff in my face, that's all."

"Did any get in your eyes?" Dad's voice sounded ready to pinch off in the middle.

"No," Lucy said at the same time that Aunt Karen grabbed her face with both hands and jerked it close to hers.

"Ow!" Lucy said.

"What? What happened?" Dad said.

Aunt Karen flipped her hair toward the door. "She's just whining. I've got it handled, Ted."

"Does she need stitches?"

"No." She squinted into Lucy's face. "What she needs is a good smack upside the head."

Lucy pulled away, wrenched the faucet on, and leaned over the sink.

"I can do it," she said.

"We're going to need tweezers ... hydrogen peroxide ..."

Lucy could hear her pawing through the basket on the table under the window.

"I can't believe you don't have any Neosporin." Huge sigh. "Yes, I can."

"What do you need?" Dad said.

Aunt Karen sighed again. "Nothing. We're fine."

"That's right," Lucy muttered. "*We* are."

If Aunt Karen got that, she didn't let on. "I'm going to need a latte after this," she said. "Can you make that happen, Ted?"

"Sure," Dad said.

Lucy heard that thing in his voice — the cut-off sound when somebody found something for him to do because they thought he couldn't handle what the rest of the grown-ups were doing. She scrubbed at her face and refused to whimper, or even wince.

When she stood up straight, her face was raw-looking, but clean.

"Let me see," Aunt Karen said, coming at her with a pair of tweezers.

"I got it all," Lucy said. "Where did you get those?"

"From the bottom of that basket. Nobody around here uses them, obviously." She lifted her eyebrows, which always reminded Lucy of very long, perfect commas. "I'll teach you how to use these on your brows at some point."

"Hello! No!" Lucy said. She pulled her head back, but Aunt Karen just shook hers. "I'm not going to do it now. I just want to see if you got all the rocks out of your face. Come here."

Lucy let her peer until she finally seemed satisfied that there were no minute particles of dust in Lucy's pores.

"I don't think you'll scar at least," Aunt Karen said. "I can't say the same for your sweatshirt—oh my *gosh!*"

Lucy tried to contract her arm up into her tattered sleeve, but Aunt Karen's fingernails snagged the cloth so she could gape at Lucy's cut as if her forearm were half-amputated.

"Don't make a big deal out of it, okay?" Lucy said between her teeth. "Dad'll just get upset."

"As well he should be!"

But Aunt Karen lowered her voice and scoured out the wound and poured what seemed to Lucy to be half a bottle of hydrogen peroxide into it. By the time it was bandaged up with strips from an old, clean pillowcase and Aunt Karen had ranted under her breath about the lack of first-aid items in "this house," Lucy was in more pain than she'd been in before Aunt Karen started doctoring. She hoped she'd still be able to write, because the first chance she got, she was going to add, "Because she calls OUR home 'this house,'" to that list of reasons.

Just in case Dad should take a full survey of her limbs to make sure nothing was broken, Lucy donned a long sleeved T-shirt and another sweatshirt before she joined him and Aunt Karen in the kitchen. They sat across the table from each other—Dad mug-less, Aunt Karen sipping from the cup with the big butterfly on it that Lucy always drank her hot chocolate from because it had been her mother's. She hugged her arms around herself to keep from snatching it, latte and all, right out of Aunt Karen's hand.

"What can I get you, Luce?" Dad said.

His eyes came up to search for her. She scooted a chair close to him and rested her head against his shoulder.

"I'm good," she said.

"Are they going to start calling you Scarface now?"

"No." Lucy grinned. "Just 'Klutz.'"

Dad chuckled. Aunt Karen didn't.

"I don't see what's funny about any of this," she said. She licked her lips. Sometimes Lucy counted how many times her aunt licked her lips in a single visit—and how many times she had to put on new lip gloss.

"She's a kid," Dad said. "Accidents happen."

"Yeah." Aunt Karen tapped the rim of Mom's mug. "To girls who go out in the desert and play chicken with ATVs."

"I wasn't—"

Aunt Karen's hand went up like a stop sign. "You know what—we've had this conversation how many times?"

Lucy grunted. *Twelve hundred.*

"Well, I'm done."

Good. Me too.

Aunt Karen pushed her latte aside and covered Dad's hand on the tabletop with both of hers. Her white-tipped, squared-off nails looked dangerous against his wrists. But her eyes went to Lucy.

"Your dad and I have been talking," she said.

"About what?" Lucy said.

"About the fact that you don't have a good female influence in your life on a day-to-day basis."

Lucy blinked. "Mrs. Gomez is a female." She didn't add that she and her teacher didn't talk to each other much beyond, "Lucy, do you have your homework?" and "No, my cat ate it."

"I said a 'good' influence," Aunt Karen said. "If she were good, she wouldn't let you stay in that special ed class—"

Lucy's neck stiffened. "It's not special ed. It's called a support class."

"It's a lazy class you are far too smart to be in."

Aunt Karen didn't know what she was talking about. Mrs. Gomez didn't think Lucy was dumb or lazy. She just left her alone.

"I know you're probably going to pitch a fit," Aunt Karen said, "but it's time for you to come to El Paso and live with me."

Lucy jerked her head up from Dad's shoulder.

"Now just hear me out," Aunt Karen said.

"I don't think so." Lucy scraped her chair back. "I have stuff to do in my room."

She didn't want to hear the rest of it. But she still could, as Aunt

Karen said, "You're growing up—you need a strong woman in your life—" and Dad said, "Luce, now wait—" and Marmalade uttered a meek meow and fled from Dad's lap. Lucy fled too—down the hall and into her bedroom and behind the slammed door. She sank to the floor and buried her face in her arms, and over and over, she just said, "I won't go. I won't go. I won't go."

A good ten minutes passed before the Dad-tap came on the door. Long enough for Lucy to move to the bed and kick the giant soccer ball off because she didn't want to be close to anything that reminded her of HIM right now. She was lying on her back, passing her real soccer ball back and forth between the feet she extended above her when he said, "Luce, may I come in?" She had to think about it.

After she didn't answer, the door creaked open and Dad put his salt-and-pepper head inside. "Is it safe, or should I duck?"

Lucy looked at the stuffed soccer ball, but the urge had passed. "Come in," she said.

"You okay?"

"Yes."

"You left in a hurry."

Lucy rolled over onto her stomach and stuffed the ball under her. "I was getting bored with that conversation," she said.

"Really."

There were no question marks in the lines around his mouth, so she didn't answer. It wasn't being rude not to answer if he wasn't actually asking her anything.

"I just found it kind of interesting," Dad said. "Is there a clear path?"

Lucy pushed the stuffed ball out of his way with her foot and checked the floor for other debris.

"You're good to go," she said.

Dad made his way to the rocking chair, barely touching the wall with the tips of his fingers. When he sat down and rested his hands on his knees, he turned his face square at her, as if he could see her. Lucy was sure somehow he could—and knew she was scrunched into a sitting-up ball with her arms wrapped around her knees.

"You start," he said, "because I can tell you're about to crack open like an egg."

"I'm fine."

"Champ, I know better."

She cracked. "How come you talked to her about me going there to live before you said anything to me?"

"Who says I talked to her about it?"

"She did."

"She said she and I were talking, which, as you know with your Aunt Karen, means *she* was talking to *me*."

Lucy unfolded. "She made it sound like—"

"I know how she made it sound, and I've already spoken to her about that."

"Is she gone?" Lucy said hopefully.

Dad smiled. "I said I spoke to her. I didn't say I threw her out."

"Oh." Lucy let her air trail away like a tired party balloon. "She always does that."

"Does what?"

"Tries to make me think you're on her side."

"I didn't know there were sides." Dad eased the chair back on its rockers.

"There are, and I'm not on the one she's on, wherever that is."

"Right now, she's getting our Christmas presents out of her car."

"That's not what I mean."

"I know what you mean—and no, Lucy—" Dad tilted his head to the side, eyes wavering. "I'm not going to send you off to live with her."

Lucy melted back into her pillows like a puddle from ice. "That would be so hideous."

"Good word," said Dad, who liked good words. "But I'm not sure it applies here."

Lucy snorted.

"Your Aunt Karen is just concerned that you don't have a grown-up woman in your life day-to-day."

"For what? You and I are just fine doing the laundry and cooking and stuff. What do we need a woman for?"

"Evidently to help you with your hair and your clothes—"

"And my eyebrows!" Lucy wriggled up to a sitting position again. "Dad—she wants to pull them out with tweezers! I bet she holds them over a fire until they're red hot and then—"

"Luce!" Dad laughed like sand pouring out of a bucket. "She doesn't want to torture you. She just wants you to know what being a girl is all about." His face went mushy. "And I can't teach you that, champ."

For the first time maybe ever, Lucy was glad her father couldn't see. She didn't want him to know that she was suddenly uncomfortable, as if he were a stranger who had just walked in on her in the bathroom. She pulled a yellow throw pillow up to her chin.

"It's true," Dad said. "I don't know anything about skirts and panty hose."

"Da-ad!"

"See? We can't even talk about it."

"It doesn't matter, because all you have to do is keep telling me about Mom and I'll grow up to be like her and I'll be fine. That's probably what's gonna happen anyway, right? I look like her, so I'm probably like her in all the other ways too."

Dad's smile looked crumply. "You come pretty close."

"Okay, so, there you go." Lucy got still. "Just as long as Mom wasn't like Aunt Karen. You said she wasn't, right?"

"Right." Dad passed a hand over his mouth and closed his eyes. He did that, Lucy knew, when he didn't want her to see what he was really thinking. "Just because they were sisters doesn't mean they were alike, trust me."

Lucy scrambled from the bed and parked herself on the floor at Dad's feet. "Tell me about Mom," she said.

"For a minute." He ran his hand over the top of Lucy's head. "And then we need to go back out there and spend some time with Aunt Karen."

"Whatever," Lucy said. "Tell me again how Mom was."

As Dad talked, she could have recited the words right along with him. For a long time when she was seven years old, after he had come home from Iraq and Mom hadn't, he sat by her bed every night and told her how he and Mom had promised each other that if war broke out there, they would leave their posts as foreign correspondents for National Public Radio and come home to Lucy. He told her over and over how Mom wasn't going to go there in the first place, but NPR had begged her, told her the people in Baghdad would open up to her because she was a woman, because people all over the world always did, because she was the best at finding out the real stories and the true feelings of folks in places where hard things were happening.

"In Afghanistan, in Saudi Arabia," Dad told Lucy many times, "your mother visited women's inner sanctums, places that were off-limits to the guy reporters. She loved you, Lucy. She delighted in you, but when she felt called to something, she became dogged and determined. She wanted you to be proud that she had courage, that she wanted people to know the truth."

But part of the truth they would never know. Why was the very hotel in Baghdad where she and Dad were staying bombed, even after most of the other news correspondents had left? Was it just chance? Or was it because Cheryl Rooney always reported the true feelings of the people and that didn't make the Iraqi government happy?

No one could tell them, Dad had told Lucy. Mom was killed and he was blinded, and they had to trust God and move on from there.

That was almost impossible. Especially the God part, since as far as she was concerned, it was God who had let it happen in the first place. But sometimes it seemed like they could move on—at those times when Dad reminded her that Mom had said she was going to start a kids' soccer program there in Los Suenos when she came back so Lucy could learn more than Mom had already taught her because—and this was the best part—she said Lucy had an "athletic gift."

"Just like her," Lucy said now.

"Exactly like her," Dad said.

Lucy picked at a loose blue thread on the rug. She wanted to tell him about the book she'd found in the storage shed, the one Mom was keeping. He would understand; he wouldn't take it away from her. She opened her mouth.

"Are you two all right in there?" Aunt Karen said from just down the hall.

"We're fine," Dad said. He ran his hand across Lucy's head again. "You were going to say something?"

"No," Lucy said. "I wasn't." Dad wouldn't take it away from her. But Aunt Karen would, she knew it.

"You can't fib to me, champ," Dad said.

Lucy groped back through their conversation. There was one thing she could talk to him about. "I don't see how I'm gonna ever get to be a great soccer player," she said. "We still don't have a soccer league here."

"I know."

"We try to play soccer at recess—me and J.J. and Oscar and Emanuel. And Carla Rosa, only she's pretty bad. And the Hispanic kids won't play with us." She grunted. "They won't even talk to us."

"That doesn't make sense to me," Dad said. "I know you're the only totally white student at school, but J.J.'s half white. So is Carla Rosa. Not that that should make any difference." He rested his hand on her shoulder. "But, Luce, you know the radio station here is one of the few places I can work where my handicap isn't—well, a handicap."

"I'm not complaining. Honest. And I *sure* don't want to move to El Paso."

"Then let's go make sure your Aunt Karen knows that." Dad stood up, and then cocked his head.

"What's that noise?" he said.

"What noise?"

"Sounds like one of the cats. Is somebody trapped someplace?"

"Oh my gosh!"

Lucy leaped across the bed and lifted the lid to the toy chest. An indignant Lollipop looked up at her and told her in no uncertain terms that she was not pleased.

"Lollipop was in the chest?" Dad said.

"How did you know it was her?" Lucy said.

But she didn't really have to ask. Dad knew by smell and sound and the little hairs on his fingers. And that was why they were just fine alone, the two of them. And it was going to stay that way.

4

Lucy and Dad made a deal: he wouldn't pack her off to El Paso, and she wouldn't let Mudge attack Aunt Karen for the rest of her stay—or do anything else evil to her.

Lucy kept her end, even though her Christmas presents from Aunt Karen were, just as she'd predicted, clothes, clothes, and more clothes, except for the manicure kit and the CD player. It didn't surprise her that everything, including the boom box, was pink.

That wouldn't have been so bad if the *coat*, too, hadn't been "Peppermint Delight," as the tag read, and with fur around the hood no less. The rest she could shove to the back of her closet when Aunt Karen left and be done with it, but a down coat she'd be expected to wear every day, especially since Aunt Karen declared her now-torn jean jacket a disaster that no niece of hers was going to be seen wearing in public. Lucy had to fish it out of the trash can after Aunt Karen went to bed.

But Lucy didn't argue the next morning when Aunt Karen popped into her room before she was even up and said, "You're going to wear your new outfit to church, right?"

"Of course." Lucy said, squeezing Lollipop to keep from adding, *I really WANT to look like a bottle of Pepto-Bismol.* Lolli mewed and scooted out from under the covers, though when she saw Aunt Karen, she made a beeline for the toy chest, where Lucy had repositioned the wooden spoon for her convenience.

"That isn't the one that tried to attack me yesterday, is it?" Aunt Karen said. She peered into the chest like there might be a collection of alligators in it.

"No, that was Mudge," Lucy said. "He's the brown tabby. Lollipop's the black one. Marmalade's orange, and Artemis Hamm is—"

"There are far too many cats in this house," Aunt Karen said. She opened Lucy's closet door and parked her hands on her hips. Dad said Aunt Karen was only thirty-something, and Januarie thought she was way hip, but to Lucy, she sure seemed like an old lady sometimes. Who didn't like cats except grouchy old dinosaur women?

"We so need to go shopping, Lucy," Aunt Karen said into the closet.

"You just brought me a ton of clothes."

"That was one outfit."

"I hate shopping."

"How do you know? You've never really done it." Aunt Karen turned to face Lucy, a delicious gleam in her eyes. "We'll go out for breakfast first and then hit the mall for your basics—then lunch of course—and then we'll go to Claire's for accessories." Aunt Karen licked her lips. "That's the fun part."

None of it sounded like fun to Lucy. Boring maybe, tiring definitely, but not fun. However . . .

"Do they have any sports stores at the mall?" she said as she climbed out of bed and tugged her too-small Brazilian soccer team T-shirt down to cover her underwear. "You know, for, like, cleats and shin guards and stuff."

"How long have you had that shirt?" Aunt Karen said. "Since you were eight?"

Seven, actually. Her mom had bought it for her just before she left. Lucy stomped past Aunt Karen for the bathroom. "Just put whatever you want me to wear on the bed," she said over her shoulder. It was going to be a very long day.

Made longer by the fact that Lucy had to spend it in pink, from fuchsia Uggs to the oversize cotton-candy-colored scrunchie in the small ponytail Aunt Karen made at the top of Lucy's head so the rest of her hair could fall down to her shoulders in curling-iron curls. With all the sprays and gooey stuff Aunt Karen put on those curls, Lucy was convinced they were going to be there the rest of her life. Fortunately, Dad was close by when her aunt mentioned tweezers.

"Leave her eyebrows alone, Karen," he said. He smiled, but there was nothing fun in his voice.

"They're getting a little bushy between her eyes," Aunt Karen said. "She definitely has your brows."

"Which are great, Dad," Lucy said. Okay, so they looked a little like Mrs. Benitez's rose bushes, but he didn't have to know that.

"I'll leave them alone for now," Aunt Karen said. "But maybe when you come to El Paso to shop we can have them waxed. That's what I do."

"Hello!" Lucy said.

"Enough with the eyebrows, already," Dad said.

Lucy was never so glad to get into church, just so she didn't have to listen to Aunt Karen talk about Lucy's fingernails or Dad's need for a new barber or anything about "this house." She'd rather listen to Reverend Servidio, and *that* was pretty drastic.

Los Suenos Community Church was on Granada Street. People sometimes came to town to take pictures of it because it was old and Spanish-mission-looking and what they called "quaint." Lucy had long ago decided "quaint" must mean lopsided and attended by thirty people and led by a pastor who couldn't seem to remember all their names. That was the only reason Lucy could think of why he always called her "kiddo" and called Dad "my friend," even though he had never been to their house, which was only two doors down from the church.

She figured he couldn't remember the words to his sermons either, because he read them from sheets of paper that he kept turning to the next one, longer than Lucy could ever listen to them. They always started out the way they did that day—about how people should come to church. *Hello.* He was talking to the people who were there every single Sunday. Then he went on about how those people—who weren't there—should stop arguing and start working together as a town. Why was Reverend Servidio talking to people who didn't show up to hear it? Why didn't he talk to her and Dad and the rest of the people in the pews?

Aunt Karen put her hand on Lucy's leg, which Lucy only then realized was jittering up and down.

" 'You have heard that it was said,' " Reverend Servidio read from

43

the next sheet he turned over, " 'Love your neighbor and hate your enemy. But I tell you, "Love your enemies and pray for those who persecute you—" ' " He looked up from beneath his straight-across crop of eyebrows but over the tops of his wire-rimmed glasses. "That is from Matthew, chapter five, verses forty-three and forty-four."

Fine, but it made no sense. Lucy looked down at Aunt Karen's hand, which was still holding her leg in place. All she could pray was that Aunt Karen would move to Australia. That was one of the reasons she didn't read the Bible—that and the fact that she really didn't like to read much of anything.

When Aunt Karen finally moved her fingers from Lucy's knee, Lucy concentrated on the two backs-of-the-head in the pew in front of her. They belonged to Dusty Terricola and Veronica DeMatteo, both sixth graders, though neither girl was in Lucy's support class. She wondered if they prayed for *her*. She didn't think they exactly considered her an enemy. They just ignored her. Maybe you didn't have to pray for those who acted like you didn't exist.

When the service was over, Lucy squeezed past Dad, who was on the other side of her, and escaped to the front steps to wait so they could go to Pasco's for lunch like they always did. She almost tripped over somebody who was already there.

"Lucy Rooney?" said the really skinny Mexican girl with the smile that never showed her teeth. "Is that you?"

"Dusty Terricola," Lucy said back. "Is that *you*?"

Dusty looked at the other girl, Veronica, and wrinkled her forehead into ridges the color of coffee with a lot of milk.

"Of course it's Dusty," Veronica said to Lucy.

She *always* showed *her* teeth, because as far as Lucy had ever been able to tell, she never closed her mouth. It simply hung open in her ruddy-brown face as if its hinges were broken.

"You're the one who looks totally different," Veronica said to Lucy.

Dusty ran her hand down Lucy's pink coat sleeve. "You look so cute."

"Doesn't she, though?"

Aunt Karen was suddenly there, rubbing Lucy's other arm. "Don't you think she should wear her hair like this all the time?"

"Yes!" Veronica said. She pulled a hunk of her own Hispanic-black hair to the top of her head and looked to Aunt Karen, who said, "Hello—adorable on you."

Lucy made a silent vow never to use the word "hello" like that again. She also vowed to get her hair back into its real ponytail the first chance she got, which wasn't going to be soon, from the sound of it.

"Okay, we are so going out to lunch," Aunt Karen said. She swept her gaze over Dusty and Veronica. "You two want to come with?"

Before Lucy could break her vow and cry out "Hello! No!," both girls shook their heads as if their necks were made of wood.

"We can't," Dusty said, while Veronica stood next to her, lower lip hanging.

Well, du-uh. Two people who had overlooked Lucy as if she were invisible since second grade were suddenly going to do lunch with her?

"We're going up to Ruidosa," Aunt Karen said.

"We are?" Dad said. He had materialized from inside the church and was tapping his white cane to find the steps.

"Dad and I always go to Pasco's after church," Lucy said. Like Aunt Karen didn't know that.

"Bye, girls," Aunt Karen said as Dusty and Veronica escaped down the sidewalk. She turned to Lucy. "Why didn't you introduce me to your friends?"

"Because they're not my friends."

Aunt Karen shaded her eyes with her hand. "They seem precious."

"Adorable," Lucy said.

That led to a discussion all the way to Ruidosa in Aunt Karen's car about how Lucy needed some girlfriends. How it wasn't healthy for her to always hang out with J.J. How Januarie didn't count because she was too young for real girl talk. And how, by the way, they really shouldn't eat at the Pasco's Café so much. The food there, she said, was so unhealthy. Lucy hoped Dad wouldn't mention that Lucy went there every day after school for a grilled cheese sandwich and two dill pickles. Aunt Karen would be calling the nutrition police next.

She seemed to forget about Dad and Lucy's diet once they reached Ruidosa, because it was Aunt Karen's idea of heaven. There was a store for everything—handmade jewelry, and art that cost more than their house, Dad said. There was even one whole shop just for sunglasses. In spite of the snow plowed to the middle of the main street so cars could get by, the place was packed with tourists, most of them from Texas. Why would anybody drive three hours to shop? Or three minutes, for that matter?

Since Dad was along, Aunt Karen shortened the window shopping that had been known to drive Lucy to the brink of hair tearing more than once and, after trying to convince them for the fifty-third time that sushi was wonderful, steered them to her second choice. Dad liked Italian, and Lucy didn't mind it, as long as Aunt Karen didn't make her try clam sauce or fried squid. They could call it "calamari" if they wanted, but it still had those little sucker things on it.

While they were eating, the owner came along to chat with them. The owner always came along in any restaurant they went to with Aunt Karen. Dad said it was because she was in public relations and was a people magnet.

"This can't be your niece," the woman gushed when she saw Lucy.

"You remember my niece?" Aunt Karen said. She pressed her hand to Lucy's back as if she were presenting her prized poodle.

"Last time I saw you, you were a little tomboy," the woman said.

"I still—"

"Isn't she a young lady?" Aunt Karen said.

"She is." Owner Lady leaned close to Lucy and winked. "Would you like your Coke in a wine glass?"

"How fun would that be?" Aunt Karen said.

Not very, as far as Lucy was concerned, but she nodded and Owner Lady swept away as if she were going to fetch a crown for Lucy. It didn't escape her that the woman hadn't even looked at Dad.

"Ted, you need to take her out more," Aunt Karen said, voice lowered.

"Who, the waitress?" Dad said.

"Lucy! She doesn't even know how to act in a restaurant."

"What did I do?" Lucy flipped up her hand, just as a waiter appeared at her elbow with a Coke-in-a-wine-glass on a tray. Coke, glass, tray, and ice flew back into his face and left him blinking.

"That didn't sound good," Dad said.

People swarmed to clean up the mess while Aunt Karen ordered Lucy to the restroom to wipe off the spot on her white-with-pink-trim sweater—a spot that could barely be seen without a microscope. Lucy stayed in the stall for a while and considered not ever coming out. Only the thought of Dad out there with people ignoring him drove her back to the table. The conversation over a tangle of calamari on a platter looked serious. Both Dad and Aunt Karen stopped talking when Lucy sat down.

"Sorry about that," Lucy mumbled. "I didn't see him."

"Neither did I, Luce," Dad said.

Aunt Karen licked her lips and folded her hands on the tabletop. "I know we said we'd hold off talking about this anymore, but, Ted, there is so much Lucy needs to know that you just can't teach her."

"Then what about a nanny?" he said.

"A what?" Lucy could feel her eyes bulging from her head like a frog's.

"Isn't she a little old for a nanny?"

"You mean, like a babysitter?" Lucy said. "Dad—I AM too old for that!"

She couldn't believe she was actually agreeing with Aunt Karen.

"Tell me some more," Aunt Karen said.

"I think you're doing just fine, Luce," Dad said. "But it might save you some embarrassing moments if you had somebody to teach you a couple of things." He smiled. "Like how to keep from taking out waiters with a single blow."

"So, you'd have somebody come in and live?" Aunt Karen said.

"No!" Lucy said.

Dad shook his head. "I haven't even formed a plan, and I obviously haven't discussed it with you, Luce, I'm just thinking out loud here."

Stop thinking! Lucy wanted to shout at him.

"What about a lady to come in after school," he said, "just for a few hours a day?"

"To do what?" Lucy got up on one knee and ignored Aunt Karen's we-don't-do-that look.

Dad's face got firm. "We'll talk about it later, you and me."

That was the only reason Lucy didn't bolt from the table, out of the restaurant, and into a snowbank.

Aunt Karen pulled out her lip gloss and slathered it on. Then she licked her lips. "That could be a good compromise. I'd like to be in on the interviewing process."

"I think I can handle it, Karen," Dad said.

Steaming plates of pasta arrived, and the waiter gave Lucy a wide berth. She didn't care if he dropped the entire tray—preferably right on Aunt Karen's head—because her aunt was making a face at Dad that clearly said she didn't think he could handle it at all.

Lucy hated it when people did that, thinking he couldn't tell they were disrespecting him. It was the biggest reason of all for Aunt Karen to move to Australia. And the sooner, the better.

She and Dad didn't talk about the nanny question after Aunt Karen left that afternoon, although Lucy did hear her say, "This isn't over, Ted."

Dad had to go to the radio station to record some "packages" for the week, but Lucy didn't go with him like she usually did. She wanted to stay away from him until he had a chance to forget the whole idea.

"Maybe he just said that to hush Aunt Karen up," she said to Artemis Hamm that night when she fished both the cat and her school binder out from under the bed.

Artemis pounced on a dust ball that came out with the notebook and seemed disappointed that it wasn't alive. She gave up on it and jumped to Lucy's dresser to survey herself in the mirror. She spent the hours when she wasn't hunting mice and lizards gazing at her own image. Lucy joined her.

Although she'd scrubbed off the makeup Aunt Karen had put on her wounds that morning to cover them up, they didn't look as red and rough as they had the day before. The ones on her nose blended in with her exactly sixteen freckles. She made sure they were all still there, because her mom had had precisely that many too.

It was the only thing that kept the thought of going back to school tomorrow from driving her under the bed with the dust balls. If she could make it to recess, it would be okay.

She opened her underwear drawer and carefully lifted the Book of Lists. She'd managed to keep it from Aunt Karen, who probably didn't even realize it existed. It didn't seem to Lucy that she understood Lucy's mom, her own sister, at all. She would probably have been surprised at the only list Mom had written.

Lucy took the book to her bed and curled up next to Lolli.

"'Things I Want to Teach Lucy,'" she read.

"'One. What it means to be a woman ... as soon as I find out myself. Two. How to play soccer like Mia Hamm, or at least like me, which isn't all that bad.'"

That was all Mom had written And that was all Lucy needed to know.

"No more messing around with ATVs," she said to Artemis. "From now on, all my adventures are going to be about soccer."

As she got ready for school the next morning, Lucy tried to make her mind follow anything good she could think of.

Aunt Karen was gone.

She didn't have to wear anything pink.

Her hair was back in its regular ponytail with a plain old rubber band.

Dad made waffles.

She could put on her broken-in denim jacket with its fuzzy lining and leave the pink down coat and its furry hood in the back of her closet. She would give it to Januarie if she didn't know Aunt Karen would demand to know where it was next time she came. Like, the minute she walked in the door.

But one good thing happened that Lucy didn't expect. When she stepped out the back door, J.J. was there with her bike.

"You fixed it!" Lucy said.

"Kinda."

J.J. hunched one shoulder up as he rolled the bike forward. The bike basically did the same thing. The new front wheel was a little smaller than the back one, which made it uneven.

"Looks fine to me," Lucy said.

She couldn't say that about J.J. himself. His hair hung in greasy groups, and his eyes were puffy. Lucy didn't ask him why. She just said, "Thanks."

"Hey—you left without me," a Chihuahua-voice whined from the other side of the fence.

"You noticed?" J.J. said under his breath.

But Lucy hopped onto her bike and pushed open the gate with it and joined Januarie on the sidewalk. She was decked out in her frog-green coat, and her eyes sparkled as if she were going to Disneyland instead of school.

"Ride slow," she said. "So I can keep up."

"Don't I always?" Lucy said.

Behind her, J.J. grunted and sped his bike past them, crossing Second Street like he was in the Tour de France. Dad asked Lucy just a few days before if J.J. was still doing his Lance Armstrong imitation.

Lucy went so slowly that her front wheel wobbled, and she had to circle around Januarie as they crossed so she wouldn't get ahead.

"I don't see why you have to ride your bike to school anyway," Januarie said. "You could totally walk just as fast."

That wasn't the point. A bike just felt freer—like you could go further if you had to.

J.J. waited for them at the rickety bike rack at the end of the sixth-grade wing of the elementary school. He'd already parked his bike between two of the bent rungs, and Lucy deposited hers beside it. Neither locked them in. Nobody was going to steal two pieces of rust-with-wheels.

Lucy looked at the empty space next to hers. "Oscar's not here yet."

"He'll probably show up about Wednesday," J.J. said. "What do you want to bet he told his mom school didn't start up again 'til then?"

"But we need him for soccer."

"I can take his place," Januarie said.

Before J.J. could open his mouth, Lucy said, "You'll get your new coat dirty. Can't have that."

J.J. pointed toward the trailer where their class met. Teachers called it a "portable"—as in portable classroom. Lucy wished it were portable enough for someone to pick it up and take it away.

"There's Emanuel and Carla," J.J. said. "We got enough for soccer."

"Man," Lucy said as they trailed to the portable. "Emanuel grew, like, a foot over the holidays."

Their friend leaned against the metal building, legs stretched out as if they came straight from his neck. His arms dangled like he didn't know quite what to do with them. Of course, he looked even longer with his dark hair pulled to the back of his head in a ponytail and the sides shaved. He was half Apache, half Hispanic, but to Lucy, he always looked like a race all his own. He was just Emanuel.

Carla Rosa ran to meet them and stood on tiptoes to throw her arms around Lucy's neck and then Januarie's. When she got to J.J., he said, "Don't even think about it."

Carla didn't look disappointed. Her face was a collection of dimples and crinkles as she grinned away. Her honey-brown eyes disappeared when she smiled, which she did all the time, so Lucy didn't ever see much of them. Although Carla wasn't fat, she seemed to be all cheeks.

"I *love* your hat," Januarie said to her.

Carla bobbed her head back and forth, jiggling the big white sequins that covered her knit cap. Reddish curls peeked out from underneath it.

"My mom got me it for Christmas," she said. "Guess what?"

"What?" they all said together. If they didn't, Carla Rosa would keep asking until they said it.

"We got a new teacher," she said.

Lucy stiffened. "For what?"

"For our class, silly."

Emanuel looked at J.J., who shrugged. Lucy craned her neck toward Carla Rosa. "You mean a substitute?"

"No, a new teacher forever."

"What happened to Mrs. Gomez?" Lucy said.

"She got sick, and now we have Mr. Alligator or something like that—Lucy, you have a big rip in your coat. And guess what?"

Nobody answered.

"We got a guy?" J.J. said. He hunched his shoulders in.

"Don't ask me," Emanuel said. "I ain't seen him."

"Guess what?"

Januarie inserted herself between Carla and Lucy. "What?"

But Lucy took her by the shoulders and moved her aside. "How do you know this, Carla Rosa?"

"Guess what—my dad's the mayor," Carla Rosa said.

"I know that—"

"Yeah, du-uh," Januarie said.

"Shut it, Januarie," J.J. said.

"That's how I know. There he is—that's him." Carla pointed. "And that's Oscar."

Lucy recognized Oscar. He was short and square and had a round, buzz-cut head, and he was currently carrying a box almost as big as he was. He looked like a cartoon robot at the moment.

But she didn't know the kid walking with him, holding a box on his shoulder like he was showing off his muscles.

"That's no teacher," J.J. said. "That's one of the high school kids."

Carla blinked, Emanuel went back to holding up the portable classroom, and Januarie whined that now that Oscar was here she was never going to get to play. But Lucy watched as Oscar and the other kid approached. The guy had a shaved face and chest hair sticking out of his shirt and a walk like he'd walked a lot of places before.

"Hey, guys," he said. "I'm Mr. Augustalientes."

"I told you it was like Alligator," Carla Rosa said.

Januarie giggled. "It is!"

It was Lucy's turn to blink as the guy put his box down and stuck out his hand.

"I'm your new teacher," he said.

5

The bell rang. J.J. and Emanuel dove into the portable as if they actually liked school. Januarie whined that it wasn't fair that she couldn't be in their class and wandered off to the lower elementary building. Carla Rosa slipped her hand into Mr. Augu-what's-his-nose's outstretched one and then ran shyly off. And Oscar shifted the box and looked like he was going to fold up under the weight. When the new teacher took it from him, Oscar escaped too.

That left only Lucy, caught in the act of sizing up this kid-who-turned-out-to-be-a-grown-up. He was shorter than Dad and had shiny, milk chocolate brown hair cut short except for a silky part that curved over his forehead. He wore sunglasses and had a very small smile, and he just stood there looking right back at Lucy.

"And you are?" he said.

She tilted her chin. "Lucy Rooney."

"Really? You're Miss Lucy?" He cocked his head. "I saw your name on my roll, but—"

He probably expected a girly-girl.

"How lucky am I, then?" he said. "And listen, Augustalientes is way too long—just call me Mr. Auggy."

Lucy groaned inside. He already thought she was too dumb to remember his actual name. Man, she hated getting a new teacher.

"Shall we?" he said, as he balanced both boxes on his shoulders.

Show-off. Lucy would rather have donned her Peppermint Delight coat than follow him into the portable. The room fell silent when they entered, which wasn't all that amazing since there were only five people

in their class. Other kids came in and out for help during the day sometimes, but these five were the permanent residents of the support class
portable.

Only it didn't look like their room right now. A gallery of posters
lined the walls, which two weeks before had held a handwriting chart,
a list of rules, and a calendar with puppies on it, none of which anybody
ever looked at.

Lucy didn't have time to survey the new display because she had
to find her seat. The former row of desks had been replaced by two
round tables and a mismatched collection of chairs. Emanuel, J.J., and
Oscar were already gathered at one table. Carla Rosa patted the empty
chair next to her at the other one and dimpled at Lucy.

"Guess what, Mr. Argentina?" Carla Rosa said.

Lucy heard J.J. grunt. Carla got on his nerves, Lucy knew. She
reminded him of Januarie sometimes, even though she was twelve.
She was kind of eight in her mind, maybe even six.

"What, Miss Carla?" the teacher said.

"I gotta question," Oscar said. He stuck his hand up *after* he asked it.

"I hope I have an answer." Mr.—what did he say to call him—Mr.
Auggy?—set the boxes on a long table Lucy had never seen before. He
leaned against his desk and tilted his head at Carla.

"You first," he said, "and then Mr.—" He raised his eyebrows at
Oscar.

"Oscar. See, that's what I don't get." Oscar twisted his face. "How
come you call us Miss and Mr.?"

"Out of respect," Mr. Auggy said. "I expect you to respect each
other, so I ought to respect you. Now—Miss Carla, you wanted to
say something?"

Carla giggled. "I forgot."

Emanuel let out a hiss—and Mr. Auggy was on him as if he'd just
spit on the floor.

"Just so you know," he said, "there will be none of that here. There
are no stupid questions, and there are no dumb answers."

J.J. folded his arms and slid down in his seat.

"Problem, Mr.—well, it's either Mr. Emanuel or Mr. Jedediah?"

Oscar spewed a juicy laugh, and J.J. punched him. Lucy cringed. J.J. hated to be called by his actual name, which was Jedediah Joseph. Lucy couldn't really blame him.

"Problem?" Mr. Auggy said.

"He likes to be called J.J.," Carla Rosa informed him. "And I like to be called Carla Rosa."

"I apologize, Mr. J.J.," Mr. Auggy said. "I'll probably make a lot of mistakes this first day."

By lunchtime, Lucy decided he had that right, at least. First, he made them each tell him something about themselves, which was a huge mistake since all Carla could do was giggle, and J.J. wouldn't say anything, so Emanuel wouldn't either, and Oscar talked until everybody was yawning and rubbing their eyes. When it was Lucy's turn, she sat up straight and said, "The only thing you need to know about me is that I love soccer and I hate school. No offense."

"None taken," Mr. Auggy said.

His next mistake was making them give him all the reasons they hated school while he wrote them on the chalkboard. It took up the whole board and what was supposed to be their time for math—the one subject that didn't make Lucy wish she was at the dentist instead. Why talk about hating school anyway? School was what it was, and there was nothing anybody could do about it.

"What would you like to change about school?" Mr. Auggy said next.

"Lunch," Oscar said.

"What do you want for lunch?"

"No chili and cheese on top of Fritos," he said. "It's gross."

"What *do* you want?"

The other kids said things like chicken nuggets and pizza and burritos, except J.J., who still wasn't participating. Lucy said she wanted sushi and calamari. Then she thought her dad wouldn't be smiling at her right now, and she wished she hadn't said it. It did make J.J. smile, though.

"What else would you change?" Mr. Auggy said, even though there was no room left on the chalkboard. He picked up a clipboard.

"I don't like doing work," Oscar said. He looked around as if he expected the rest of the class to congratulate him on a brilliant answer. Mr. Auggy actually wrote it down. Okay, as long as they were being ridiculous—

"I want a sports program," Lucy said.

"Ah, Miss Lucy, our soccer player."

"Except there's no soccer team. There's not even any soccer balls—"

"And all the basketballs are old. They don't even bounce."

The class stared at Emanuel. He almost never talked, especially in class.

"What sports do you have?" Mr. Auggy said.

"None at our school," Oscar said. "Huh, Lucy?"

Lucy lifted her chin. "None. They have some boys' teams at the middle school and the high school—baseball and basketball and football, but the girls can't even try out for those."

"Girls have that thing where you punch the ball over the net." Carla Rosa frowned and looked at Lucy.

"Volleyball," Lucy said. "My mom was going to start a soccer league in Los Suenos."

"Why doesn't she?" Mr. Auggy said.

"She's dead," Carla Rosa said.

"Shut up!" J.J. said.

Mr. Auggy cocked his head at J.J., but Lucy shook her ponytail. "It's okay. She can't help it."

Mr. Auggy didn't say anything for a minute, and J.J. slid back down in his chair.

"My dad asked about the school having a soccer team," Lucy said. "But they said there wasn't enough money."

"I see," Mr. Auggy said. He had stopped writing things down. It figured. Whenever somebody said there wasn't any money, that was usually the end of whatever needed to be paid for.

Mr. Auggy committed a few more flubs before lunch—like giving them each a clump of clay and telling them to make something, which ended in a major clay-ball battle—but as far as Lucy was concerned, his worst mistake came during recess.

They gobbled their lunches as usual—in four bites Lucy downed the peanut butter and pickle sandwich Dad made her—and raced out to the playground, stopping only at her cubby in the main hall of the sixth-grade wing to get the soccer ball she kept there. Cubbies lined the walls on both sides and served as lockers, but no one ever took anything from anybody's because, Lucy always figured, nobody had anything worth taking. In her case, no one else in sixth grade except her little team had any interest in soccer equipment.

Just as Lucy was tucking the ball under her arm, a female voice behind her said, "What happened, Lucy?"

She turned to Veronica, who stood, hang-lipped, on the other side of the hall next to Dusty.

"What?" Lucy said.

"Why aren't you wearing that cute pink coat you had on yesterday?"

Dusty nodded. "That one looks like you ran over it or something."

"I'm saving the pink one," Lucy said.

"That lady you were with was nice."

Lucy wasn't sure which one of them said that, and she didn't care. What was up with them noticing her all of a sudden? "You guys ready?" she said to her group.

Veronica and Dusty turned to their side-by-side cubbies, filled with color-coded pastel binders that said SOCIAL STUDIES and ENGLISH in perfect fat letters. They never had to come to the support class. Lucy reminded herself to make a list of all the reasons she was glad. Them paying attention to her couldn't be a good thing.

Once she was out on the playground with Emanuel and Oscar and Carla Rosa, however, she forgot all about them. She could even ignore Januarie, who sat on the ground with her lower lip poking straight out, bleating like a small goat because they wouldn't let her play.

"We could use her for the ball," J.J. muttered to Lucy.

"You want to hold my jacket for me, Jan?" Lucy said.

Januarie settled for that, though she kept her lip standing out.

Lucy pointed to a space near the fence. "Be goalie, J.J. Oscar, you be the defender—"

She doled out the positions—midfielder to Carla Rosa, and forward to herself and Emanuel. That made it basically J.J. against everybody else, but there weren't enough of them to make one team, much less two. Besides, J.J. was the best player, except for Lucy.

"Ready?" she said.

Heads bobbed, and Lucy set the ball down, took a step forward, and smacked it squarely in the middle with the inside of her foot so her leg looked like a hockey stick. That was the way her mom had taught her, the way she'd watched players on TV do it, and the way she'd practiced in her backyard until her feet were black and blue.

"To you, Emanuel!" she shouted.

He stuck out a long, spindly leg and caught the ball with his toe. It popped up and spun back toward him. He flailed at it again with his foot, missed, and said, "To you, Lucy."

"No!" Lucy waved her arms at him. "I can't touch it again until somebody else does."

Emanuel looked at Carla Rosa, who blinked at him.

"That's why you need me!" Januarie said.

"So why aren't you playing, Miss Thing?"

Lucy stopped in mid-lunge toward the ball and stared at Mr. Auggy, who was crouching beside Januarie.

"They won't ever let me," she said, pitifully.

Carla Rosa chose that moment to whack at the ball with her foot. Lucy trapped it with hers and dragged it back behind her with her sole.

"Okay, let's start again," she said.

"Pass it here," Mr. Auggy said. "I'll throw it in."

Lucy didn't move.

"I love a pickup game. It looks like you could use another player." He looked down at Januarie. "Two, even. You want to be on my team?"

J.J. grunted. Carla Rosa giggled. Oscar and Emanuel shrugged at each other. Lucy kicked the ball hard toward Mr. Auggy. It was trapped and in his hands so swiftly, Lucy barely saw how he did it.

"Go on in, Miss Thing," he said to Januarie, who was jumping up and down and squealing.

She bounded onto their playing space, nearly knocking Emanuel over, and turned to face Mr. Auggy. Leaning forward with one leg, he raised the ball over his head and threw it gently to her feet.

"What do I do?" she cried.

"Kick it to me," Mr. Auggy said as he jogged onto the "field."

"No, kick it here!" J.J. said.

When she turned her head to him, Emanuel got his foot between hers and snagged the ball.

"Here!" Lucy said, running toward the goal.

But from somewhere, a high-pitched sound came. All heads turned to Mr. Auggy, who let a silver whistle drop to his chest on a cord. He waved his hand for them to gather around him. Carla Rosa bounced over like she was going to hug him. J.J. gave Lucy a dark look.

"Listen," Mr. Auggy said when they'd formed a half circle around him, "I like your spirit, but no fair taking advantage of the new kid." He gave Januarie his small smile. She looked back like he'd just given her the last cookie. "What's your name, Miss Thing?" he said.

"Pain in the Tail," J.J. muttered.

"Is that your brother?" Mr. Auggy said.

Lucy felt J.J. growl, but Mr. Auggy was still smiling.

"Yes," Januarie said. "And he's evil. And my name's Januarie."

"All right, Miss Januarie. Let me give you a few basics."

It was all downhill from there. Lucy and the others got to play for five minutes while Mr. Auggy explained the entire point of soccer to Januarie. Then he made them play against the two of them and J.J., barking out instructions and stopping the game to give them pointers at least every seven seconds.

"Great game!" he said when the bell rang.

The only other person who seemed to agree was Januarie. Even Carla Rosa had drawn her mouth into a straight line.

"I'm bad at soccer," she said to Lucy as they headed back to the portable.

"No, you're not," Lucy said, even though Carla Rosa was the worst, next to Januarie. "He's just B.O.S.S.Y."

Carla wrinkled her forehead.

"Bossy. And he doesn't even know anything," Lucy said, even though he obviously knew a lot.

"Everybody go to the main wing for water," Mr. Auggy said from behind them. "Stay hydrated."

"I'm not thirsty," Lucy said, even though she was.

And then she spent the rest of the school day pretending it didn't feel like she had the entire desert inside her mouth.

"It was way more fun when we played by ourselves," Lucy told J.J. when they were at Pasco's Café after school.

"When we didn't have to play with Januarie." J.J. glared at his sister. She was on the other side of the room playing checkers with old Mr. Esparza who ran the museum next door that hardly anybody ever went to, especially in the winter.

"Who even asked him to play anyway?" Lucy said.

"Nobody had to ask him. He's the teacher. He can do whatever he wants." J.J. grunted. "Just like parents."

Lucy ripped a corner off the grilled cheese sandwich Pasco had just put in front of her. It felt good to rip something. She'd been wanting to all afternoon.

"He made Emanuel feel like a dork," she said. "He probably won't even want to play tomorrow."

"Are you going to eat both of those pickles?" J.J. said.

Lucy shook her head. "Carla Rosa got her feelings all hurt. We were doing just fine giving her the ball once in a while so she thought she knew how to play."

"Nobody knows how to play," J.J. said, green juice spilling over his lips.

"I was teaching us! This is our thing. I was gonna get it started and get everybody playing better. And now this Mr. Auggy person is ruining it." Lucy pushed the plate toward J.J. "You can have the rest of this."

"Am I going to have to tell your father you're not eating what he's paying for?"

Lucy looked up at Pasco, who was standing at their table, hands on his own opposite shoulders like he was afraid they were going to get away. He was shaped like a playing card and always wore his hair brushed straight back and shiny as Aunt Karen's car. He smiled at the end of every sentence, whether there was anything to smile about or not.

"J.J.'ll eat it," Lucy said.

J.J. stuffed half the grilled cheese into his mouth before Pasco could think about grabbing the plate.

"You didn't like it?" Pasco said, his very big dark eyes clouding over the smile. "You want me to make you a quesadilla? A burrito?"

"I'm not hungry," Lucy said.

J.J. jammed the other half of the sandwich in and chewed with his eyes sparkling. "Your father wants you to eat." Pasco smiled—at nothing—and moved back to the counter. Lucy hauled in a big breath that smelled like chiles and coffee beans.

"He'll probably just go away," she said.

"The teacher?"

"Yeah. He's not gonna stick around that long."

"How do you know?"

Lucy leaned in. "He's all excited about being a teacher. Those kind always leave or they get like Mrs. Gomez and don't care that much anymore."

"Didn't you save anything for me?"

This time it was Januarie at the table. She was more like a begging Chihuahua than ever.

J.J. narrowed his icy eyes at her.

"Want the rest of my pickle?" Lucy said.

Januarie wrinkled her nose. "I wanted some sandwich. I bet you ate it all, J.J. I'm telling."

J.J. looked around. "Who you gonna tell? Old Man Esparza?"

Januarie didn't answer but hiked herself one bottom-cheek at a time onto the chair next to Lucy and scooped up some melted cheese from Lucy's plate.

"Who invited you?" J.J. said.

"Mr. Auggy," Januarie said.

"Huh?" Lucy and J.J. said in unison.

"He said you had to play soccer with me."

"That doesn't mean you get to hang around with us all the time," J.J. said. The "time" climbed up into outer space.

"Go order us another sandwich," Lucy said to Januarie, "and I'll split it with you."

Januarie's eyes grew rounder. "Your dad must be so rich. You get to order anything you want."

"Don't forget napkins," Lucy said.

When Januarie had skipped happily away, Lucy leaned into the table again. "Don't be too hateful to her, J.J. You'll get in trouble."

J.J. aimed his gaze at Januarie's back. "You better be right about that teacher going away, 'cause I'm not playing with her."

"She's really not that bad," Lucy said.

"You don't know." And then J.J.'s mouth closed, and Lucy knew the conversation was over.

"Don't worry," she said. "Mr. Augus-whatever won't have recess duty tomorrow. They only have it every other day. We won't even see him on the playground."

"Do we want double cheese?" Januarie called from the counter.

"You just better be right," J.J. said.

6

By Wednesday, it was clear that Lucy was not right. Mr. Auggy played soccer with them three days in a row, even when there was another teacher on the playground for recess duty. He kept calling what they were doing a "pickup game."

"I've played pickup games all over the world," he told them Wednesday as he was herding them toward the water fountain for a break—like Lucy hadn't already taught them to drink plenty of fluids when they did sports. "But this is the most fun group I've ever played with."

Carla Rosa beamed. Emanuel kicked at a rock. Oscar had to know what foreign countries he'd visited. Had he been to California?

While Mr. Auggy patiently explained that California was part of the United States, J.J. nodded Lucy away from the group.

"I thought you said he would go away," he said.

"I thought he would."

J.J. grunted, sounding like it was all Lucy's fault that this pushy teacher had appointed himself their soccer coach.

"I want to throw in this time," she heard Januarie say.

"You got it," Mr. Auggy said. "Is your side ready, Miss Lucy?"

J.J. looked like he wanted to spit.

Back on the field, Lucy, Emanuel, Oscar, Carla Rosa, and J.J. waited while Mr. Auggy instructed Januarie on how to throw in properly. "Both feet on the ground when you let go of the ball.... Throw it equally with both hands.... Both hands start from behind your head and come all the way over.... Your body faces the way you're throwing."

Januarie didn't get it.

After the fifth time she messed it up, when even Carla Rosa was looking bored-out-of-her-braces, Mr. Auggy said, "Miss Lucy, demonstrate for our Miss Januarie."

"Me?" Lucy said.

Mr. Auggy gave her his small smile. "Yes, you." He pointed to the place he wanted her to stand and looked at Januarie. "You watch Miss Lucy—she has perfect form."

Lucy felt a strange flush as she planted her feet and pulled the ball back. It sailed lightly toward Oscar, who was startled and bonked it with his head.

"All right!" Mr. Auggy said. "You rock, Miss Lucy."

She almost felt like grinning as she ran onto their tiny field and, with her foot like a big squishy pillow, trapped the ball that rolled randomly toward her.

"Next time I'll teach you to direct the ball on the first touch," Mr. Auggy said to her.

She hated to admit it, but whatever that was, she wanted to learn it.

She didn't have the same feeling once they were back in the classroom. Mr. Auggy told them all to take out a piece of paper and think about a person they considered to be their hero.

"You!" Carla Rosa said.

Lucy thought of Dad, of course. And then she thought of the obvious next thing, which was having to *write* about why he was the bravest person on the planet.

She didn't rock at writing.

"This is not for a grade," Mr. Auggy said as Lucy pulled a piece of paper out of her notebook one wire spiral at a time. "I just want to get an idea what your writing is like."

She could tell him that. It stunk.

"Start now," Mr. Auggy said. "Simply put your thoughts on paper."

Lucy stared at the blank sheet in front of her. She studied a stray fleck of ink from where the lines were printed. She noticed how the ripped places hung out like flags where it had been torn out. She counted how many lines there were on the page. She wondered why the lines were blue and the margin marker was pink. Anything but pink would have been better.

She did everything but write on it.

What was the point? Mr. Auggy was probably only going to scribble all over it in red when she was done. Or circle the words she didn't spell right, which would be half of them.

That was the other thing. Why even try to write about "My Hero" when the words she wanted to use—like *courageous* and *insurmountable*—she couldn't even begin to spell. She knew why her dad was her hero. She didn't have to write it down. She couldn't write it down.

So why try?

"I can see those wheels turning in your head, Miss Lucy," a voice whispered near her ear.

Lucy jumped and hunched over her paper, pencil clenched between her knuckles, so Mr. Auggy couldn't see its blankness.

"There's so much going on in there," he said, "I bet it's hard to catch it."

Lucy curled harder over her table. When he moved on, she sneaked a glance around the room. Carla Rosa was carving into her paper with her pencil, slowly, as if she were cutting up a steak. Emanuel was erasing a hole in his. Oscar shook his hand and huffed and puffed like he'd been writing for hours. J.J. had his head on his arms on the tabletop.

"Okay," Mr. Auggy said. "I know what I need to know now."

"That we're dumb?" Oscar said. "I coulda told you that."

"Shut up," J.J. muttered into his arms.

Lucy didn't listen to the rest. She just wrote her name on her paper and handed it in.

She skipped having grilled cheese at Pasco's that afternoon because Wednesday was her day to go to the market for groceries. Dad went on Saturdays. Since they didn't have a car, they couldn't get all the stuff for a whole week in one trip.

Lucy would have liked going to the market if it weren't for Mr.

Benitez. He was the owner, so he was always lurking there, spying as she went up and down the skinny aisles with her handbasket like he was sure she was going to steal something. He wasn't a fat man. It just seemed to Lucy like he had thicker skin than most people, and that made him big and fleshy. It also made his eyes almost impossible to see, but she could feel him surveying her anyway.

Otherwise, the market was fun. On Tuesday nights, she and Dad made a list of what they were out of—usually cat food and milk and bread and Captain Crunch, which they both ate a heaping bowl of almost every morning, and microwave popcorn, their best bedtime snack. When it was her turn to shop, she always got the buttered kind. Dad bought the plain. That was their deal.

Once the "needs" were taken care of, she was allowed to get some "wants"—as long as she didn't go over the budget. She didn't have to add things up in her head anymore. She just knew that if she had to buy tortillas that week, she couldn't get Nesquik too.

She was deciding between creamy and crunchy peanut butter, always a tough decision, when she heard Mr. Benitez clear his throat. He did that so much, Lucy sometimes wondered if he had hair balls like her cats.

"Your father called," he said. It sure *sounded* like he had a hair ball in there.

Lucy selected the crunchy p.b. and put it in the basket.

"He said to tell you to get tea bags."

"Tea bags?" Lucy scrunched up her nose. "We don't drink tea."

"I don't care whether you do or not. He said to get tea bags."

Mr. Benitez pulled a box from the shelf above Lucy's head and dropped it on top of her peanut butter. Then he peered in until Lucy felt like he was peeping into her brain.

"You don't have enough money on your account for all of that," he said. "Put something back."

"I know how much money I have," Lucy said, and then added, "Thank you, Mr. Benitez."

Dad said she had to be polite to him no matter what because he let them have an account and nobody else in town got one.

Still, she gave his thick face an I-told-you-so smile when she didn't go over the limit on her items, including the mysterious tea bags. She wondered about those until she got closer to the house with her two full-to-overflowing bags and saw a faded red pickup truck parked in front.

She slowed her steps. A repairman? No, nothing was broken this week. Somebody returning one of the kitties who'd wandered off? None of their cats ever actually left town, and who in Los Suenos had a truck like that?

Lucy was no closer to figuring it out when she peeked through the window in the back door while she balanced both bags on one hip to turn the knob. The person sitting across from Dad at the table was a total stranger.

Only, even from where she stood, Lucy could see that she didn't act like one.

The woman sat in the chair like a perfect L, making her short self look tall and important. In spite of the fact that she wore her black-pinstriped-with-gray hair in a straight-at-the-chin cut like a child in an old picture book, she wasn't little-girlish at all, not with a face as square as a box and a mouth that pulled inward like she was sucking herself in. Anybody that serious couldn't be there for a good time.

"Come in, Luce," Dad called.

Lucy pushed open the door and deposited the bags on the counter and peeled off her backpack and extracted her arms from the sleeves of her jacket—until Dad finally said, "Enough with the stalling. Come say hello to Senora Herrera."

"Inez," the woman said.

Her voice was as dead-sober as her face, which was why Lucy was surprised as she crossed to the table to see that the woman wore a bright-white blouse with life-size red hibiscus flowers embroidered on it, and a yellow skirt that matched the flowers' centers. Two strands of pearls followed the ring of wrinkles around her neck.

"This is Lucy," Dad said, sounding as if Lucy had already been a main topic of conversation before she came in.

"Hi," Lucy said, and stuck out her hand to the lady, because Dad would tell her to anyway if she didn't.

The hand she put into Lucy's had calluses that scraped like toothbrushes on her palm. She looked at Lucy with small, black, smart-looking eyes, like she knew things she wasn't about to tell.

"I'll put the groceries away," Lucy said.

"They'll keep," Dad said. "Did you get the tea bags?"

"Uh-huh. What did we need them for?"

The lady — *did she say her name was Inez?* — stood up. She was only as tall as Lucy, but Lucy felt as if she were shrinking in front of her.

"Do you have the tea kettle?" she said. She spoke like English wasn't the first language she learned.

"I don't know," Lucy said.

"In the pantry, top shelf, all the way to the left," Dad said. "Get the step stool, Luce."

Lucy was glad for an excuse to retreat to the pantry so she could collect her thoughts, which were now scattered like confetti. What was with the Mexican lady who had Dad buying tea and pulling out kitchen stuff Lucy didn't even know they owned? If this Inez person thought she was going to cook it, or whatever it was you did to make tea, in Lucy's kitchen, she better think again —

From the top of the step stool, Lucy spotted a bright yellow pot with a lid and a spout, which she pried out from behind two other mystery pots they never used. It was greasy-feeling and coated in dust, and she sneezed as she carried it to the sink. Inez stood still and pot-like herself and watched Lucy wash it off.

"That was your mother's," Dad said. "She was a tea drinker."

Lucy cradled the lid in her hand and stared at it. How come he'd never told her that before? It made her feel cold to think there was something about Mom she didn't know — something she would have known by now if she were still here.

Lucy dried the pot and the lid with exaggerated care, but she couldn't put off the obvious question any longer.

"How do I make tea?" she said.

"Why don't you let Inez make it?" Dad said. "She knows how she likes it." He chuckled as if he were entertaining an old friend. "Die-hard tea drinkers are persnickety about their brew."

Lucy would rather have given Inez her soccer ball than to let go of her mother's tea kettle, but she handed it over and turned to the door. "I gotta find Mudge and feed him," she said.

"In a sec," Dad said. "Come sit."

Lucy sank into the chair next to his and tried not to look as if she were paying attention to how tea was made. She hoped it wasn't too disgusting, because she was going to have to become a tea drinker if Mom had been one.

"Inez is going to be your nanny," Dad said.

Lucy sucked in air. She'd forgotten all about Dad's ridiculous suggestion about a nanny. He'd only said it to get Aunt Karen to stop bugging him, hadn't he?

"After-school companion," Inez said.

Lucy didn't care what she called herself. She didn't need her.

"Like we talked about," Dad said. "She'll be here when you get home from school to get you started on your homework, help you with all that girl stuff I don't know anything about, make sure you have a good snack." He nudged Lucy with his elbow. "No more rubber sandwiches down at Pasco's."

She liked Pasco's.

"She's going to do the grocery shopping for us too, so you can have more time to do girl things." Dad chuckled again. "Whatever they are."

She liked grocery shopping.

She liked making things at their stove.

She liked everything just the way it was.

Dad eased back in his chair and folded his hands on his tummy. "I'm waiting for the whistle," he said. "Bet you didn't even know tea kettles whistle, did you, Luce?"

"No," she said woodenly.

"I love that sound."

She didn't know that either. Had she been the blind one all this time? Didn't Dad like the way things were, the way she thought he did?

"So—" Dad said.

"Sure," Lucy said. "Fine. I'm gonna go find Mudge."

She got almost to the door without anyone stopping her. Even then, Inez only said, "You want to say something to me?"

Lucy swallowed. There were no colors in the person's voice. It was hard to tell what she really meant. But Lucy knew what *she* meant, and the woman *had* asked.

"I just want to say one thing," Lucy said.

Inez nodded.

"Lucy Rooney doesn't wear pink."

And then instead of going to look for Mudge, Lucy took the carpet ride down the hall to her room and carefully closed the door behind her without any tantrum sounds. That way Dad wouldn't come in when Inez was gone and ask her what was wrong.

And this *was* wrong. She did not need a nanny or an after-school companion or anybody else to show her how to be a girl. She was going to be a girl like her mom—brave and strong and a soccer player who rocked.

Only when Lollipop leaped from under the pillows with a frightened mew and dove into the toy chest did Lucy realize she'd said it out loud.

She wanted to dive in after her and hide, but that wasn't what her mom would have done. Lucy opened her underwear drawer and dug under the pile of rolled-up socks and pulled out the Book of Lists.

Mom would make a list. Maybe while she was drinking tea.

Lucy slid the pen from its holder and began to write.

Things I Miss about Having a Mom

— Having somebody brush my hair, even though I never liked it that much, but I would now if I could have her back.

— Giggling. Dad doesn't giggle. He can't. He's a man.

— Teaching me about soccer — instead of Mr. Auggy.

— Having somebody say, "When I was a little girl . . ." so I could roll my eyes.

— Having somebody to say "Mo-om!" to. Anytime I want. Or ever.

7

Inez cooked dinner for Lucy and Dad before she left—another thing Dad said he was going to have her do on the weekdays from now on. As they ate, Lucy swallowed more of what she wanted to say than she did of the enchilada she pushed around on her plate.

Don't you like it when we cook together? she choked back.

Do you think our enchiladas are icky? Do you think I'm icky all of a sudden and you need somebody to change me?

When Dad finally said, "What did you think of Inez?" Lucy just shrugged.

"Whatever that answer was, I didn't hear it."

"She was okay," Lucy said.

"Just 'okay'?"

"I don't even know her. I guess she's fine."

Dad chewed for longer than it took anybody to soften up a tortilla, but Lucy didn't fill in the blank space. She felt the same way she did in class, staring at that too-white piece of paper and not knowing what was right to put on it.

"I tell you what." Dad felt for his checkered napkin and swiped it across his mouth, making a smile appear. "We'll just give her a try, and if it doesn't work out—"

"How long of a try?" Lucy said. She came up on one knee.

"How does two months sound?"

Two months? She could grow an inch in two months. Or be well on her way to failing sixth grade. Or—

"Luce?"

But it was better than forever. And in two months she could also show him, and this Inez woman, and Aunt Karen, that she already knew how to be a girl.

"Hello?" Dad said.

"Okay," Lucy said. "Two months."

"Good. Now let's talk about some ground rules."

"Dad." Lucy gave her best elaborate sigh. "I know the rules."

"New rules." Dad put down his fork and held up a finger. "No letting the cats loose on her."

Oh.

Another finger came up. "No disappearing for hours on end with J.J."

Rats.

"Three."

"I know. No sneaking hot chili pepper into her tea."

Lucy poked her fork into her enchilada and watched the sauce drool out.

"Well," Dad said, "that's all I need to say. You and Inez will work things out."

What things? Lucy wanted to shout. Yesterday or the day before, she would have said it. She could have asked Dad anything and not been afraid. But now things were different, like someone had whispered something to Dad that had changed how he thought about her.

And that changed how she thought about him too.

At least Mr. Auggy didn't give their papers back with big red Fs on them the next day. He didn't even mention the assignment all morning, and by the time recess came around, Lucy could even get a little bit excited about playing soccer. Maybe Mr. Auggy would teach her about that thing he'd mentioned yesterday.

But when she ran onto their little playing field, ball tucked under her arm, J.J. stopped her with a jerk of his head. His eyes were colder than the air.

"What?" Lucy said.

"What's he doing here?"

Lucy twisted to see where J.J. was directing his icicle stare. A big, dark-haired boy stood with his back to them, talking to Mr. Auggy. Lucy put the ball up so she could make a face at J.J. behind it.

"That's Gabe," she said.

"Duh," J.J. replied.

"Did he get in trouble?" Lucy peered hopefully over the top of the ball. "Is Mr. Auggy yelling at him?"

"I don't hear any yelling."

"Lucy." There was a tug at her sweatshirt sleeve. Januarie was using the Chihuahua voice.

"Not now," J.J. said.

"No—listen. Mr. Auggy's telling that mean kid he can play with us."

Lucy watched J.J.'s eyes turn to ice cubes. Lucy was sure her own eyes weren't a whole lot warmer.

"I don't want to play with him," Januarie said. "He called me a name one time."

"Only once?" Lucy said. "You got off lucky."

"I'm not playing with him," J.J. said between his teeth, and he slunk, head down, to the nearest wall and stuck himself against it.

"Are you playing, Lucy?" Januarie said. "'Cause if you're not, I'm not."

Lucy watched as Mr. Auggy dropped a ball to the ground. Where had that come from? She always brought the ball. He said something to Gabe, who tapped it with the side of his foot and caught it lightly with the other one, dribbling several feet before Mr. Auggy smiled his small smile and captured the ball from him.

"He knows how to play," Lucy said, more to herself than to Januarie.

Mr. Auggy blew his whistle, and the little team straggled toward him, all except J.J. Lucy saw Oscar and Emanuel and Carla Rosa casting cautious glances at Gabe, who ignored them all as he bounced the ball off his knee.

"*Are* you?" Januarie said. She was pulling so hard on Lucy's sleeve it was sliding off her shoulder.

"He won't want to stick around for very long," Lucy said. "I guess I'll play."

Januarie gave a final yank and held most of Lucy's sleeve in her hand. "Don't let him hurt me."

It occurred to Lucy that Mr. Auggy wouldn't let Gabe hurt anybody. He was all about rules and being fair. Lucy grunted. Everybody was about rules these days.

"You all know Gabe?" Mr. Auggy said when they'd gathered around him in a ragged circle.

Nobody looked at Gabe. They just nodded at the ground. Lucy sneaked a peek at him as he swept his gaze at the tops of their heads and shrugged, like it didn't matter whether they knew him or not. Lucy looked back at the still-icy J.J., frozen to the wall.

She tilted up her chin. "Yeah," she said. "I know him. He almost ran over me with an ATV one time."

Carla Rosa gasped. Mr. Auggy's eyebrows went into upside-down *V*s. Gabe muttered something about being sorry he'd missed. If Mr. Auggy heard it, he didn't show it. Of course not. No teachers ever came down on Gabe. He was in the smart classes, and he was never mean to white kids in front of the faculty. Besides, he was the sheriff's son.

"Nobody's going to be running over anybody on my soccer field." Mr. Auggy danced his eyes over them. "Understood?"

Everybody gave an automatic nod.

"Then let's play some soccer!"

So now it was "his" soccer field. And his ball. And his choice of players.

What was up with everybody taking over everything that was hers?

"Lucy—throw in," Mr. Auggy said.

And then the ball was in her hands, and she was sailing it over her head, and Gabe was trapping it with his thigh. Then Mr. Auggy was calling for Oscar to pass the ball—to plant it first and then—

They were playing soccer.

As Mr. Auggy darted back and forth among them, he captured the ball and taught them the push pass, and then he let them practice driving the ball up and down the field. Carla Rosa fell down a lot.

Januarie mostly stood there and squealed happily. Gabe passed fast and crisp and got the ball to somebody every time. Emanuel and Oscar sometimes actually got control of the ball. After the first time, when Gabe smirked and told Lucy under his breath that she played like a girl, she never missed it.

"Lead your teammate!" Mr. Auggy called to Gabe. "Don't pass it to where she is now—think about where she'll be in two seconds."

Lucy knew where she wished Gabe were, but she didn't pass it all the way there—to Texas. It was too good, keeping up with this kid who thought he was David Beckham. It was way good.

"You guys rock!" Mr. Auggy said when the bell rang.

"What about us girls?" Januarie said.

Gabe hissed through his teeth, but Mr. Auggy high-fived the breathless Januarie. "You are all gonna rule the field pretty soon if you keep this up."

The rest of the group headed for the water fountain, except for Gabe. He sauntered off to the regular sixth-grade wing, and Lucy expected him to kick back dust like a dog.

"So, Miss Lucy." She looked at Mr. Auggy, who was now strolling beside her, twirling the soccer ball on his finger. "What's up with J.J. Do you know?"

Lucy shrugged.

He stopped twirling. "Guess I'll have to ask him."

"No," Lucy said. "I'll ask him."

The mood J.J. was in, he was sure to get himself thrown into detention if Mr. Auggy even said his name.

J.J. was only just beginning to peel himself away from the wall when Lucy reached him. She didn't have to ask a single thing.

"I can't believe you played with Gabe," he said.

Lucy stared. "You're mad at *me*?"

J.J. jammed his hands in his pockets and stalked toward the portable with Lucy on his heels.

"I didn't ask him to play," she said.

"Whatever."

"J.J.!"

He stopped just short of the metal steps that led up to their class-room. "I'm done," he said. "I'm not playing with Januarie or him. You can. I'm not."

Lucy stood at the bottom and watched somebody she didn't know disappear through the door. Had everybody in the world decided to have personality transplants, all at the same time?

The next day, she decided they had. Not only did J.J. sulk at the wall again when recess started, but as Lucy arrived with the ball—just in case they needed two—she saw two female figures flanking Gabe like a pair of giggling bookends.

"Will he let us play?" Veronica said, lip hanging almost onto Gabe's shoulder. "Even if we don't know how?"

Oh, nuh-*uh*.

"I know how," Dusty said. She waggled her head back and forth on her skinny neck. "Well, sort of."

"Nobody else knows how to play either," Gabe said. "'Cept me."

Lucy chomped right down on her lip to keep from yelling, "Hel-lo-o!" She didn't want to sound like the two who were practically drooling on Gabe's shoes and scooping their hair into ponytails as if they were actually going to do something athletic.

"Did you bring more recruits?" Mr. Auggy stopped juggling the ball with his thigh, to Carla and Januarie's squeals, and tipped it to Oscar. He tried to catch it with his chest, and dumped himself straight to the ground on top of it.

"Is that how you do it?" Veronica said.

"I told you they don't know how to play," Gabe said to Dusty.

"To you, Mr. Gabe." Mr. Auggy suddenly had the ball and was kicking it, high, to Gabe. He had no choice but to try to head it, but it bounced off the top and went straight up into nowhere.

"I guess we could all use some lessons," Mr. Auggy said.

Lucy smothered a smile. Okay. She'd give him a point for that.

"You ladies want to play?" Mr. Auggy said.

Lucy felt her face stiffen again as Veronica and Dusty looked at

Gabe and giggled and nodded and basically acted more like they were going out on a date than out on the soccer field.

"A few basics, then," Mr. Auggy said.

While he was starting all over with them, Lucy took her own ball and motioned Oscar, Emanuel, and Carla Rosa over. Januarie stood watching Dusty and Veronica as if Hannah Montana and her sidekick Lilly had just joined the team.

"Let's do that one juggling drill he taught us," she said. "Get in a circle."

"Hey," Gabe said.

"What?" Lucy said. She bounced the ball off her foot once, twice, three times.

"How come your boyfriend isn't playing?"

"I don't have a boyfriend." Lucy sent the ball to Oscar with her thigh.

"You missed," Carla Rosa said.

Gabe trapped it with his foot and bounced it up to his thigh where he kept it going for four, then five bounces. "He's your boyfriend," he said, and made a kissing sound.

"Then those two must be your girlfriends," Lucy said.

The ball came at her. She caught it with her chest and started a juggle with her foot.

"They worship me," Gabe said.

"Excuse me while I go throw up." Lucy passed the ball to Emanuel, but it went past his foot and rolled to where Mr. Auggy was cheering Veronica on in a clumsy dribble.

"Hey, Mr. Aug—!" Oscar put his hands on his stocky hips. "Why can't we just play?"

"You throw in," Mr. Auggy said. "Miss Dusty, you're on my team with Miss Januarie and—" He looked back at the wall, where J.J. was pretending to be asleep. "Mr. E.—you come over to my side."

Why couldn't he take Gabe? Now it was her, Gabe, Oscar, Carla Rosa, and Veronica. She'd rather stick her hand in a blender.

"Choose a goalie!" Mr. Auggy said, over Januarie's whining that she wanted to be on Lucy's team.

"You," Gabe said, pointing to Oscar. "With all that fat, you should be able to block a ball."

Lucy looked at Mr. Auggy, but he was huddled with his team. They came out shouting, and Januarie headed for the cones at the other end of the area. It was pretty clear he didn't expect anybody to get close to making a goal.

"Do you think Gabe is cute?"

Lucy turned to find Veronica's lips almost at her ear. She was twiddling with her blackish ponytail, which hung down one side of her head.

"Huh?" Lucy said.

"Gabe. Do you think he's cute?"

"No. Ick."

Ickety-*ick*.

"Heads up!" Mr. Auggy shouted.

The ball came out of nowhere, and Lucy ran right into it and kept going, that is, until a foot came between hers and she was on the ground spitting out playground dust. Above her, a whistle blew.

"There will be none of that," Mr. Auggy said.

Lucy scrambled up in time to see Dusty blink at him as if he were speaking Chinese.

"Tripping," he said. "That's a foul. The other team gets a direct kick."

"I didn't do it on purpose," Dusty said.

"That's good to hear," Mr. Auggy said. "Because, seriously, if a fight breaks out, the game stops. Who wants that, right?"

"Not me!" Carla Rosa said.

There were some other mumbles. Gabe looked like he would love nothing better.

"I just want to play soccer," Lucy said.

"Then let's do it." Mr. Auggy tossed her the ball. "You know what to do."

After school, Lucy was on her way to Pasco's—thinking it would be the last grilled cheese sandwich before that Inez lady started on Wednesday—when Januarie caught up to her. She looked over both frog-green shoulders before she whispered, "The pizza has—aw man, those things that start with an A. Auggies? No—"

"Hand it over," Lucy said. She held out her palm.

Januarie shook her head. "He got in trouble for taking the pizza menu off the refrigerator last time. He just said to tell you something."

Lucy stopped on the dirt path that lined Granada Street. "What did he say?"

"He said not to tell you until you shared a grilled cheese with me."

"He did not!"

"But I'm hungry!"

"Oh, come on." Lucy curled her fingers around Januarie's backpack strap and pulled her along. "You can have the whole thing. Just tell me what he said."

"Promise?"

It took swearing with spit on her palm and two bites of the sandwich for Januarie to finally spill J.J.'s message.

"He said that Dirty girl—"

"Dirty?" Lucy said. "You mean Dusty?"

"Yeah. He said she did trip you on purpose."

"That didn't take a rocket scientist to figure out." Lucy nodded at the plate. "Take the pickle too."

"I don't like pickles. But could we get ice cream?"

"Not until you tell me the rest."

Januarie stretched her arms up over her head, for no particular reason that Lucy could see, revealing a roll of flesh that she took her time covering back up with her sweater. Lucy felt a little guilty about promising her ice cream, but this was about J.J.

"Well?"

"He said he bets the Hispanic kids are gonna gang up on you."

"How does he know?"

"I don't know." Januarie suddenly leaned forward, squishing her belly against the table. "If they do, I could get back at them for you and nobody would know it was me."

Lucy's jaw dropped so hard she knew she must look like Veronica. "What?" she said.

"I know how. I get away with stuff all the time. J.J. never does." Januarie poked a piece of sandwich into her round mouth and talked as she chewed. "Like right now—he's grounded because he took one of our dad's bicycle wheels out of our yard. I take stuff and nobody knows, ever—"

"J.J. got in trouble for that?" Lucy said.

"Yeah. That's why he's not here."

Lucy sagged against the chair.

"It's only 'til my dad isn't in a bad mood anymore," Januarie said. "I can take care of that too, if you want me to."

"Don't do anything to Dusty or Veronica," Lucy said. "I mean it." She pulled the plate toward her. "No more 'til I've heard it all."

"J.J. said he'll come back and play soccer, but only so Gabe and them can't beat up on you. Now?"

Lucy let her have the sandwich. J.J. really thought they wanted to bust her. What did that mean, exactly? And why? She just didn't get it.

"J.J. hates playing with me," Januarie said. She pulled the last of the melted cheese off the plate with her finger and twirled it like an expert before she stuck it in her mouth. "Do you?"

"Do I what?"

Januarie looked suddenly shy. "Do you hate playing with me?"

Lucy's heart tied itself into a knot. "No," she said, even though she did.

Because for the first time ever, she thought she might know how it felt to be Januarie.

8

Reasons Why I Want to Flush Our Soccer Team
Down the Toilet and Start Over
— Veronica looks at Gabe more than she looks at the ball.
— Dusty only looks at the ball when I have it. To her, a goal is seeing me fall down.
— Carla Rosa tells me every time I fall down that I just fell down.
— Januarie tells Mr. Auggy every time I fall down, even though he can see that I'm on the ground.
— Gabe just passes the ball right over me while I'm lying there.
— Mr. Auggy blows his whistle every seven seconds, when all I want to do is —

"Look at you go."

Lucy spread both hands over her paper. Mr. Auggy squatted beside her.

"I'm not reading over your shoulder," he said in his private-conference-with-a-student voice. "I don't like somebody reading my first drafts either."

"What's a first draft?" Carla Rosa said from across the table. Evidently the private-conference voice wasn't soft enough.

"The sloppy copy," Mr. Auggy said.

Carla Rosa cocked her cap-topped head, sending the big white sequins dancing. "All my copies are sloppy." She went back to engraving her paper.

Lucy slid hers into her lap. It wasn't any kind of copy. It was just a list she was making to transfer into her book later, so Mr. Auggy would think she was doing the assignment in class. They were supposed to be brainstorming about "My Biggest Problem." At the moment, her biggest problem was *him*.

He stood up and tucked his fingers into the back pockets of his jeans so that his elbows stuck out like chicken wings.

"Remember, this is just brainstorming. It doesn't have to be neat—or written in complete sentences. It doesn't even have to make sense to anybody but you."

"That's good," Oscar said. He grinned. "'Cause this don't make no sense at all."

Lucy waited for Mr. Auggy to correct him.

"Everybody have some ideas written down?" he said instead.

They all nodded. Except for J.J., who turned his paper over and pushed it back and forth with his pen. He didn't rock at writing either.

"Now you're gonna make us turn it into them sentence things, right?" Oscar said.

J.J. glared at him. "Quit giving him ideas."

"Yeah," came the echo from Emanuel.

"Actually, no." Mr. Auggy reached under his desk and produced one of the boxes from his first day and dumped it onto the table. Slick magazines slid out, spilling their bright colors into a cheerful pile. He spread them with his hands.

"I'm going to ask you to turn them into pictures."

"Huh?" Oscar said.

"Why don't you shut up and let him explain it?" J.J. said.

Mr. Auggy made a loud buzzing sound that turned all heads in his direction. "'Shut up' is now a taboo word."

"J.J. doesn't know what taboo is," Carla Rosa said.

"Shut up!"

Mr. Auggy buzzed again. "From now on, if you tell a classmate to shut up, it's going to cost you."

Carla Rosa jiggled the sequins as she shook her head. "We don't have any money."

"No, but you do have integrity." Mr. Auggy smiled the small smile. "It's just buried."

"What's—"

"Knowing right from wrong and doing it," Lucy said, "even if you don't want to."

Heads swiveled toward her. "What are you, the dictionary?" Oscar said.

Her face felt like someone was coloring it with a red crayon. Things just seemed to pop out of her without permission lately.

"My dad says that," she muttered.

"Ding-ding-ding!" Mr. Auggy said.

Oscar shook his head. "You are so weird, Mr. Auggy."

"Ding-ding is the opposite of—" Mr. Auggy buzzed again. "When you get buzzed for dissing a classmate, you have to try to perform an act of integrity until you hear—" He made the bell sound.

Oscar twisted to look at J.J. "So do something integrity."

"Shut—"

"Watch it now," Mr. Auggy said.

J.J. slid his backbone down in his chair.

"What's he s'posed to do?" Oscar said.

Lucy closed her eyes. She didn't want to see what was going to happen if Mr. Auggy tried to make J.J. do *anything* right now. J.J. sitting on his own shoulder blades was a signal Lucy knew well.

"He just needs to show who he really is," Mr. Auggy said. "And he doesn't have to do it this minute."

He brushed a hand across J.J.'s shoulder and moved to the magazine table.

"Between now and recess, go through as many of these as you want and pull out pictures that remind you of your problem—the one you were just brainstorming about."

Faces crumpled up, and "Huh?" and "I don't get it," erupted from mouths. Lucy looked at J.J. He tucked his hands into their opposite armpits.

"Just give it a try," Mr. Auggy said.

Lucy went to the table and scooped up two armfuls of magazines. She deposited one stack on the table in front of J.J.

"Just pretend," she whispered to him. "That's what I do."

Then she sat down, flipped open a copy of *Sports Illustrated*, and tore out the first picture she found: a girl with her face all set like she was going to smack somebody. Maybe a lot of somebodies.

She showed it to J.J. He nodded and slowly opened the magazine on the top of his stack.

Mrs. Gomez always just let J.J. sit and do nothing if he wanted to because she was too busy trying to keep Oscar in his seat and make Carla Rosa hush up. But this Mr. Auggy person wasn't leaving anybody alone. And sometimes, J.J. just had to be left alone.

She watched him pull something out of his *Soccer World*, and she let out the breath she didn't know she'd been holding.

"How's it going, Miss Lucy?"

"Fine," Lucy said, and she ripped out a picture of a leg in the air with muscles like bungee cords.

Then she found a soccer ball. A mascot dressed up like a coyote. An Olympic gold medal.

The ripping and tearing and Carla Rosa's questions and Oscar's comments on every single thing he saw filled the room. Mr. Auggy leaned against his desk and nodded like they were all solving the mystery of the comma. Oscar was right. He was very strange.

Lucy found a picture of some fans with their faces painted in their team's colors and carefully eased it out. And then there was one of a girl looking all sweaty and pleased with her sweet self—

When the bell rang for lunch recess, Lucy was surprised.

"Good work, team," Mr. Auggy said.

Lucy looked around. Each person had a clutter of pictures in front of them, even J.J.

But he still hadn't earned a ding-ding-ding, and from the way he hurled the ball onto the field after lunch, he wasn't going to get it anytime soon. It hit a startled Gabe square in the nose before he could even get his neck forward to head it. Mr. Auggy blew loud and long on the whistle.

"That'll be a do-over, Mr. J.J. " He fake-punched J.J.'s shoulder. "Glad you decided to join us, though. You'll be on my team."

J.J. looked at Januarie, lifted his lips, and narrowed his eyes.

"Problem?" Mr. Auggy said.

J.J. shook his head and threw in again. Lucy quickly cut in front of Gabe and ran through the ball, directing it toward Carla Rosa, who let it fall beneath her. She stared at it as if it had just arrived from another planet.

Veronica called out something in Spanish and smacked the ball with the side of her foot. Lucy chased it and passed it back to Carla Rosa, who made a wild, flailing kick, lost her balance, and fell against Dusty.

"Isn't that one of those foul things, Mr. Auggy?" Dusty's cheeks became blotches of purple.

"Hel-lo—yes!" Veronica said.

Lucy couldn't help rolling her eyes. Like Veronica actually knew what a foul was.

"Purely an accident," Mr. Auggy said. "Let's focus on some teamwork."

He held his arms out for them to gather, and Lucy gritted her teeth. Were they ever going to just play?

"Take three minutes in your team," Mr. Auggy said, "and come up with a name for it."

He steered Dusty, Januarie, Emanuel, and J.J. into a circle and squatted with them. The rest stood looking at each other and looking away. It was sort of like being in an elevator with strangers.

Carla Rosa poked Lucy. "What's our name?"

Oscar wiggled his eyebrows. "The Assassins."

"Ewww." Veronica wrinkled her nose and scooted up next to Gabe. "What should we be called?"

Gabe juggled the ball off his head—once, twice, three times. Show off. Lucy waited for it to bounce away so she could—

"The Banditos," he said.

"Cool!" Veronica said.

Lucy rolled her eyes again. "That's almost like Assassins, and you said 'Ewww' to that."

"It sounds better in Spanish." Veronica sent Gabe a sideways smile. "At least when you say it."

Maybe Gabe was right. Maybe she did worship him. Ickety-ick.

"Teddy Bears," Carla Rosa said.

"Lame," Gabe said.

"Bandito Assassins," Oscar said.

"Okay, you know what?" Lucy snatched the ball—her ball—from Gabe and stuck it firmly on her hip. "It should actually sound like a soccer team. Like there's the Atlanta Beat and the Carolina Courage and the Philadelphia Charge—"

"The Los Suenos Lame-o's," Gabe said. "Gimme the ball, Lucy Goosey."

Lucy shoved it behind her back.

"Let's call it Lucy's Gooses," Carla Rosa said.

Gabe tried to slap at the ball. "Not like I really care, but I'm *not* being a goose."

"We better hurry." Carla Rosa pointed to Mr. Auggy's group, which was currently high-fiving.

Lucy pressed her lips together. All the names she'd dreamed up for soccer teams, like Galaxy and Fire and Power, ran and hid in her mind. They were too special to waste on this—this—posse of—

"Posse. Yeah."

Lucy clapped her hand across her mouth. Had she done it again?

Gabe knocked the ball out of her other hand and dribbled it away. Veronica went after him, squealing, silky hair flying out behind her.

"Tell them our name," Mr. Auggy said.

"Los Amigos!" Januarie cried. "What's you guys's?"

"The Posse." Gabe dribbled the ball into the clump of kids, faking from one side to the other so the still-giggling Veronica couldn't get it. "We're the Posse."

"Excellent." Mr. Auggy clapped him on the shoulder. "Now we're starting to think like teams."

Who, Lucy wondered, was he calling "we"?

"Los Amigos?" J.J. said on the way home that afternoon. He jerked the front wheel of his bike back and forth like he wished it was some amigo's head. "They aren't my friends. 'Cept Emanuel, kinda."

"Lucy's *my* friend," Januarie said. "Only—could you slow down?" Her moon face was the color of a setting sun as she skipped beside Lucy's bike.

J.J. stopped at the edge of Second Street, and Lucy pulled up next to him.

"Januarie, go home," he said.

"Why?" She slipped a meaty hand over Lucy's on the handlebar.

"Because if you don't, I'll—"

"Because I need you to be a lookout," Lucy said. "Go see if there's a red truck parked in front of my house."

"Who is it?"

"Just see if it's there, and if it is, watch it until I come." Lucy lowered her voice and tried to look serious. "It's really important."

Januarie nodded solemnly and chugged across the street. Lucy turned back to J.J., brushing off her hands.

"You owe me," she said.

"She's a pain," J.J. said.

"So, what did you want to say that she can't hear?"

J.J. tossed his hair away from his face, but the wind slapped it back again. "I got an idea."

"Ye-ah," Lucy said slowly. "Last time you had an idea, I about got run over by an ATV."

"That's what I'm saying. There's another place we can play soccer—without Gabe or those two girls."

"At school? They'll just find us, and Mr. Auggy will make us play—"

"This is a place we can go after school and on weekends and stuff. Just you and me and Emanuel and Oscar. Maybe Carla Rosa." J.J. rolled his bike a few rotations. "We don't even gotta tell Januarie. Come on—I'll show you."

"Aren't you still grounded?"

J.J. waved that off.

"It's not out by Little Sierra Blanca, is it?" Lucy said.

"No—this is—just come."

Lucy cocked a foot onto a pedal and hopped up on the seat again. She could already feel a hopeful smile taking shape on her face.

"Lucy!" It was a Chihuahua whine. Januarie charged toward them, not even looking as she bustled her round self across the street. "That red truck's there," she said.

"Just go back and keep an eye on it," Lucy said.

"No—there's a lady at your house, and she said to tell you to come in."

"She's not the boss of Lucy," J.J. said.

Januarie planted her hands on her hips and looked like somebody's fed-up mother. "Her dad is. And that lady said Lucy's dad said to come in before she went anywhere." She gave a period-at-the-end-of-a-sentence nod.

"You're lying," J.J. said.

"No, she's not." Lucy turned her wheel toward the house. "It's this nanny my dad hired."

"A babysitter?"

"Don't worry. She'll be gone in two months."

"Two whole months?" J.J. said.

Lucy took off slowly. "Maybe sooner," she said over her shoulder. "I'll catch up in a couple minutes."

"Aw, man." Lucy heard him wheel off away from Granada Street.

"He's gonna get in trouble again," Januarie huffed out as she tried to keep up with Lucy. "He's still on groundation."

Lucy chewed at the inside of her mouth. Okay, so she'd check in with Inez and then go look for J.J. and bring him back. Januarie must not have gotten Mr. Cluck in a good mood again like she said she could.

She leaned her bike against the fence on the outside, so she'd be ready for a quick takeoff, and picked up Mudge, who was in his usual spot behind the century plant.

"Are you gonna let him bite that other girl?" Januarie said.

Lucy backed into the gate, Mudge filling her arms, and pushed it open. "What other girl?"

"The girl that's with that lady that's in your house."

Lucy stopped. "There's a girl in my house?"

Januarie nodded importantly. "She's, like, ten, or maybe eleven—okay, more like twelve. And she's Mexican or something—Dusty Mexican, not Veronica Mexican—and she wears magazine clothes."

"Magazine clothes?"

"Like—"

"Never mind." Lucy pushed the gate to close it. Januarie squeezed her face near the crack.

"Did I do good?" she said. "Spying for you—did I do good?"

"You did awesome. I'll let you do it every single day."

The last thing Lucy saw as she shut the gate was Januarie's very-significant-person smile.

The *first* thing she saw when she opened the back door was a girl in silky blue pants and a white jacket with a stand-up color that announced MORA on the back of it in shiny embroidery. She held a cell phone in one hand while a long finger on the other pointed its white-tipped nail at Inez.

"I am SO not coming here if I can't get reception," she said.

Inez picked the cell phone from the girl's hand like it was a peach on a tree, and dropped it into the pocket of her own red sweater.

"You do not need the reception. Everybody you need to talk to is here." She nodded at Lucy.

The girl twirled around as if she were about to launch into a dance, led by her thick fudge-colored swirl of hair. She faced Lucy with brown eyes so big they barely seemed to fit on her face. She didn't smile. Januarie was right about one thing. Her skin was the shade of coffee-with-cream like Dusty's, not cola-colored like Veronica's.

But she was definitely Hispanic, just like everybody else who looked at Lucy the way this girl was looking at her.

"This is Lucy," Inez said in her flat voice.

"How do you talk to your friends if you don't get reception?" the girl said.

Lucy blinked. "I don't have a cell phone."

"That is just wrong."

"What do you mean it's wrong?" Lucy was glad she was still holding Mudge, because she suddenly wasn't sure what to do with her arms. "What do I need a cell phone for? I see my friends at school."

"How do you even talk to them in school if you can't text message them?"

"Mora." Inez looked at Lucy with her lips pressed together, so that two dimples appeared that Lucy hadn't seen before. The girl had them too. "This is my granddaughter, Mora. She will come with me every day."

"Until my mom comes back from California, which better be soon." Mora picked up a green-and-white polka-dotted purse with orange leather trim from the counter and pawed through it, fingers flying. Lucy had never seen such long fingers, or such perfect fingernails, at least not since the last time Aunt Karen was there.

Mora pulled out an iPod. "It is so boring here."

"Not for long." Inez had the iPod out of Mora's hand and into her other pocket before Lucy even saw her do it.

"I need music!" Mora said.

"You need the manners. Both you sit at the table. I have the snack ready."

Mudge popped his head up and licked his kitty-lips.

"No snack for you," Lucy said to him. She opened the back door to let him go and used it as an excuse to stand on tiptoe and look over the fence. There was no sign of J.J. He could be halfway to Alamogordo by now.

She poked her head inside. "Thanks, but I can't stay. I'm not that hungry anyway."

"Sit," Inez said. "Eat. Your father give the orders."

This woman was such a liar. Dad never gave "orders."

At least he didn't used to.

"Take the jacket off. You are staying."

Lucy closed the door with her foot and felt the kitchen grow strangely small. She let her backpack slide to the floor and took off her coat and trudged to the table, all the while watching Inez glide from the stove to the cupboard to the refrigerator, as if she knew where everything was and had, in fact, put it there herself. As Lucy sank into a chair, she checked to make sure this was the same table where she and Dad had breakfast that morning.

Mora leaned against the counter and stuck one leg up on the other thigh like a flamingo.

"Sit," Inez said.

"I want to eat mine in front of the TV," Mora said. "Oprah's on." She pointed one of her endless fingers at Lucy. "You do have a TV, don't you?"

"Sit," Inez said again.

Mora flounced over to the table and plopped herself next to Lucy. A yowl rose from the chair that sent her flying almost into Lucy's lap.

"You sat on Marmalade!" Lucy dove past Mora and swept a bundle of orange and white stripes into her arms. Marmalade poked his head into Lucy's armpit. Mora thrust a hand against her chest.

"Oh—my—gosh," she said. "Does it bite?"

Lucy couldn't quite get her head to shake. Dad had said she couldn't turn the cats loose on Inez. He didn't say anything about letting granddaughters think—

"He's never actually attacked anybody," Lucy said. "But we keep a very close eye on him—just in case."

Mora yanked back the hand she was stretching toward Marmalade's fur. "In case what?"

"Let's just say he had a very traumatic kittenhood before we got him. If he feels threatened—" Lucy lowered her voice "—well, just watch your fingers."

"Why?"

"And your toes."

"Your father says you like the grilled cheese," Inez said, and set a plate with two golden quesadillas snuggled next to scoops of guacamole on the table. "I told you sit, Mora." She gave her a push into the chair.

"That cat—"

"He'll be fine if you let him sit on your lap," Lucy said.

"But you said—"

"It's either that, or he'll be watching your toes the entire time."

Mora's already-huge eyes got bigger. "Okay," she said.

Lucy placed Marmalade onto Mora's thighs and stroked his back cautiously until he, of course, curled into a contented ball and went back to his purring-wheezing-snoring. Mora pulled her arms above the table and looped her feet back over the rung of the chair.

"Is this okay?" she said.

"That should do it," Lucy said.

She reached for a quesadilla and watched Mora out of the corner of her eye. The girl kept glancing into her lap and curling her fingers into her palms.

"Mom takes me to Starbucks in Alamogordo after school," she said to Inez. "They have free wireless."

"I know," Inez said in a voice like a dial tone.

"Wireless what?" Lucy said.

For a second, Mora seemed to forget about the Terminator Kitty. "Tell me you don't have a computer either."

"I don't have a computer."

Mora flattened her palm against her forehead. "I can't even deal with this another minute."

And definitely not for two months, if Lucy had anything to do with it. She tried to put some hope in that as she sank her teeth into a quesadilla.

9

Inez cooked dinner before she left—pork asada, she called it, and salad and black beans that Lucy refused to admit were the yummiest things she'd ever put in her mouth. She'd seen how many chiles Inez had put in the salsa, though, and she gave that a wide margin at the dinner table. She had to get Dad a glass of water after he slurped some up on a homemade tortilla.

"That's hotter than the surface of the sun," he said when he could speak. "What color is it?"

"Green."

"Ah." He took another gulp out of his glass. "We could use that to clean the drains too."

"She doesn't have to fix dinner."

"She's a good cook."

"We're good cooks," Lucy said.

"This is kind of nice though, isn't it? Just sitting down and relaxing over a meal?"

He looked so much like he wanted the answer to be yes that Lucy said, "Sure."

Dad dabbed at his eyes with a napkin. "I hear you actually got your homework done."

"Dad, she practically chained me to the table. Me and her granddaughter."

Dad chuckled. "You weren't so crazy about Mona?"

"Mora. She thinks we're boring because we don't have a computer and satellite."

"You don't have to be best friends with her."

"That's good because it isn't gonna happen." Lucy suddenly felt squirmy. "Can I be excused?"

"You're done already? I haven't even started. Keep me company." Dad put his hand right on the plate of sopapillas that were oozing butter and sugar, as if he saw them with his nose. "Have some of these—it smells like she stole them from heaven."

"I don't want dessert."

Dad's eyebrows lifted. "Okay, who are you, and what have you done with my daughter?"

"Da-ad."

"Lu-uce."

Lucy picked up her plate. "I'm gonna clean up."

He laughed out loud. "Now I know you're avoiding me. Sit down. Have a—what are they—sopapillas?"

Lucy plunked back into the chair, but she forced herself not to reach for one of the white puffs she'd watched Inez create at the same time she was drilling Mora on her vocabulary words and checking Lucy's fractions.

"Talk to me," Dad said. "Did you like Inez?"

Lucy saw her chance and formed her words carefully. "She told a lie."

Dad's eyebrows went up even farther. "And that was?"

"Are you ready for this?" Lucy got up on one knee. "She said that you said that I had to sit down and have a snack before I did anything else. No, she said you 'ordered' it."

She sank onto her foot and waited for him to call for Inez to be fired immediately. He tapped his plate with his fork.

"I need coordinates," he said.

Lucy leaned across the table. "Meat at twelve o'clock. Beans at three. That evil salsa at six o'clock. Salad at nine. Don't you even care that she lied to me?"

Dad tasted the pork before he answered. "That was the truth. I wanted you to have something more nutritious than Pasco's."

"We don't care about nutritious!"

"We do now."

Lucy poked her finger into a sopapilla.

"I take it you didn't sick Mudge on her."

Marmalade chose that moment to hop onto Dad's lap and twitch his whiskers at his plate. Lucy felt a small twinge of guilt. But only a small one.

"Keep your paws off, pal," Dad said.

Lucy pulled her hand out of the dessert. "I was good. But, Dad, I'm almost always good. Which is why I don't need a nanny. Pasco watches out for me — and Mr. Benitez isn't going to let me get away with anything, and—"

"We've already been there." Dad closed his eyes and eased a forkful of beans into his mouth. "That's heaven too."

"Whatever."

His face grew still, and all trace of angels faded from it. "You promised to give this a fair try for two months."

"One month and twenty-nine days," Lucy said.

The only way she was going to get through it, she told Lollipop later as they snuggled with the big stuffed soccer ball on her bed, was if J.J. really did have a place for them to play without Gabe and the Gigglers. And that bossy Mr. Auggy.

"Okay," she said to the purring face that was nose-to-nose with hers. "So he said I rocked. But he makes us play with people who don't even care about soccer."

She relocated Lolli into the pillows and knelt to look out the window. The lights in J.J.'s house tried to shine through the bedsheets Mrs. Cluck draped across the windows for curtains. J.J.'s, on the second floor, was dingy white, perfect for hand signals if he pointed his flashlight at it.

She watched, chin resting on the tile windowsill, but no message appeared from J.J.'s fingers. And Januarie didn't show up with a pizza delivery. Lucy felt very much all by herself. Dad could probably use some company listening to NPR—

But Lucy pulled the Book of Lists from her underwear drawer and hugged it to her until the next list idea came to her.

WHY I DON'T NEED INEZ

1. Pasco can make my afternoon snack.
2. Mr. Benitez won't let me buy too much junk food.
3. I do enough homework so I don't flunk, and I'm going to be a soccer player anyway, not a doctor or something.
4. I can cook dinner as good as she can. Okay, almost. All right, maybe not, but Dad never complained.
5. I can do about anything a grown-up can do except drive a car or spit in the gutter, which I think is gross anyway (the spitting, not the driving).
6. The only thing good is that she's better than living with Aunt Karen.

Number Six made it easier to go to sleep.

J.J. just grunted the next morning when Lucy met him and Januarie outside the gate. He wasn't on his bike, so Lucy walked hers. Januarie chattered away, but Lucy studied the side of J.J.'s face. It was stiff as the frost inside Dad and Lucy's freezer—the one Aunt Karen always said they needed to replace with the kind that defrosted itself.

Finally, when Januarie ran off to join the third-graders, Lucy said to J.J., "Well?"

"What?"

"New place to play today?"

"No. Saturday."

"Why?"

"Januarie and her big mouth."

"Grounded?"

Grunt.

The warning bell rang, and Lucy hurried into the sixth-grade wing to put her soccer ball into her cubby. Late as it was, the hallway was empty, except for one person. Lucy groaned inside when Dusty turned from her perfect lineup of color-coded notebooks.

"Hi," she said.

Lucy shoved a nest of papers into the back of her cubby and pushed her soccer ball carefully in front of it. What was Dusty up to now?

"Hi," Lucy said into her cubby hole.

"So — who was that lady that was with you at church that one day?"

"My aunt. You want her?"

"Huh?" Dusty said.

Lucy set her backpack on the floor so she could pull out the books she needed, and Dusty came to stand above her.

"Where did you learn to play soccer?" she said. "You play pretty good, for a white girl."

Lucy stood up, backpack in hand. "For a white girl? Haven't you ever heard of Mia Hamm — Julie Foudy — Michelle Akers?"

Dusty wrinkled her nose. "What smells?"

"Not me." Lucy whirled to head the other way and nearly ran into Mrs. Nunez, the principal. She was so close that Lucy could see the line she'd drawn around her lips to fill her orange lipstick in. Lucy turned, jammed her lunch into her cubby, and tried to get to the door without looking at her again.

"You need to work on that cubby, Lucy," Mrs. Nunez said in that voice that always sounded like she was talking to one of the kindergartners.

"The bell's about to ring," Lucy told her, as she hurried down the hall.

"You could take a few lessons from Dusty."

Lucy pushed the door open and imagined Dusty looking like she'd just scored a goal. Yeah, they definitely had to get away from her. Saturday couldn't come fast enough.

There were two more days of recess soccer to get through — with the usual giggling and tripping and whistle-blowing that drove Lucy nuts.

And two afternoons doing homework over beany burritos while Mora told Lucy she was practically a cavegirl because she somehow survived without the Internet and a camera phone. And Mr. Auggy's assignment, which involved putting all her pictures on a piece of poster board in a big puzzle called a collage, which didn't have anything to do with English, as far as Lucy could tell. But as long as it kept her from having to make a fool of herself trying to write a paragraph, she was willing to cut and arrange and glue all period.

J.J. still didn't earn a ding-ding-ding, but Lucy was ready to give him one herself when Saturday morning finally came. He was waiting outside the gate when she finished her litter box emptying chore — the one thing Inez refused to do — blue eyes glowing warm in spite of the bite of the New-Mexico-winter air.

"Hurry," he said. "Before she gets up."

Januarie-less, they biked down Granada Street, past the church and Mr. Benitez's store and his house with the now-naked rose bushes napping and waiting for spring. Pasco's wasn't even open yet, and neither was Claudia's House of Flowers with its Valentine boxes in the windows or Gloria's Casa Bonita with the shades drawn on the hair dryers and rows of nail polish bottles which Lucy didn't want to see anyway. She liked the town early in the morning, before it woke up and Mr. Benitez swept his sidewalk and glared at Pasco, who didn't sweep his, and Claudia complained that the smells of Gloria's perms were wilting her orchids, and Mr. Esparza just stood in his doorway looking disappointed because no one ever came to see the dusty pottery.

But when J.J. biked across Highway 54, she stopped at the corner and called out to him, "I don't know if I'm allowed this far."

"Just a little farther," he said over his shoulder.

A car swished by and then left only the sound of the cottonwood leaves chattering under their breath. Only because an almost-smile teased at the corners of J.J.'s mouth did Lucy follow him across and past a pistachio grove and onto a gravelly road she'd never been on, tasting the dust he spewed out from his tires. When they rounded a sharp curve, she was glad she had.

At first, she saw a chain-link fence with dents where cars had missed the road and bounced off of it. But that disappeared at the sight of a long, long brown-grassy rectangle with a rusty metal frame and tattered net at either end. On one side was a set of bleachers, empty but expectant, and on the other was a cement block building with a boarded-up window that begged to be opened for refreshments.

"This is a for-real soccer field," Lucy said.

"I know." J.J. pointed to a sign, taller than they were, that stood as if one leg were shorter than the other. The letters were chipped and faded, but Lucy could still read what was left of "LOS SUENOS SOCCER FIELD."

"It was worth my dad—" J.J. stopped.

"Grounding you," Lucy said.

"Nobody owns this—I asked Pasco."

"He knows everything about the whole town."

"Duh." J.J. pulled his front wheel up. He didn't look at Lucy.

"Then I say we take it over," Lucy said.

"Yeah?"

"It's like a sin to let it just sit here. Look at it." Lucy got off her bike and let it fall against the battered fence. "It's begging us to bring it back to life."

J.J. didn't answer. But he did smile, an actual smile.

He said he wanted to round up Emanuel and Oscar immediately and start playing. But inside the fence, Lucy took one step across a now almost-invisible painted sideline on the weeds and heard a crunch. The remains of a brown bottle smashed under her foot.

"We have to clean up," she said, hands on hips. "This place is a mess."

It felt good to say that, made it feel like they were grown-ups surveying a room little kids had trashed. Somebody obviously didn't know what a sacred space a soccer field was, and they did.

"First, we get it in shape," she said. "Then, we play."

They spent the rest of the day picking up crumpled wrappers and broken glass and withered plastic bottles. J.J. went on his bike to the Mini-Mart on Highway 54 at noon and brought back two Twinkies and a 16-ounce Coke for them to share for lunch.

Lucy was too excited to take more than a bite and a sip. The more she collected into a pile for future trash bags, the more there seemed to be to pick up. But all she had to do was look behind her at the cleared dirt, litter-less and waiting, and she could almost hear the smack of a soccer ball against a foot and someone calling, "To me, Lucy!"

They stripped off their jackets and sweatshirts after lunch, the way you could sometimes on a New Mexico winter afternoon, and let the sun soak into their T-shirts as they yanked out the biggest weeds and clumps of sagebrush.

"Somebody will definitely trip over those in pursuit of a goal," Lucy said.

J.J. flipped his hair back. "Sometimes you talk like your dad. Like, smart."

"He's a radio announcer," Lucy said. "He has to talk smart."

She flung a hunk of sagebrush onto the pile and felt comfortable with J.J. He was really talking to her. "I never hear your dad talk that much," she said.

"Me neither," J.J. said. "I don't listen to him that much."

"Is that why you get grounded a lot?"

J.J. grunted. End of conversation.

Lucy had that all-by-herself feeling again. She pulled the last of the big weeds and wiped off the falling-down sign with the bottom of her T-shirt and kicked a clump of dirt from the bottom row of bleachers. Then she felt better.

The sun was settling down behind the mountains when Lucy untied her sweatshirt from around her waist and pulled it on and retracted her hands into the sleeves. The goal frames made shadows across the clear space of dirt.

"We could play tomorrow," she said.

J.J. walked along the bench behind her, arms out like he was on a tightrope. "What time?"

"After church. And after lunch. And after I go to the station with my dad."

"Too late."

He was right. It would be 2:00 by then, and that would only leave a couple of hours of sunlight and warmness. But Sunday was her day with Dad.

"I'll get Emanuel and Oscar," J.J. said. "And Carla Rosa. Januarie's not coming though." His voice went up and away like it did when he was really into something. She hadn't heard it that way in a while.

"I'll hurry after I get done with stuff." Lucy swiveled around and looked up a long leg. "Don't start without me though."

"'Kay."

"Swear?"

"Dude, I swear."

They got their bikes then and put on their jackets and headed down the gravel road that, to Lucy, was now the best street in town, even without nut trees and rose bushes and sleepy shops. At the curve, J.J. stopped, and so did Lucy. He shaded his eyes with his hand as he twisted back toward their soccer field.

"Pretty cool," he said.

"Very cool," Lucy said.

Reverend Servidio's sermon the next day was the longest ever. Maybe because he talked about Jesus healing a blind man, which Jesus seemed to do about sixty times in the Bible and which was Lucy's most un-favorite story of all of them, since Jesus hadn't chosen to heal Dad. Hello.

Besides, she had things to do. Reverend Servidio went on for so long about whose fault it was that the guy was blind in the first place that Lucy thought she would stand up and shout, "What dif-ference does it make? He can't see — there's your problem!" Dad put his hand on her arm, which made her wonder if she'd actually said it out loud.

"So what was up with you in church?" he said when they were settled at their usual table at Pasco's with a pile of chicken nachos. "You haven't squirmed that much since you were four."

"He just kept saying the same thing over and over." Lucy caught some melted cheese with her finger and twirled it around. "I got it the first five times he said it."

"And what exactly did he say, do you think?" Dad got his smooth-faced, we're-about-to-have-a-good-conversation look.

Lucy opened her mouth, but nothing came out. She stuffed a hunk of tortilla chip and chicken into it.

"Pretty deep," Dad said with a chuckle.

"It was something about Jesus spitting in some dirt and putting it on a blind guy's eyes to make him see, which doesn't work now, so what does that have to do with me?" She glanced at her watch. It was already 11:15. J.J. probably had the team at the field by now.

"Lucy."

She looked up at her father. His face was sober.

"You don't see what Jesus' healing love has to do with you? Seriously?"

"Dad, I'm eleven. I don't exactly need any healing." She didn't mention that he did, and so far, Jesus hadn't shown up with it. "You done?" she said.

"Done? He's barely started." Pasco was standing at the table, giving his automatic smile. "First you ditch my grilled cheese—now you're boycotting my nachos." He smiled again, that quick thing he did at the end of every sentence. "I'm deeply wounded."

"Not to worry, Pasco," Dad said. He didn't raise his face. "We'll finish it up."

Pasco gave Dad a long look before he left their table. Lucy didn't blame him. Dad was being very un-Dad at the moment. His voice was serious, like they were talking in the bank.

"The Bible," he said. "You don't see anything in there that you can use in your life?"

"I think I'm supposed to say 'yes, I do'." Maybe if she did, she could move this along.

"But you don't?"

"I will when I grow up," Lucy said.

"And right now you're in a rush to get off somewhere."

She stole another glance at her watch. If she could hurry him to the radio station, they could still do their thing, and she wouldn't hurt his feelings —

"Maybe your Aunt Karen is right about one thing," Dad said. "I've neglected a lot more than I thought with you."

Lucy's backbone went prickly, and suddenly she didn't care about his feelings so much. "I want to go play soccer," she said. "J.J. found a real field —"

"Where?"

"Over across 54. We got it all cleared off, and I CAN get across the highway without getting run over by a truck because I'm not a stupid little baby —"

"Whoa, whoa." Dad put up his hand and darted his eyes all over the tabletop. "Where's all this coming from?"

It's coming from you treating me like a bad kid when I didn't even do anything wrong, she thought. But for once, she kept her lips pressed together so it wouldn't come out where he could know it.

"Sorry," she muttered.

There was a silence, like a stranger had suddenly sat down at the table with them. Lucy didn't want to be there with it.

"Okay," Dad said finally. "Go play soccer."

"After we go to the station."

"Go now. I'll be fine."

Lucy looked hard at him. There was no pointy anger around his nose, no sharpness to his mouth.

"I'll be back before dark," she said.

"Take care of what I love," he said.

Lucy ran all the way down Granada Street and collected her bike and her soccer ball and raced across the highway with her mind tumbling over itself. Only when she saw them — her team — all lined up on the bottom row of the bleachers, waiting, did it fall into a soft, good place.

"Hey!" she said. "Let's play soccer!"

10

One hundred yards long and fifty yards wide. It was so big, even Lucy couldn't kick the ball far enough for them to use the whole thing.

It was enough space to shout across and not be heard. To swing a kicking leg for a long instep pass or take a running start and slide into the ball. There was room to play, and no one was blowing a whistle to stop them every seven seconds.

Even Carla Rosa could pass the ball a couple of inches—and Emanuel dribbled without getting tangled up in his long legs—and Oscar threw himself in front of the goal like he was trying to stop a train.

"This is the best, the best, the BEST!" Lucy cried—just after she smacked the ball past Oscar's fingertips and sent it right into the ragged net. It didn't matter that the frame leaned like the old men at Pasco's, or that there was no one but Oscar to try to keep her from scoring a goal. She did it, on a real soccer field, for the very first time. A hundred people cheering in the bleachers couldn't have made it better.

Unless her mom had been there. Lucy turned for a second toward the team bench and imagined her, the tip of her nose like a cranberry from the cold, Lucy-blonde hair whipping in the wind—

"Aw, man—what are you doing here?"

J.J.'s voice brought Lucy straight back to now. Had Gabe and the Gigglers found them?

"I followed you," Januarie said. She looked small on the sideline of the big field, swallowed in the greenness of her scarf and hat and gloves, with only a scarlet face showing.

"I been waiting under there." She pointed a wooly finger toward the ramshackle bleachers.

The others gathered around her.

"Guess what?" Carla Rosa said. "You have snot coming out of your nose. It's frozen."

"Waiting for what?" J.J. shook his head. "Never mind. Just go home."

"If you make me go home, I'll tell Daddy where you are."

Everyone's heads swiveled from Januarie to J.J. and back again. Lucy felt her middle sag. J.J.'s dad didn't know where he was? That never turned out to be a good thing.

"I was waiting for Lucy," Januarie said.

"Why?" J.J. said.

"'Cause I knew she would let me play."

"You don't know nothin' about soccer," Oscar said. "At least we been learnin' from Mr. Auggy."

"I have too!" Januarie's whine wound up. "Haven't I, Lucy?"

"Um, not so anybody could tell," Lucy said.

The round face fell and took Lucy's heart with it. But they'd just gotten a real field. They had a chance to be actual players now. Januarie could mess it all up.

"Go home," J.J. said. "Tell Dad—I don't care—just get out."

"Guess what," Carla Rosa said. "She's gonna cry."

Januarie's face indeed puckered.

"See. She's crying."

"There ain't no cryin' in soccer," Oscar said.

"You don't see me cryin'," Emanuel put in.

Okay, if Emanuel was talking, this team really was worth saving. Lucy had an idea.

"We should let Januarie try out for the team," she said.

"Try out?" J.J. said.

Carla Rosa crunched her forehead. "We didn't have to—"

"New members do," Lucy said. "Januarie, you get between J.J. and me out on the field. We'll pass the ball back and forth to each other. If you can get it away from us before we get to the goal, you can be on the team."

"And you can't use your hands," Carla Rosa said.

"Then how am I supposed to get it?" Januarie said.

Oscar gave a loud "Ha." "I told you you didn't know nothin' about soccer."

"If you can't get it away from us," Lucy said, "you have to go home and not tell your dad where we are."

"How come your dad can't know you're here?" Carla Rosa said.

"Because," J.J. said.

"Because why?"

"Shut up!"

Oscar buzzed. Then J.J. jumped him. Then Carla Rosa hopped up and down and waved her hands and said, "Don't fight. I hate fighting!" and went purple in the face.

Once Lucy got that all sorted out and everyone standing up, she turned to Januarie. "There's one other choice."

Januarie managed to squeeze a "What?" from her pouted-out mouth.

"You agree not to play, and be my personal assistant instead. I need somebody to bring me water and wipe the sweat off me—"

"What sweat?" Carla Rosa said. "Guess what? It's freezing."

Januarie stomped her foot, nearly taking out Emanuel's toe. "No. I want to play. Mr. Auggy lets me."

"He's not here. This is our team." J.J. jammed a thumb into his chest. "Ours." He glared at Lucy. "Don't even let her try out."

"It's only fair," Lucy said, although she knew it really wasn't. There was no way Januarie was going to get the ball away from them. Not with all the tricks Mr. Auggy had taught them that Januarie never got because she was, well, Januarie.

It turned out to be true. Lucy used a long, lofted pass to get the ball to J.J. over Januarie's head. When she ran for it, he took a few dribbles and called "Wall!" to Lucy. As the ball came toward her, Lucy trapped it while J.J. ran around Januarie. Feeling like Mia Hamm herself, Lucy passed it back to him. By then they were so far ahead of the poor kid that she sat down on the dirt and burst into tears.

"Not fair!" she wailed.

Lucy trotted over to her and put a hand down to pull her up. Januarie turned her streaked face away and continued to blubber.

"Cry all you want," J.J. said, "but you gotta get off the field. Go home—and remember—you can't tell—"

"I *am* telling!" Januarie struggled to her knees and then her feet. "I'm telling that you—" She thrust a hand toward Lucy. "—won't let me play because you think I'm too fat."

"Huh?" Lucy said. She swiped her bangs back with her hand. "I never said you were fat."

"Yes, you did. They told me you did. And I didn't believe them, but now I do."

Carla Rosa was right about one thing. There was a lot of stuff coming out of Januarie's nose. And the crying screech made Lucy wish for the Chihuahua whine.

It howled out of Januarie as she stomped off the field and down the road. That's when it occurred to Lucy that Januarie had walked all that way to be with them—and that she was going to cross the highway by herself.

And that she really was going to tell J.J.'s dad.

"We better go after her," Lucy said.

"I hate that kid," J.J. said.

"We'll fix it somehow. But if she gets run over by a car—"

"Guess what," Carla Rosa said in her matter-of-fact voice. "She'll get killed."

J.J. muttered something about that being fine with him. Lucy herself would have at least let Mudge loose on her if he'd been there.

They caught up with Januarie at a bent sign that seemed to have once said SLOW CHILDREN PLAYING. She was sitting against it, huffing and puffing, and the crying started again as soon as she saw them. Lucy hushed her up with a Jolly Rancher she found in the pocket of her sweatshirt and a promise that Januarie could spy for her the next day—just as soon as Lucy needed her.

"I still want to play," Januarie said stubbornly when Lucy said good-bye to them at the gate.

"You get to play at school," Lucy said. "And as soon as you get good enough, you can join our team."

J.J. grunted. But Lucy found herself warming up. "See, our team is secret. And so is the field. That's what makes it special. It's not an honor to belong to it if you don't have to work to get in on the secret."

Januarie wiped her nose on her sleeve. Fortunately, the jacket was the same color as what came out.

"It's so special," Lucy said, "Gabe and Veronica and Dusty aren't even good enough to be on it yet."

That was actually not true, Lucy knew. But "good" could mean a lot of things. As in good sport, which they so were not.

"If you tell," J.J. said, "that ruins the whole team, and you'll never get to be on it." He glanced at Lucy, who nodded at him.

Januarie looked as if she were eating his words with her eyes, tasting them for truth. "But when I'm good enough, I will be on it," she said. "Right? You said that."

"Yes," Lucy said quickly, before J.J. could point out that the chances of her ever being good enough didn't exist.

"All right then." Januarie drew her finger across her lips and pressed them together so tightly they turned white.

"What was that?" J.J. said.

"I'm zipping my lips," she said, barely opening them.

J.J. grunted again. "That's the smartest thing you ever said."

Dad was sitting in his special cracked-leather chair in the almost-dark living room when Lucy got inside with an armful of Mudge. Marmalade was snoozing on his lap, and Lollipop sat in a curl on the tile in front of the fireplace, face to the flames like she was trying to get a tan. Artemis Hamm crouched with her whiskers to the corner near what Lucy and Dad called the Napping Couch, where you could nap, as opposed to the Sitting Couch, where you could sit. Lucy suddenly wanted to be with Dad again.

"Artemis Hamm is stalking something," she said.

"I hope it's not alive," Dad said. "You have Mudge with you."

"How do you always know?"

"Because Marmalade's heart rate just went up about twenty notches."

Mudge gave a low growl and leaped out of Lucy's arms, straight for Lolli. She rolled under the Sitting Couch, so Mudge tore after Artemis, who hissed and spit—and then retreated to the windowsill.

"Outside with him," Dad said in his dry voice.

Lucy scooped Mudge up and shut him in the kitchen with his food, which she could hear him eating between grumbles.

"Why is he so evil to the other cats?" Lucy said as she perched on the arm of Dad's chair.

"That's his job," Dad said. "They all have their jobs."

"Artemis's is definitely to hunt. Tell me about when she first came." She'd heard it six thousand times, of course, but happy as she was with the day, she was in the mood to hear it again.

"She just strolled up to our back door one day with a snake in her mouth."

"Dead, right?"

"Yes, or your mother would never have let her in. She wanted to exchange it for food." He gave his special chuckle. "You have to be good to catch a snake, which is why Mommy named her Artemis."

"The goddess of the hunt in mythology," Lucy said. "But I got to give her the middle name Hamm."

"Your mother was so proud that you knew about Mia Hamm. Of course, she was telling you about female soccer players when other moms were talking to their daughters about fairy princesses."

Lucy shook her ponytail. "Artemis Cinderella wouldn't be a very good name."

"Doesn't exactly roll off the tongue. Artemis Hamm. Did you ever notice how she won't come running for her food if you don't say the whole thing?"

"Sometimes she doesn't even come then if she already ate something. Something gross. Like a kangaroo rat. Those things are nasty."

"Like you said, that's just her job." Dad eased his hands down Marmalade's sides. "Marmalade's is to sleep, and Lollipop's is to cuddle with you."

Lucy peered under the Sitting Couch where Lollipop was still puffed up. Her eyes were almost as big as Mora's at the moment.

"She's mad at me because I brought Mudge in. What's his job?"

"To be grouchy. That's why his name is Curmudgeon, a grumpy old man." Dad tilted his head back. "Am I turning into a curmudgeon, champ?"

Lucy didn't answer right away, and Dad laughed. "I guess that answers that question."

"You're not grumpy," Lucy said slowly. "Like you didn't care that I was gone all day playing soccer." She slid down from the arm of the chair so she could get comfortable on the thick, nappy rug. "It was awesome, Dad. We all played so good on that big field."

"Excellent." Dad said.

And then he waited. He was never fooled by a Lucy fast change-of-subject. Lucy dug her fingers into the rug. You're not grumpy, Dad, she wanted to say. But—

The phone rang on the table next to him, and Artemis shot off the windowsill and pounced on it. That cat would hunt anything. Lucy laughed, until she heard Dad say, "Karen, hi."

So much for the happy mood.

Lucy started to crawl across the floor, but Dad stopped her with his foot. She flattened her face on the rug and closed her eyes. Maybe if she pretended to be asleep she wouldn't have to talk to her.

"We're good," Dad was saying. "Yeah, that's working out fine. She has a granddaughter Lucy's age."

There was a long pause in which Lucy could imagine Aunt Karen asking if this granddaughter was a good influence on her. Like, did she wear pink and look in the mirror every minute?

"She's formed her own soccer team," Dad said.

Lucy opened her eyes. His voice sounded kind of proud.

"No, it's just a bunch of kids from school—"

Lucy sat up and tugged at Dad's pant leg. "Don't tell her," she whispered.

Dad felt for the top of her head and tugged at her ponytail. "Really? Well, she's pretty excited about this one—"

Another long pause. Lucy flopped back to the rug and propped her feet on the arm of the chair. Aunt Karen was probably telling Dad Lucy's team should wear pink uniforms.

Uniforms. She hadn't thought about that yet. What should their colors be? Something very cool, but not too flashy. Blue, maybe, and red. Blue pants and red shirts—

Dad nudged her with the phone. "She wants to talk to you."

Lucy made a face.

"Be nice," Dad said.

Sometimes she was just sure he only pretended to be blind. With a hidden sigh, Lucy put the phone to her ear.

"Hi, Aunt Karen."

"Okay, here's the deal," Aunt Karen said, instead of "hello." It was like she was always too busy for friendly. "They have a great community soccer program here in El Paso. My company sponsors a team."

In spite of herself, Lucy said, "What does that mean, they sponsor it?"

"We pay for their uniforms—"

Here we go.

"—provide money for them to travel when they win championships, and they have the company name on the back of their shirts."

Lucy couldn't imagine anything but her players' own names on their shirts. Maybe they could all have soccer nicknames. Not Lucy Goosey for sure—

"I'm going to look into it." Aunt Karen's voice was business crisp.

"Look into what?" Lucy said.

"The soccer program. If it's as good as I think it is, I'm going to bring you down here to see some games, introduce you to the coaches. You know, show you real soccer." Aunt Karen actually took a breath. "You aren't going to get it in that town."

"That town," "this house." It was like she was saying, "those germs."

"Okay, well, I gotta go," Lucy said. "We have to start supper."

"I thought the nanny was doing that."

"It's Sunday."

"Oh. Right."

"Here's Dad," Lucy said, and handed off the phone.

How did Aunt Karen know Inez was cooking the dinners? Had that been her idea?

Lucy gathered herself up off the rug and headed for the kitchen. They were having their Sunday Night Special — macaroni and cheese out of a box, which she knew how to make by herself. There were some things that weren't Aunt Karen's idea. Sunday night supper and her soccer team were two of them.

And she was going to keep it that way.

11

Oh, nuh-*uh.*

Inez had *not* just said they were going to do *Bible* study.

But the fact that on Tuesday afternoon two worn-out-looking leather Bibles appeared on the kitchen table next to the quesadillas was proof that she had.

So was the bug-eyed, open-mouthed expression on Mora's face. She looked as if Inez had just suggested the three of them get up a game of basketball in the middle of Highway 54.

Lucy would have preferred that. At least it would put her closer to the soccer field, where J.J. and the rest of the team were probably practicing their passing like she'd told them to do until she got there.

As she snuck a glance up at the clock over the sink, she caught a glimpse of a round face peeking in the window of the back door. Even Lucy's little spy was in place, ready to alert her should Gabe or the Gigglers come on the scene.

"One half hour," Inez said.

Mora flung her hands in the air. "I'll miss *Oprah!*"

"I do not like you watching that."

"Well, I would watch Hannah Montana, but she—" Mora flapped a finger toward Lucy. "—doesn't have cable."

"It's not like that's a crime." Lucy turned to Inez. "I ate. I did my homework. How come I have to spend another thirty minutes doing Bible study?" She fanned the pages of one of the books. "I go to church. I already know about the Bible."

Inez made her eyes go level like her straight-cut bangs. "Not so much, your father says."

Lucy stopped fanning. "My dad said that?"

"He says do the Bible study, so we do the Bible study." Inez pointed to the plate. "Are we finished here?"

Lucy nodded glumly. When Inez had her back to them, Mora leaned across the table, eyes still bulging like a frog's.

"The man is blind," she whispered. "Can't you just tell him you read it?"

"He's blind, not stupid," Lucy said.

Besides, he would quiz her over supper if she knew him—which she wasn't entirely sure she did at the moment.

Inez pulled a sleeping Marmalade off the third chair and deposited him in an empty laundry basket on the dryer. Mora stared.

"He mostly goes for younger women," Lucy said quickly. The lie didn't feel like it fit, but, then, what did?

Inez pushed a Bible toward each of them. Her hands, usually so swift in their busyness, were gentle on the covers, as if she were handling china tea cups.

"Open," she said. "Book of Ruth."

"I don't see why I have to do this just because her dad says she has to." Mora's fingers flew to punctuate every pronoun.

Lucy was momentarily fascinated. She'd never seen anyone talk with her hands so much. But Lucy's eyes went again to the back door, where Januarie was giving hand signals of her own.

"I just need to do one thing," Lucy said to Inez.

"You need to open to the book of Ruth."

"As soon as I—"

"Old Testament. Right after the Judges, just before the First Samuel."

"Huh?" Mora said.

As Inez opened Mora's Bible for her, Lucy leaned back and stretched her arms over her head. Closing and opening her hands, she flashed ten fingers three times and hoped Januarie would get it.

Januarie's brow furrowed into Tootsie Rolls. She obviously didn't.

Lucy pointed to her chest, made her fingers walk and do a kick, and then pointed at her watch. Januarie looked as if she were trying to understand brain surgery, but she finally nodded and disappeared from the window. Lucy listened to the gate opening and closing and heard Mudge meow. If Januarie got even half that message to J.J., it would be a miracle.

"It's on page 289." Mora tapped Lucy's Bible with a long, busy finger.

"Like you knew that," Lucy said.

She fumbled through the pages, thin as the skin of an onion, and located a section with "The Book of Ruth" printed at the top in letters with pictures wound around them. Pretty—but for Pete's sake, they weren't in Sunday school.

"Read," Inez said.

Lucy stumbled silently through the first part of the first sentence.

In the days when the judges ruled, there was a famine in the land, and a man from Bethlehem in Judah—

Lucy felt a yawn coming on. If the Bible didn't sound like some history professor wrote it, people might actually read it.

—together with his wife and two sons, went to live for a while in the country of Moab.

Lucy rubbed her eyes. "How much of this do we have to read?"

"Mora," Inez said, "you read out loud."

Lucy groaned inside. Out-loud reading was like a funeral in her class.

"The man's name was E-lim-e-lech," Mora read—pretty smoothly—"his wife's name Naomi, and the names of the two sons were—" She lifted her big eyes. "Who wrote this stuff?"

"Dr. Seuss," Lucy muttered.

Mora gave a soft snort.

"Close the Bibles," Inez said.

"We're done?" Lucy said hopefully.

"We have not yet started." Inez folded her hands in front of her on the tabletop, fingers in a tidy stack. "Listen," she said.

Lucy propped her elbows on the table and dropped her chin into her hands. Mora picked up a pen and fiddled with it.

"You ever been hungry?" Inez said.

"Yes," Mora said, "for a biscotti at Starbucks to dunk in my mocha."

"Sorry?" Lucy said. "I don't speak Starbucks."

"Very hungry," Inez said. "So hungry your stomach it feels like it eats itself because it has nothing else."

"Ewwww!" Mora said.

Lucy was quiet. Dad talked sometimes about the starving children in the places he and Mom had worked. But what did this have to do with anything?

"Think of day after day of that," Inez said.

"No thanks," Mora said.

Lucy wished she would hush up so they could get this over with.

"It is that way in Bethlehem, so Senor Elimelech, he takes his family—his esposa, Naomi, and their two *hijos*—to Moab."

"It didn't say 'Senor'." Mora made quotation marks with her fingers when she said "Senor."

"I see my world in there when I read the Bible." Inez ran the side of her hand down the page in front of her. "You will learn that senora Naomi has to leave everything she knows—her family, her amigas, her church."

Lucy pulled a foot up under her and sat on it. Okay—maybe if she learned it today, they could be done with this. All right—Naomi leaving everything—that might be what it would be like if she had to go live with Aunt Karen. Lucy sighed. That wasn't going to happen, so why even think about it?

"More worse," Inez was saying, "Senor Elimelech dies and leaves her with the two sons. It is not so easy raising children alone."

Okay, okay, so that was like Dad raising her. Which he was doing just fine until Aunt Karen made him think he wasn't doing a good job, and now here she was doing Bible study with a lady who obviously—

"They marry women from Moab," Inez said. "And then, the hijos died too." She shook her head as if the two hijos were relatives of hers. "Naomi decides she will go back to Bethlehem where her family might provide for her."

"Why didn't she just get a job?" Mora said.

"Women did not get jobs in those days."

Then what did this have to do with them? Lucy looked at the clock and pictured Januarie announcing who knew what to her team.

"Naomi's two daughters-in-law—Ruth and Orpah—"

"Oprah?" Mora said. She actually looked interested for a second.

"Or-pah," Inez said, stretching her lips like a rubber band. "But forget her. She does not go to Bethlehem with Naomi. Only Ruth."

"That's why the story's named after her," Lucy said. "I get it. Can I go now?"

Inez didn't even look at her. "Naomi tells them stay in Moab with their own people, but Ruth refuses to leave her. She says wherever Naomi goes, that was where she will go too."

Inez leaned in as if she were about to share a secret. Mora leaned with her.

"Ruth says Naomi's people will be her people, and Naomi's God will be her God."

Mora looked blankly at Lucy and then at her grandmother. "That's it? That's the big deal?"

Inez scowled. "It was the great thing to give up her future to be loyal to the old woman. She will be an outsider in Bethlehem. She will look different, and they will ignore her, maybe even hate her."

A picture of Veronica and Dusty looking right through her, and another picture of Gabe sneering at J.J., popped up in Lucy's mind. She could almost hear Januarie telling her, "J.J. says they're out to get you." Too bad she couldn't tell Inez she got that part and pass this whatever-it-was test so she could go play soccer. Still, she had to ask—

"So what happened when she got to Bethlehem? Were they evil to her?"

Mora glared at her. "If you ask questions, we'll be here for decades," she said between her teeth.

"We are finished for now." Inez pulled the Bibles back to her and ran her hands over their covers as if to wipe away Mora and Lucy's disdain.

"Do we have to do this every day?" Mora said.

"One time a week," Inez said.

Mora looked at the ceiling, hands together as if she were praying, and said, "Thank you."

"Mora." Inez's voice pricked Lucy to attention. "You will not mock the Lord."

"I don't even know what that means."

"Pray with your heart. Never pretend."

"Whatever."

"Mora."

"Okay, okay. Sorry."

Lucy wasn't sure she was. She calculated—one month and three weeks—that was seven more times they'd have to do this.

"You may watch the television, Mora," Inez said, "while I cook the supper."

Mora shot to the living room. Lucy reached for her jacket.

"You are going somewhere?" Inez said.

"Yes."

"How far?"

"To the soccer field. It's just—"

"I do not know any soccer field in Los Suenos."

Lucy jammed her arms into her jacket sleeves. "It's kind of new."

"Where is it?"

"My dad lets me go—"

Inez turned to the cutting board. "Where?"

"On the west side." Lucy jerked at her zipper. "Across the highway."

She waited while Inez chopped a tomato into obedient cubes.

"I have to check with Senor Rooney," she said finally. "Not today."

"He totally lets me!"

"I totally do not. Not until I talk to him."

Lucy marched to the phone on the wall.

"I will speak with him when he comes home," Inez said.

Lucy snatched up her backpack and stomped to the hallway. Inez could talk to him—but *she* might never speak to her father again.

She did, of course. The minute he came through the door, Lucy squared off with him in the kitchen.

"Please tell Inez I can go to the soccer field after I finish the fifty million other things I have to do after school now."

Dad unzipped his jacket. "Watch your tone, Luce."

What other tone was there for this huge injustice?

"How's it going, Inez?" Dad said.

"Da-ad—can you please tell her?"

Dad's face went stiff. "If you expect me to do it before I get my coat off, then no. I won't."

Lucy slapped one arm over the other across her chest and breathed in short chops. Inez moved soundlessly back and forth to the table with dishes and silverware.

"Tell you what, Luce," Dad said, "why don't you take your attitude to your room and shake it out a little. I'll be there in a minute."

Lucy felt her chin drop.

"I don't hear footsteps."

She gave him footsteps, hard loud ones that would have put Januarie's to shame—all the way down the hall to her room.

What had just happened?

There was a lot of we're-talking-so-the-kids-can't-hear murmuring in the kitchen before Inez and Mora left. Then Dad tapped on Lucy's door.

"How's the 'tude?" he said.

He sounded like a stranger trying to make friends. Lollipop fled to the toy chest.

"It's the same." Lucy sat up on her bed and hugged her soccer ball and waited for him to come in, to ask if she'd cleared a path. Then they would get this sorted out.

"Okay," he said through the door, "let me know when that changes. Then we'll talk."

He moved off down the hall. Lucy heard him rattle plates and forks, smelled the tamales, felt the aloneness of her room. She was just there with Lollipop and the soccer ball and her attitude. And she wasn't even sure what an attitude was.

Dad insisted around 7:30 that she come out and eat. While she pushed beans and rice around on her plate with a fork, he told her he'd rather she didn't go all the way to the soccer field while she was under Inez's care.

"Da-ad!"

"I'm done, champ," he said. And he was.

"Why?" J.J. said when she told him the next morning.

"Because of Inez."

"The babysitter?"

"She's not a—" Lucy stopped at the door to the portable. "Yeah. Her."

"That stinks."

Lucy started through the doorway.

"It's like at my house," J.J. said.

He followed her in and folded into his chair. Even though the conversation was over, Lucy wished she could sit at his table.

"All right, team," Mr. Auggy said. "Everybody take your chair to your collage."

"Our what?" Carla Rosa said.

Lucy noticed for the first time that their pictures-on-poster-board were all tacked to the wall in various places around the room.

"And take pencil and paper with you."

"I knew we was gonna hafta write," Oscar said.

Yeah. Everything good eventually turned into something that did not rock.

Putting the pictures of her "problem" into words—just words, not sentences yet—did one thing for Lucy. When recess came around, she decided she knew what "attitude" was. She'd have to write it in the book later:

Feeling like you collided with a cactus on your inside.

Waiting for somebody to say one wrong thing to you so you can rip their lips off.

Outside, Lucy chipped the ball against the wall while the group was gathering around Mr. Auggy. And then suddenly Dusty was there, trying to intercept it with her head, and Lucy knew whose lips she wanted to rip. She grabbed the ball and walked away so she wouldn't. In the process, she almost tripped over Januarie, who sat on the ground at the edge of their field, face in her pudgy hands. Her shoulders went up and down like someone was filling them with a bicycle pump.

"You should get up, Januarie," Lucy said. "Somebody's going to step on you."

"They can't miss me," she said into her fingers. "I'm too fat."

"Would you get over it?" Lucy set the ball on the ground and perched on it. "I did not say you were fat."

"They told me—"

"They lied. Who are 'they' anyway?"

Januarie shook her head, jittering her ponytails against each other. Mr. Auggy's whistle blew, and Lucy latched onto her sleeve.

"Come on. Tell me."

"No. If I do, I can't play."

"What are you talking about?"

Januarie raised her face. Her eyes were puffed out like Inez's so-papillas. She'd been crying for a while.

"We can't tattle and fight, Mr. Auggy said. We have to get along or we're out."

The whistle chirped again.

"The Posse and Los Amigos are missing some players," Mr. Auggy called out.

Januarie stuck a hand up and let Lucy pull her to her feet. She didn't let go as she whispered, "Am I too fat to play, Lucy?"

Lucy felt something give in her chest. "No," she said.

Okay, so maybe she was. But what gave "them" the right to decide who was fat and who was pretty and who was anything?

"We're going to play Double Jeopardy today," Mr. Auggy said. "We need two even lines—about this far apart. And to make things a little more interesting, you don't have to play as Los Amigos and the Posse; you can get in whatever line you want."

The space looked small to Lucy, compared to what she and her real team were now used to. She wound up next to Dusty, across from Veronica. Even a kid in a support class could figure out who told Januarie a whopping lie.

"One ball on each side," Mr. Auggy said. "You'll pass the ball back and forth. The line that gets both balls on one side is the winner. Miss Lucy, may we use yours?"

Lucy tossed the ball to him, but her eyes were on Veronica. She could tell Veronica she looked dumb with her mouth always hanging open like that. But what good would that do? One more reason Lucy wasn't one of them. Huh. Like that Ruth person.

The whistle blew, and Mr. Auggy tossed the balls to each team. Gabe rushed in and booted theirs past Januarie. J.J. trapped it. Lucy kept her eyes on the ball Veronica whacked at several times with her foot before she got it across the line.

Lucy swung from her hips and smacked the ball squarely in the middle, right back at Veronica. She was staring, gape-mouthed, at Gabe and let it hit her in the side.

"Foul!" Veronica yelled.

Mr. Auggy blasted his whistle.

"Lucy hit me with the ball on purpose!" Veronica said. She left her lower lip hanging at the end.

"You weren't watching the ball," Lucy said.

Mr. Auggy crouched next to Veronica. "Are you hurt?"

"Maybe." Veronica stroked her side.

"Can you give yourself a big hug?" Mr. Auggy said.

Veronica giggled and wrapped her arms around herself.

"She was fakin'," Oscar said.

"Was not!" Veronica shot back.

"Guess what? They win."

They all looked at Carla Rosa, who was pointing at Emanuel. He had both balls between his feet.

Gabe stuck his arms out to his sides like the wrestlers on TV. "That's cheating."

"Shut up," J.J. said.

Lucy put her hands over her ears. These were not the sounds of soccer, not like she'd dreamed them, not like she knew they should be.

"Could I have my ball?" she said.

Emanuel passed it to her. She picked it up and turned toward the building.

"What's up, Miss Lucy?" Mr. Auggy said.

"I just want to play soccer," she said. "This isn't soccer."

"So you're going to take your ball and go home," Gabe said.

"Yeah," Lucy flung over her shoulder.

But since she couldn't go home, she got as far as the sixth-grade wing so she could put her soccer ball in her cubby—for the last time. She was so done with them. She and her own friends had their own soccer field. If she ever got to go there again.

She rounded the corner and stared. All her papers were on the floor, and her backpack lay in a heap on top of them. Her jacket hung halfway out of the cubby, the tear in the sleeve open like an angry mouth that wanted to tell her who had done it.

Like she didn't already know.

"You're not the neatest student we have, Lucy," said a voice behind her, "But this is out of control, even for you."

Lucy barely glanced at Mrs. Nunez.

"I didn't do it." Lucy said. She shoved her jacket into the back of the cubby and stuffed her soccer ball in after it.

"You're saying someone else got into your things?" Mrs. Nunez's kindergarten voice sounded like she didn't believe it. "We don't usually have that problem here."

You do now, Lucy thought.

Mrs. Nunez leaned over and picked up Lucy's backpack. Her nose twitched.

Lucy took the pack from her. "It wasn't like this before recess. I've been out playing this whole time."

She crammed it into the cubby and stood with her back to it, arms folded, eyes down. She was afraid she'd burn a hole through the principal if she looked at her.

"All right, then. Any idea who would have done this?" She sneezed. "Or why?"

Idea? How about a fact?

Lucy heard a nervous giggle near the door. Great. Now they had an audience.

Besides, what was the point? Mrs. Nunez wasn't going to believe her over Dusty and Veronica. They had names like Terricola and De-Matteo, not Rooney.

"Lucy?" The principal was actually tapping her booted foot.

"I don't—" Lucy started to say. But then it all seemed to happen at once. Januarie ran in crying, "I'm not fat! I'm not!," and Dusty and Veronica were behind her, looking so innocent they could have won an Academy Award. That's when the words tumbled out of Lucy's mouth, all by themselves.

"They probably did it," she said. "Dusty and Veronica. They hate me and everybody else who isn't—like them."

Januarie wriggled her warm, round self under Lucy's arm and made it easier to stay standing under Mrs. Nunez's suddenly pointed face. Until she heard Carla Rosa say, "Guess what—see—"

The big sequins on the white hat shivered as Carla Rosa let go of Mr. Auggy's hand in the doorway and pointed at Lucy. "She's in trouble."

"Well, somebody is," Mrs. Nunez said. She sneezed.

"Not me!" Dusty said.

"Me neither," Veronica said, and folded her long arms like pretzels.

They were getting more convincing by the minute, with the start of tears in Veronica's eyes and clenched fists at Dusty's sides. Both of them chattered things in Spanish to Mrs. Nunez, who made a wall with her hands.

"I do not have time for this." Her voice now matched her face in pointiness.

"I do." Mr. Auggy stepped forward. His hands were parked lazily in his sweatshirt pocket, but his eyes looked anything but laid-back. "I think I know where this is coming from. You want me to handle it?"

Mrs. Nunez hesitated, and then she sneezed again, three times. "All right, yes," she said. She sent one more look at Lucy's offensive cubby that could have withered a cactus. "And I want that backpack cleaned before you bring it back to school." She rubbed her nose. "It smells."

"I'll do it," Januarie said.

"Would you?" Mr. Auggy said. "I need to talk to Lucy."

Me? What about the Gigglers, who were still looking like someone had gone through their *stuff and dumped it all over the floor?* They turned from Lucy and marched off down the hall, heads bent together so they looked like one person.

"Let's take a walk, Miss Lucy," Mr. Auggy said.

And since it wasn't in a tone that left her any choice, Lucy followed him outside.

12

Lucy blinked as she and the coach walked out into the afternoon sunlight. No cloud faces smiled from the sky today. It was a happy blue that didn't match Lucy's "attitude."

Mr. Auggy led her to a bench by the wall at the end of the sixth-grade wing, a place no one ever sat because it was full of splinters. He took off his sweatshirt and spread it on the seat and motioned for Lucy to sit on it. She plopped herself down. With his foot on the bench and his forearms resting on his knee, he looked straight into her eyes.

"Miss Lucy," he said, "did you actually see Dusty and Veronica mess up your cubby?"

She shook her head.

"Did you dust for fingerprints and find theirs on your belongings?"

"No!" Was he serious?

He appeared to be, as he searched her face with his eyes. "Do you have any other evidence that they're the ones who did it?"

"No. I just know."

"Female intuition?"

"Huh?"

"It's that thing girls get inside that they can't explain. Or so they tell me." Mr. Auggy tilted his head so the silky part of his hair slid across his forehead. "Is that what tells you Dusty and Veronica are the culprits?"

"I don't think so," Lucy said. "I'm not, like, your average girl."

"I know that." Mr. Auggy sat beside her. "You're better than the average girl."

Lucy gave a nod. "Better at soccer."

"Better at a lot of things. Better than a girl who would accuse somebody for any other reason than that they actually did it."

"Who else would do it?" Lucy heard herself blurt out. "They hate me because I'm not Hispanic—only that was never a big deal before because they just left me alone, but now that I have to play soccer with them—" She turned her face away from his. "You've seen how Dusty makes me fall down on purpose every chance she gets—only you never blow your whistle at her."

"Because I've never seen that."

Lucy looked at him sideways. He had his hand over his heart like he was about to say the pledge. "Honest."

Then he wasn't a very good referee. She sighed.

"What's the point anyway? I'm not going to play soccer here anymore, and then I don't have to deal with them. Maybe we can just go back to leaving each other alone."

"You're better than that too."

"Better than what?"

"Better than somebody who quits without trying to work things out."

Lucy shrugged. "What's to work out? I'd have to learn Spanish or dye my skin or something."

"Did you know I went to college in France?"

Lucy blinked. What did that have to do with anything?

"I butchered the French language. I must have sounded like a baby just learning to talk. But this one guy—his name was Alain—asked me to play on a soccer team he was getting together." The small smile appeared. "He didn't care that I called everything the wrong name. He wanted me because I knew how to pass and shoot."

"Oh," Lucy said. She was kind of interested.

"Alain put guys from about ten different countries together, and some of them had governments that were practically at war with each other. But when we were on the field, we just concentrated on the game."

"Did you win a lot?"

The smile turned into a grin, though still small. "We kicked tail. And we got to be friends. George, a guy from Africa, I didn't trust him at all when we first started. I thought he hated my guts because he hated all white people. But I just went to see him last month for Christmas."

Lucy felt her eyes widen.

"Sometimes I think about what I would have missed if I hadn't learned to focus on what was really important. I kind of think wars would stop if everybody just got out there and played soccer. You think so?"

"Me?"

"You're a better than average girl. I know you have a lot of thoughts in there that you just aren't saying."

Lucy grunted. "I think that's kind of a good thing most of the time."

Mr. Auggy laughed.

"So—" Lucy drew a circle in the dirt with her toe. "I should come back and play soccer with Dusty and Veronica? Even if they hate me?"

"I can guarantee you they don't hate you. I have a white mother, and they don't hate me—and they might, especially because I'm a teacher telling them what to do." He lowered his voice almost to a whisper. "Lucy, as into the way things look as those two are, it would drive them batty to see a cubby throwing up on the floor like that right across from theirs. I don't think they're guilty."

"Then who did it?"

"Don't know—but I do suggest you apologize to them."

"Do I have to?"

"As a better-than-average girl—yes, I think you do. But it's up to you. I can't squeeze it out of your mouth."

Neither could she.

"I will say this, though." Mr. Auggy rubbed his hands up and down on the tops of his legs. "You'll need to do it before you come back out for soccer. And you're cheating yourself if you don't, because, Miss Lucy, you are a natural-born soccer player."

He stood up and hooked his thumbs into his belt loops, and Lucy remembered she was sitting on his sweatshirt. As she scrambled up, he gave her the small smile and said, "I want to teach you everything I know."

So after school, Lucy waited by the neat, color-coded binders in Dusty and Veronica's cubbies until they appeared, and she did squeeze out an apology, even though she would rather have been at the dentist having a tooth filled without any novocaine. They looked at each other, and Dusty said, "Okay," and Veronica nodded, with her mouth, of course, open. Lucy was sure that conversation wasn't going to stop any wars.

But at least it meant she could play soccer at recess, and she had to. Mr. Auggy said she was a "natural-born soccer player." Besides, since Dad was making her stay home with Inez and Mora after school, she would only get to play twice a week—on Saturday and Sunday with her own team—if she didn't participate at school.

J.J. wasn't having a good time. Lucy could tell that, even though he didn't talk about it much—or about anything else, really. He spent most of his time on the soccer field trying to keep from being hit in the head, the shoulder, the backside by balls shot at him by Gabe. Mr. Auggy didn't catch most of that, and even though Carla Rosa pointed it out—"Guess what—he did that on purpose"—J.J. always shook his head and crammed his jaw down hard and kept playing. And Gabe kept smiling like everybody worshiped him.

Maybe it worked in France, but it wasn't working in Los Suenos, New Mexico. Lucy tried to focus, though, on passing and dribbling and kicking. Every day she learned something new and figured she was pretty close to being taught everything Mr. Auggy knew, like he said. Once she got everything down, it was going to be all about her team on their big dream field.

Finally, at the speed of a herd of turtles, Saturday came. Lucy shoved most of the debris in her room under her bed, cleaned Marmalade's litter box, and put away all the clothes Dad folded.

Dad felt the stickers in their squares on the chore chart and, except for telling her to take care of what he loved, didn't say much. Lucy felt a little lonely as she stuffed a bottle of water and her soccer ball into her backpack—which now smelled like school bathroom soap—but once she met J.J. and Januarie on the sidewalk and kissed Mudge on the nose, it was all about soccer.

"How come that cat lets you touch him and nobody else?" Januarie huffed as she struggled to keep up with them on her bike.

"He loves me, I guess," Lucy said.

"Do you love him?"

"Uh-huh."

"Better than all your other cats?"

"I love them all the same amount—I just love them different."

"But do you love him the MOST?"

"Januarie—" J.J. said.

"I brought cookies," Lucy said quickly. J.J. wasn't snarling, yet, and she'd like to keep it that way. There should be no snarling in soccer.

And there wasn't much. It felt so free to run down their bigger-than-life-itself field on that seamless-sky morning without having to worry that Dusty was going to trip her, or that Gabe was going to pick a fight with J.J. She could practice the words Mr. Auggy taught them to use with each other without a worry in the world.

Sort of.

"Cross it!" she called out to J.J., which meant "send a ball, high in the sky, to the center." But there was no one there to trap it.

She wanted to try "man on," which meant, "hurry up, there's a player on you," only there was never anyone on anyone else. In fact, they looked pretty lost out there with only five players.

Lucy pulled J.J. aside when they called for a water break, and Januarie was serving it in plastic cups just big enough for a swallow.

"We need more people," she said to him in a low voice.

"We're okay just like we are," he said.

"No, seriously. We can't use all the stuff Mr. Auggy's teaching us with just us."

J.J.'s eyes narrowed down so that they almost seemed to meet over his nose. "I'm not playing with Gabe."

"Did I say Gabe?" Lucy said.

"Then who?"

"I don't know."

"And not Januarie."

Lucy glanced over at his round sister, who was currently telling Oscar he could not drink out of the only bottle she had.

"Don't be such a pig," Lucy heard her say. Mr. Auggy would be buzzing his head off.

"We're okay," J.J. said. "We keep Januarie quiet with my dad, and we just play. That's what we always did before, only this is better." He jerked his head toward the field—and froze.

Lucy did too.

Three figures stood at the edge of the field, the afternoon sun shaping them into silhouettes of Gabe and the Gigglers. Lucy's team stared over their cups.

"Who told them we were here?" J.J. said.

Lucy chewed on her thumbnail. This could ruin things worse than Januarie ever could.

"Did you?"

Lucy looked up to find J.J. slicing her with his eyes.

"Me?" she said. "Why would I do that?"

"You just said you wanted more people."

"Not them!"

By then, Gabe was coming across the field with the two girls trailing behind and Lucy's team bringing up the rear. J.J. was doing his hands-in-his-armpits thing. Januarie was whimpering like a wounded Chihuahua. And Lucy was tired of everybody messing up every single thing. She stepped in front of J.J. and waited for Gabe and the Gigglers to get to her.

"This is our field," she said.

Dusty peeked around Gabe. "Hi, Lucy."

Lucy ignored her. "We found it. We cleaned it up. And we don't have to play with you here."

Gabe lifted his chin at her. "Does my old man know you're hanging out here?"

"Your what?" Lucy said.

"His father," Veronica said. "He calls him his old man."

"Shut up," Gabe said.

Behind him, Oscar gave a loud buzz.

"What does you father have to do with it?" Lucy said.

"Guess what? He's the sheriff." Carla Rosa gave Gabe a wary look and stepped backward into Emanuel, who also stepped back and let her dump to the ground.

"Okay, so he's the sheriff. Big deal." Lucy folded her arms. "He doesn't own this field."

"Neither do you." Gabe shrugged his too-big-for-him shoulders. "But he says who gets to hang out in vacant lots."

"It ain't vacant," Oscar said.

Gabe smirked. "It will be if I tell him it is."

"Oh, puh-leeze," Lucy said. "You do not tell the sheriff what to do, even if he is your father. I'm so over you." She nodded at Januarie. "Give me the ball. We're playing soccer."

"Not for long if my dad thinks it's too dangerous."

"It's not dangerous. What's dangerous about it?"

Gabe grunted. "He'll find something."

Suddenly he sounded like every other kid complaining about his parents. Dusty stepped up next to him.

"His dad's kind of a control freak," she said. "But, anyway, why can't we just play with you?"

"Why?" said Lucy. "Because you'll take over. Because you'll trip me and make me break my face. Because Gabe will finally make J.J. mad enough to stop backing down, and he'll go off on Gabe with all the mad he has stored up inside him—and it won't be fun. I just want it to be fun."

"Okay," Dusty said. "So I won't trip you—not like I ever did—and Gabe will be nice to J.J." She gave Gabe a poke in the side. "And we'll have fun because that's all me and Veronica want anyway."

Lucy stared. Had she actually said all of that out loud? She was going to have to start putting duct tape over her own mouth.

"Okay?" Dusty said. Lucy noticed for the first time ever that Dusty's face was the shape of a heart and that her eyes were more gold than brown. At the moment, they looked hopeful and nothing else.

Lucy was hopeful too that someday—soon—they could play real soccer.

"Okay," she said. And without looking at J.J., she took the ball Januarie had tossed to her and ran onto the field. "Same teams as at school," she said to the air.

"Me too?" Januarie cried.

"No!" everyone said.

Lucy was sure that was the only reason J.J. joined them. His eyes were in slits like knife slashes, and his jaw was set hard, but he was there.

It went okay at first. Dusty stayed far away from Lucy, and Gabe seemed to concentrate more on getting the ball past Emanuel, the Amigos' goalie to replace Januarie, than on bopping J.J. in the head with it.

With more players, Lucy felt the challenge of scoring a goal surge through her. Playing right midfield, she tried to move up. That was when the trouble started.

"Play back," Gabe called to her.

She pretended not to hear him.

"Lucy Goosey—play back!"

Lucy directed the ball Veronica passed her on first touch and moved up.

"Are you deaf?"

"Gabe's talking to you," Veronica called as Lucy dribbled the ball forward.

Lucy passed to Carla Rosa, who, of course, flailed at the ball with her foot.

"Back to me!" Lucy said.

But Gabe was suddenly there, smacking the ball away from Carla Rosa and heading for the goal.

"Heads up, Emanuel!" J.J. shouted.

Emanuel squinted from the goal line as if he couldn't believe a ball was actually coming his way. Then to Lucy's amazement, he got down on one knee. He was actually defending the goal—and Lucy didn't want anything more than for her team to get the ball past him, right between the posts.

J.J. came from behind just as Gabe was getting the ball into position for a shot.

"Gabe—man on!" Lucy cried.

She hoped Gabe remembered that meant, "You don't have time to settle the ball. There's a player on you."

Gabe gave the ball a direct kick. Although Emanuel flung himself at it, hands out, he stumbled over his feet and fell face down. The ball shot into the far left corner like a bullet.

"Woo-hoo!" Lucy hooted.

Veronica and Carla Rosa tore with her to Gabe, who stood at the goal line grinning, as if he scored one every day.

"Cool," he said.

"Very cool," Lucy said.

"Wait—was that a foul or something?" Veronica looked back at Emanuel, who was still on the ground.

J.J. grunted and stuck his hand down to help him up. "It was foul, all right," Lucy heard him mutter. He shot her a look that poked her hard on the inside.

"I had to help my team," Lucy said to him as Carla Rosa ambled to the sideline for the throw-in.

"Which team?" he said.

Lucy put up her hand to Carla Rosa and said, "Everybody come here."

"Who died and left you in charge?" Gabe said. But he joined the circle around her, and so did the Gigglers.

"Did you know," Lucy said, "that if people just played soccer and concentrated on the game instead of who they hate, there wouldn't be any wars in the world?"

Carla Rosa's eyes widened. "Really?"

"No," Oscar said, and then he looked at J.J. "Is that true?"

"What are you asking him for?" Gabe said. "He's in the dumb class."

"That's what I mean," Lucy said. She took a huge breath. Maybe they'd think she was trying to be the boss of everyone, but she had to say it. "If we would stop thinking about how you hate J.J.—for who knows what stupid reason—and how Dusty and Veronica can't stand me—and how every Hispanic person thinks every person who isn't

Hispanic is like dirt or something—and we just played soccer like Mr. Auggy says—we could be awesome."

"And there wouldn't be any wars?" Carla Rosa shook her head. "I don't get it."

Gabe shrugged and looked at Lucy. "I don't care about wars. All I want is for you to play back when I have a shot."

"Fine," Lucy said, "if *you'll* move back and cover *me* when *I* run up to shoot." She gave him a hard look. "And I do care about wars, because my mother was killed in one."

Everything went quiet, and Lucy was sorry she'd said it.

"Did she get shot or something?" Veronica said finally.

"Shut up," Dusty said.

Nobody buzzed. J.J. grunted again and marched away, off toward the bleachers.

"Where are you going, J.J.?" Januarie whined after him.

"Home," he said.

"Why?"

He didn't answer. He didn't have to. Lucy knew that stiff walk, that silence like a wall. He was mad at her again. Only this time she wasn't sure she cared.

Januarie turned to Lucy, hands on her hips, face crimson. "He's not gonna play anymore. I can tell. And that means I can't come either."

"Sorry," Lucy said. She was still watching J.J. retreat, climb on his bike, look back, and growl, "Get over here, Januarie."

He sounded like his father.

Januarie started toward him, and then she stopped again. When she faced Lucy, she raised her round chin. "I can make him come back tomorrow," she said. "And I will if you'll let me play."

"Would you just—no!" Lucy said.

This time, she didn't watch Januarie stomp off. She snatched up the ball and looked at the rest of them.

"I think I'll go home," Carla Rosa said, and ran.

Oscar, for once, didn't say anything, and Emanuel, for once, did. He said, "Are we coming back tomorrow?"

"I am," Lucy said.

"Whatever." Gabe said. He jerked his head at the Gigglers.

Veronica followed him across the field, but Dusty hung back. She looked like she'd just gotten caught doing something she wasn't supposed to be doing.

"I'm sorry your mom got killed like that," she said. "I don't see what it has to do with soccer, but I'm really sorry."

Lucy didn't answer. A very old knot was forming in her throat, and she wasn't sure she could speak, even if she'd known what to say.

When they were all gone, Lucy looked up and down the field. *Her* field—whether Gabe's sheriff father said it was or not. Right this minute, it was hers, and with it all to herself, she dribbled—for as far and as long as she could without missing the ball.

Everything else disappeared except for the roar of the crowd she could imagine in the bleachers, which in her mind were no longer half falling down and prickling with splinters but sparkling under fresh paint and strong enough for the throngs of people who came to cheer her team on.

As she shielded the ball from imaginary opponents and fooled them with her fancy turns and faked those who came full speed, right at her, there was just Lucy and the goal, and when she made her shot—right at the edge where the goalie couldn't possibly reach it—her crowd stood as one, and her mom's voice rose over all the others. "That's my little champion. That's my champ!"

Again and again Lucy drove the ball down the field with dynamite dribbling—that was what Mr. Auggy called it—and made perfect shots around even the toughest of goalkeepers.

"Don't tip the boat!" she could almost hear Mr. Auggy shouting to her. That, she remembered proudly, meant stay in your position. She did. She did everything right.

Until on the final drive down the field, feet moving so fast she could hardly see them, she was about to make her shot when her foot hit something that wasn't the ball. She felt herself leave the ground, and before she could stop herself, she slammed forehead first into the metal frame.

She had watched characters in cartoons hit their heads and then see stars spinning in a circle above them. She saw those same stars now, and she had to wait for their light to snap out before she could even think about standing up.

When she did, the whole soccer field spun. In near darkness. Another minute passed before she realized the sun was almost down. She tried to run for her bike, but the ground slanted up to meet her. She sank to the dirt again, and then got up, more slowly this time. If she put one foot very carefully in front of the other, she didn't fall down, and she made it to her bike.

"I hope I didn't dent the goal," she said out loud. Talking hurt her head. So did riding her bicycle. She grasped the handlebars and walked it, still going slowly and carefully as if she were on a tightrope. At this rate, it was going to be completely dark when she got home. And she was going to be in trouble.

That was fine, she decided, when she finally crossed Highway 54. Dad could ground her for being late, but she didn't want him to know about the head-banging incident. Maybe she could just tell him she was tired and go straight to bed. Lying down, going to sleep—those things sounded wonderful right now.

As she neared the house, her heart sank. Every light in the place was on, which wasn't like Dad at all. He never turned on lights—he didn't need them. Had he already called the sheriff or something?

She shuddered at the thought and made her way slowly down the last block. Just don't let there be anybody there who can see me. Just let it be Dad—just let him take away all my privileges—except soccer—but don't let somebody see that I can't stand up straight.

Lucy leaned against the inside of the gate and took some deep breaths. With one last big one, she headed for the back door. It opened, and a kind-of-familiar figure stepped out onto the stoop.

"Miss Lucy?" Mr. Auggy said. "Is that you?"

13

Lucy couldn't move.

Her teacher was at her house? Teachers didn't even call parents unless you were totally flunking or you were a "behavior problem." You practically had to rob a bank for one to come to where you lived.

Was that thing in the cubby hall with Dusty and Veronica that bad? Wasn't an apology good enough?

With visions in her head of Dusty and Veronica's mothers storming the school, screaming Spanish at Mrs. Nunez and demanding that Lucy be hauled into court, she walked toward the back door. She knew if she moved any slower she'd go backward. She wasn't sure being a natural-born soccer player was going to count for anything when she got there.

Especially when she saw Dad behind Mr. Auggy, face pinched around his triangle nose. She hadn't seen it do that since the very first day he came home without Mom. She felt sick.

"Are you okay, Miss Lucy?" Mr. Auggy said. The small smile didn't appear.

"Sure," Lucy said.

He seemed to let out all his air and stepped back into the kitchen, leaving Dad like a silhouette in the doorway.

"You're not hurt," Dad said.

Not if you didn't count the headache. "No," Lucy said.

"Come on inside."

She would actually rather have spent the night in the toolshed. Even Dad's voice was pointy, and that almost never happened. But she trudged up the steps and followed him into the kitchen. She heard Mr. Auggy talking in the living room.

"Who *else* is here?" she said.

"No one." Dad leaned against the counter as if he were very tired. "It's dark, Lucy. We have a rule about that."

"I know—I lost track of time—you aren't supposed to wear a watch when you play soccer so I—"

"You couldn't look up at the sky?"

"Sorry. I won't do it again."

"No," Dad said. "You won't."

Lucy glanced over her shoulder toward the living room where Mr. Auggy was now quiet. Couldn't they discuss this when her teacher wasn't there to hear her get grounded for the rest of her life?

"J.J. and Januarie got home two hours ago," Dad said.

"How did you *know* that?" Something big shifted in Lucy's head. She held onto the counter and waited for the room to stop spinning.

"What's wrong?" Dad said.

"I'm fine." The table slid back into place, and her eyes cleared. She moved closer to her father. "Dad, why is Mr. Auggy here?"

"He was out jogging when I was outside worrying about you."

"He just happened to be in the neighborhood?" Lucy said.

"At the right time. J.J. and Januarie passed us when we were talking, so we waited for you," Dad's face darkened. "We were about to get his car and come looking when you finally got here."

"Oh," Lucy said. The room took another tilt. "I'm gonna go put my stuff away, okay?"

"Let's go in the living room first. We have something we want to discuss with you."

Wishing the room *would* turn upside down and dump her out somewhere, Lucy followed Dad into the living room. Mr. Auggy sat in Dad's chair, murmuring to Lollipop, who was curled up in his lap. There was something very wrong with that, especially if he had come there to ruin Lucy's life. Mr. Auggy ran his hand down Lollipop's back, and she melted right into it. The traitor.

Dad sank into the Sitting Couch, and Marmalade appeared from nowhere to fit herself into his lap. Lucy would have headed for the Napping Couch, but she knew Dad wouldn't have it.

"Luce," Dad said, "I'm going to ask you something, and I want you to tell me the absolute truth, even if it means breaking a promise to somebody else."

The pinch was gone from his face, and he put out his hand to squeeze her wrist. His skin was cold and damp, the way hers got when she had to take a test.

"Okay," she said.

"Does J.J. have permission to go to the soccer field?"

That knot she couldn't swallow formed in her throat again.

"I think that answers that question," Dad said.

"His dad never lets him do anything," Lucy said. "So he just didn't ask him."

"It's easier to ask forgiveness than permission," Mr. Auggy said.

It took Lucy a minute to figure that out. When she did, the knot got bigger. Not much forgiving went on at J.J.'s house.

There was a silence in the room Mr. Auggy and Dad could have filled with a thing they weren't saying. Lucy was sure of that. Mr. Auggy looked out the front window as if he were watching for something. Lucy felt dizzy again.

"I know you want to help J.J.," Dad said finally, "but it isn't really helping when you do things with him he doesn't have permission to do."

"What am I supposed to do? You want me to go tell on him?" Lucy closed her eyes so the room would settle down again. "I don't mean to be disrespectful, but—"

"I know. It's a tough spot to be in." Dad squeezed her wrist once more. "How about we talk some more over supper? I invited Mr. Auggy to stay."

Lucy almost screamed, You *what?*

"I didn't accept yet," Mr. Auggy said. "I wanted to see how you felt about that."

"Um—"

"Give it a minute." He smiled the small smile. "It's gotta blow your mind to find a teacher sitting at your table."

Dad stretched his arm on the back of the sofa and touched Lucy's shoulder. "Mr. Auggy says you're a great soccer player."

"One of my best," Mr. Auggy said.

Dad tried to find Lucy with his eyes. They were softer now, as if something hard was over with. She wanted to keep it that way, at least until she had a chance to talk to J.J.

Lucy turned to Mr. Auggy. "Do you like pizza?" she said. "That's what we're having for supper."

"I'm diggin' it."

"I'll go turn on the oven," Dad said.

Lucy uncoiled to spring off the sofa, but Dad squeezed her shoulder. "You two visit."

It was the weirdest thing she had ever experienced, but it might also be a perfect opportunity.

"Hey, Dad," she called. "Can I ask J.J. to come over for supper?"

Silence from the kitchen. Mr. Auggy's eyes went to the front window again.

"I don't think tonight is a good night," Dad said. "Why don't you throw a salad together, Luce? Impress Mr. Auggy with how nutrition-minded we are."

If that wasn't a bad try at distracting her, she didn't know what was. Mr. Auggy himself sprang from the chair, to the disgust of Lollipop, who padded indignantly toward Lucy's room. He headed for the kitchen, saying, "Great! I chop a mean tomato." Whatever was going on, nobody was going to tell her.

Lucy managed to get to the kitchen without falling over. She was emptying a bag of greens into a bowl and listening to Mr. Auggy talk about how the Amigos and the Posse reminded him of his team in France when the phone rang. She got to it first. A voice like a hammer asked to speak to Ted Rooney.

"Mayor Rosa," Dad said after he'd listened for a second. "To what do I owe the honor?"

Evidently it wasn't an honor, because Dad's face grew stiff, and Lucy could hear the hammer pounding away even from across the kitchen.

"Is that Miss Carla's father?" Mr. Auggy whispered to her.

Lucy nodded and all but put up her hand for him to hush up.

"I'm equally concerned." Dad said. He was now using his radio voice. "I've already begun to speak to Lucy about—"

Lucy's heart started to dive.

"Absolutely—and here's what I suggest. I'm happy to spend part of Saturday on the field with the kids so they do have some adult super—"

There was more pounding, and Lucy watched Dad's face take on the same look it did when waiters ignored him and Aunt Karen acted like he couldn't even boil water. It was all she could do not to snatch the phone from him and put it down the garbage disposal.

"I see your point," Dad said. He was no longer the radio announcer. "We'll have to keep looking at that—I don't think we need to make a final decision right this minute—"

Lucy noticed that Mr. Auggy had stopped chopping, and his mouth was pulled into a small ball. When Dad hung up, Lucy and Mr. Auggy both looked at him expectantly.

"The mayor says no more soccer practice on the old field unless there's an adult present. I volunteered my services—"

"But he thinks it won't do any good because you're blind," Lucy said. "What is wrong with these people?"

"Watch it, Luce," Dad said.

She didn't want to watch it, and she might have said more if Artemis Hamm hadn't sprung across the kitchen and down the hall toward Lucy's room. She heard the toy chest slam shut.

"Is Artemis stalking Lollipop again?" Dad said.

"I'll go see." Lucy dropped the tongs in the bowl and slid all the way to her room. This could mean there was a "pizza delivery."

With the door shut behind her, she leaned for a second to get the room upright and then opened the window. Januarie stood below, hatless and shivering. Her chubby cheeks wobbled, and even in the dark, Lucy could tell it wasn't just from the cold.

"What's wrong?" Lucy said.

"I—I have a message," Januarie said in a squeak Lucy could barely hear. A Chihuahua itself couldn't sound that forlorn.

"You want to come in?" Lucy said.

Januarie nodded and hiccupped out a sob. Lucy opened the window the rest of the way and stuck the top half of her body out into the night.

"Hold on to my shoulders and walk up the wall," Lucy said. "I'll pull you in." It had been a while since Januarie had come in this way, but she definitely didn't want to bring her in through the house, not with whatever else was going on with Dad and Mr. Auggy and all the questions about J.J.

With Januarie's arms clinging to her like a baby monkey's, Lucy backed slowly into the room, pulling Januarie with her. Januarie squeezed her eyes shut as she put her head through the window and held on harder.

"You can let go now," Lucy said. "You have your top half in. Now just wiggle in."

She lowered herself to her bed and waited for Januarie to pop through and bounce down beside her.

"I can't."

"Sure you can." Lucy glanced over her shoulder. There were still man-mutters in the kitchen. "I'll pull."

"No." Another hiccup. "I'm stuck."

"No, you are not."

Lucy slid her hands under Januarie's armpits and gave a yank. She got nothing but a yip.

"Okay, wiggle back out, and I'll meet you at the front door. My dad's in the kitchen with—"

"I'm stuck that way too!" The tiny-dog voice went up another notch, and Januarie's face crumpled.

"Okay, okay, don't freak. I'll get something to pry you out."

Lucy grabbed the wooden spoon that usually propped the toy chest open, but she dropped it. Not big enough. What *was* big enough? This wasn't like getting the first pickle out of the jar.

"Is this because I'm fat?" Januarie said.

"It's because the window's not big enough," Lucy said. "That's not your fault." It was *her* fault. Why had she even tried it this way?

"Okay, here's what I want you to do." Lucy put her face right up to

Januarie's so she could whisper. The voices in the kitchen had gotten lower. "Take the biggest breath you can and hold it, and when I tell you, pretend you're a balloon with all the air going out of it. Okay?"

Januarie nodded.

"Go."

The round cheeks puffed out, and her face flushed the color of a strawberry. Lucy gathered as much of Januarie as she could into her arms, braced her feet on the wall, and said, "Go."

There was a big whoosh of air, and Lucy pulled. Something came with her as she fell backward onto her bed. The door opened, and she got an upside-down view of Mr. Auggy. Dad right behind him.

"What's going on, Lucy?" Dad said.

She wasn't sure. The room wouldn't stop going around and around. Besides, with Mr. Auggy there, it was clear she had to give it up. "I had to get Januarie through the window," she said.

"I'm still stuck!"

"What on earth—"

Mr. Auggy dodged past Lucy, who saw that she held only Januarie's frog-green jacket in her hands.

"Is she okay?" Dad said. He felt his way into the room and promptly tripped over Lucy's Uggs. He staggered forward, and Lucy lunged for him. They both tilted against the wall, in time to hear Mr. Auggy say, "Ted, do you have a screwdriver? We're going to have to take out this window."

Januarie bawled anew.

"I do," Dad said over her. "Lucy—get our tool kit—it's outside—"

With Januarie's yelps from the window ringing in her ears, Lucy felt her way through the house and out the back door into the darkness. But the ground came up to meet her, and she slammed into the side of the toolshed with her shoulder. Somebody—probably Mudge—yowled—and somebody else whispered hoarsely, "You're okay, right?"

Lucy slid down against the shed. J.J.'s face looked fuzzy in front of her.

"What are you doing out here?" she managed to get out. Her voice sounded furry too.

"Hiding."

"From what?"

"Everybody."

"Januarie came over—"

"Tell her to shut up and go home. I'm spending the night here."

"She's stuck in the window." Lucy closed her eyes so that maybe J.J. would stop twirling like a dust devil. "You're spending the night with us?"

"In your shed."

"What?"

"I do it all the time. Tell Januarie to shut up."

"We're not allowed to say 'shut up,'" Lucy heard herself say. Then she let out a long buzz, just before everything went black.

14

Lucy felt like a character in a comic book again. The faces of the people in her thoughts popped up all around her head and talked to her.

Dad's face begged her to wake up. Mr. Auggy's said he was going to call 9-1-1. Januarie's just cried. There was no J.J. face, but Lucy couldn't quite wake up enough to tell them he was in the shed, having a sleepover.

Things got clearer when a tiny flashlight shined into her eyes and another face asked her what her name was and what day it was and who was the president of the United States. She told him who it was but that she'd rather talk about soccer players. People laughed like they'd been waiting for hours for something to be happy about.

She finally came all the way awake when somebody wrapped a thing around her arm and squeezed it. She found herself on the Sitting Couch, looking at Dad and two people in uniforms. They were all searching her face as if they were looking for clues to a major mystery.

"What happened?" she said.

"That's what you need to tell us," the Lady Uniform said. She pulled a stethoscope out of her ears. "You have a concussion. Did you hit your head today?"

Lucy almost didn't answer her. She was using that too-loud voice like people used with Dad. Only Dad said, "Luce—" and his face and voice were both pinched in tight.

"Yes," Lucy said. "I tripped over a rock on the soccer field and hit my head on the goalpost thingie."

From somewhere, a small dog whimpered. Lucy's eyes found Januarie sitting on Mr. Auggy's lap in Dad's chair.

"You got unstuck," Lucy said.

"Lucy—focus," Dad said.

She closed her eyes.

"Don't go to sleep," the Man Uniform said. "Stay with us. Did you black out when you hit your head?"

"No," Lucy said.

She felt a hand on her forehead. "No bump," Lady Uniform said, "but there isn't always one."

Lucy wiggled down farther on the couch. She was so sleepy.

"We have to ask you some questions." Man Uniform took her by the shoulders and sat her up. "Do you feel nauseous?"

"Like I'm going to throw up?"

"Yeah."

She tried to shake her head. "Now I do. A little."

"Does your head hurt?"

"Some."

"Do you know where you are?"

Lucy gave him a look. He grinned at her. He had a mustache and twinkly eyes, and he didn't look like he was going to give her a shot. It might be a good idea to try for a smile herself.

"There you go," he said. "Okay—are you still dizzy?"

She opened her eyes wide. The room was still, but it could go any minute. "Not so much," she said.

He snapped off his flashlight and turned to Dad. "I don't think we need to take her to the hospital."

"Hello!" Lucy cried.

Lady Uniform put a hand on Lucy's shoulder, "If you stay quiet. For at least three days. No soccer."

"For three *days*?"

"Here's the deal." Man Uniform swept his eyes over both Dad and Lucy and back at Mr. Auggy. "If you injure your head again before this concussion heals, you could suffer more serious damage."

"Like I could be retarded?"

The mustache twitched. "Something like that."

Januarie began to wail as if Mr. Auggy had stuck her with a pin.

"Did she get hurt in the window?" Lucy said.

"Where?" Lady Uniform said.

"She's fine," Mr. Auggy said. "Hey, Miss Januarie, how about some pizza?"

They disappeared into the kitchen, and Lucy watched the two Uniforms look at each other as if this were a very strange place.

They gave Dad instructions — wake her up every few hours, make her rest for two days, and don't let her play soccer for another three. At least they didn't treat him like he had a concussion, so Lucy decided they knew what they were talking about.

When they were gone, Mr. Auggy brought Januarie back in, carrying a piece of pizza on a paper towel. Her face was still red and tear-puffy.

"Tell Lucy what you told me, Miss Januarie," Mr. Auggy said when she was once more enthroned on his lap like one of the cats.

Dad, who was on the other end of the sitting couch with Lucy's legs in his lap, sat up straighter. This must be the thing they'd been tiptoeing around earlier.

"I came to tell you J.J. ran away," Januarie said. "And then I got stuck in the window — and then J.J. came and told us you were dead in the backyard — "

"Dead!"

"So, Miss Lucy," Mr. Auggy said. He looked at Dad. "May I?"

"Absolutely."

May he what? Lucy suddenly wished she'd go into that concussion thing again so she wouldn't have to answer this.

"He disappeared again. Do you know where he might be?"

Dad squeezed Lucy's foot. "Luce — " he said. "You have to help J.J. — really help him."

Lucy sucked in air. "Okay. He might be in the shed."

"Our toolshed?"

She nodded, and things did get funny again. "I want to lie down," she said.

"I'm on it," Mr. Auggy said.

He left, and Lucy drifted off. When she opened her eyes, a pale J.J. stood over her, hair hanging around his face like curtains.

"See?" Dad said. "She's okay. Mr. Auggy's going to take you home."

"I don't want to go home," J.J. said. And his eyes told Lucy it was all her fault that he had to.

"It'll be okay," Mr. Auggy said.

Somehow, Lucy didn't think so.

Dad went with Mr. Auggy and J.J. and Januarie to the back door, and then Lucy heard the bathroom door close. She wasn't quite so sleepy now. Thoughts of J.J. and Januarie going home to the yelling that was sure to be waiting for them there—those thoughts brought her eyes wide open.

She didn't hear anything in the bathroom. Maybe Dad would be in there for a few minutes. Lucy stood up as if her head might topple off if she made any sudden moves. She hung onto the Sitting Couch and Dad's chair and made her way to the window. With her chin resting on the sill, she could see J.J., Januarie, and Mr. Auggy at J.J.'s front gate—and then there was Mr. Cluck, as if he'd been hiding in one of the old washing machines, just waiting. He started to yell, but Lucy couldn't make out what he was saying. She slid the window open a few inches and pressed her ear against the cold air.

Mr. Cluck's words came out like the voice on the other end of the speaker at the McDonald's drive-through in Alamogordo. Some were muffled. Some she heard all too clearly.

"Where ... have you been ... told you not to move ... Who ... are you?"

Mr. Auggy had both hands up. Januarie tried to slip past her father, who grabbed her by the back of the coat and held on.

J.J. just stood like a stick.

"Is Mrs. Cluck home?" Lucy heard Mr. Auggy say.

Lucy grunted. She probably was, but they wouldn't be seeing her. She never came out when Mr. Cluck was yelling like this. She could probably hear him just fine from inside the house.

Lucy glanced over her shoulder. Things were still quiet in the bathroom. She opened the window a little wider.

Mr. Cluck kept yelling—about how J.J. was an idiot and a loser and some other things that made Lucy's heart beat hard for her friend. *He's not any of that*, she wanted to scream at his father. *You're the one—*

"It may seem like that to you." The sound of Mr. Auggy's voice surprised Lucy. It was like a big rock. "But there are reasons for that, Mr. Cluck."

J.J.'s dad spit out some things Lucy didn't understand. J.J. obviously did, because he grew even stiller. Lucy was sure he wasn't even breathing. She wasn't either.

"I would be willing to work with J.J. after school," Mr. Auggy said, as if Mr. Cluck weren't now screaming so loud that Mr. Benitez's porch light went on. "Maybe I can help him learn how to stay out of trouble. Would that be all right with you?"

"Go right ahead," Mr. Cluck shouted. "Knock yourself out."

"Lucy."

Lucy jumped and nearly bonked her head again. Dad was behind her, and he didn't look happy.

"Close the window, and get back on the couch," he said.

"Sorry, Dad," she mumbled.

He kept a hand on her shoulder as she went and then tucked the blankets in around her and sat again with her feet in his lap.

"I'm sorry you heard that," he said finally.

"I've heard J.J.'s dad yell before—sort of."

"He was especially out of control tonight. I'm surprised Mr. Auggy got a word in."

Lucy rubbed at her head. She was starting to get sleepy again, and she didn't want to.

"What did J.J.'s dad mean when he told Mr. Auggy to knock himself out?" Lucy said. "Does he mean get a concussion like I did?"

"No—he's just saying he doesn't think Mr. Auggy can help J.J. because *he* sure can't." Dad's voice had a bitter feel.

"How come J.J. has to stay after school?" Lucy said. "When it's his father who's being stu—Well, you know."

Dad patted her leg. "I don't think Mr. Auggy spending time with J.J. is going to be a punishment. Who would you rather hang out with—him, or Mr. Cluck?"

"Hel-loo," Lucy said.

That was the last thing she remembered until the next day—a day so strange she would have called anyone who said it would happen as it did a liar-liar-pants-on-fire.

They didn't go to church. In fact, Dad wouldn't even let her get off the Sitting Couch where she had slept all night, except for the three times he woke her up and then told her to go back to sleep. What was that about?

He made her walnut waffles and did everything but feed them to her, and the whole time, he looked like he was about to burst into tears. She felt so guilty she could hardly eat her breakfast, except that would have hurt his feelings, so she choked it down.

Because they didn't go to church, Dad sat at the end of the Sitting Couch and said they were going to talk about the Bible lesson for the day. He scanned his braille New Testament with his fingers, and Lucy frowned. They never did this at home. Church was church, and home was home. Except now that Inez was doing Bible study.

"Okay," Lucy said, "but let's not do the ones Reverend Servidio does. Can we just talk about Ruth? I get her."

Dad closed his Bible and nestled it into his lap as if it were Marmalade. She'd never seen him do that before. He treated it the way Inez treated hers.

"So tell me about Ruth," he said. "Why do you like her?"

Lucy pulled the fringe on the edge of the Navajo blanket through her fingers. "She stuck with Naomi even when Naomi told her not to. She didn't let anybody tell her what to do—she just did what she had to do."

Dad chuckled. "I can see why you'd relate."

"And then when she got to Bethlehem—only she was a Mo-balite—or a—"

"Moabite?"

"Yeah." Lucy stopped pulling on the fringe. "How did you know that?"

He smiled his sunlight smile. "I read it somewhere. So go on."

"Yeah—she was like the only foreigner, but she just took care of

Naomi and didn't get all freaked out if the other girls ignored her or treated her like she was weird."

Something went out of Dad's smile. "Does that remind you of anything?"

"Uh, hello—yes! I'm the only 'foreigner'—" She found herself making quotation marks with her fingers like Mora did. "And the Hispanic kids used to ignore me. Till now. Which—having them pay attention to me isn't all that great." Lucy held her arms out to Lollipop, who jumped onto her chest and curled up.

"What else does it remind you of?" Dad said.

"Huh?"

"Ruth taking care of Naomi—does that remind you of your life?"

Dad's voice made her feel squirmy.

"You mean, like me helping you?" Lucy said.

"Exactly."

"I guess so," Lucy shrugged. "But that's just the way it is, Dad. It's not like I mind."

He didn't answer right away, and that made Lucy feel even squirmier.

"I like it that way," she said.

"Yeah," he said. Now he sounded like *he* had a knot in his throat. "Tell me what you think when you and Inez do the next part."

She grinned. "I have a concussion—I don't think I can do Bible study tomorrow."

"You'll be right here on this couch, so what else are you going to do? Inez will be here before I leave for work."

Lucy was ready to protest, but the next strange thing happened. There was a knock on the kitchen door, and the next thing she knew, Mr. Auggy was back in Dad's chair. Lollipop jumped from Lucy to him like the turncoat she was.

Dad fixed tea—which lifted Lucy's spirits some, although it seemed weird to her that an athlete like Mr. Auggy also liked tea—and Mr. Auggy chatted away like he belonged in their living room. Lucy was sure he was going to dive into the Sunday comics next, but he finally said, "I have news about J.J. and Januarie."

Lucy didn't care then if he moved right into their spare bedroom.

"They still get to play soccer," he said.

"On the big soccer field?" Lucy said "On weekends?" She didn't add, *And do I?*

"As long as I'm there," Mr. Auggy smiled his small smile. "Which I will be every Saturday. No Sundays. I think we all need to kick back one day if we're going to practice five days at recess and all day Saturday."

Lucy could feel her heart sinking. Mr. Auggy was totally taking over.

But the sinking stopped at her belly button. Without Mr. Auggy, they wouldn't get to use the big soccer field. And they wouldn't have Gabe and Dusty and Veronica so they could play real soccer, because J.J. for sure wasn't going to play with Gabe again if somebody didn't make him.

"You have any problem with that, Miss Lucy?" Mr. Auggy was looking at her with his head tilted, as if he were worried at what she might say. The day just kept getting stranger. "Now's the time to speak up. It started out as your team after all, so you should have some say in how it's run."

She wasn't sure whether to believe him or not. And yet—

"I do have one problem," she said. "And that's Januarie." She rearranged herself under the Navajo blanket. "J.J. hates playing with her because, well, she stinks at soccer."

"Luce!" Dad said.

"We-e-ll," Mr. Auggy said, "she's not an athlete, I'll give you that."

Ya think?

"I have to include her at school. As a teacher, that's my job. But on Saturdays—" Mr. Auggy blew some air out of puffed-up cheeks. "What would it take for you to consider her un-stunk?"

"She has to be able to keep up—dribble more than, like, two inches—pass to actual people instead of into nowhere—not get in the way when you're trying to get to the goal." Lucy sighed. "Like that's ever gonna happen. And it's not just because she's too fat—"

"Lucy Elizabeth!" Dad said.

156

"Dad—she got stuck in a window. Let's be honest here. But I would never say that to her—not like some people."

Mr. Auggy looked like he had antennae going up in his brain. "Someone told her she was too fat to play soccer?"

Lucy stopped. "I didn't hear it myself, but she says it was—well, you'd have to ask her."

"Ding-ding-ding!" Mr. Auggy said.

Dad looked confused.

"Tell your dad why I do that," Mr. Auggy said.

"You get a ding-ding when you do something that has integrity in it." Lucy felt her cheeks get warm. "That's my first one."

Mr. Auggy leaned toward Dad, to Lollipop's obvious annoyance. "Your daughter gave us a definition of integrity in class. One of the reasons I came by yesterday was that I wanted to meet the man who taught her that."

Dad gave his sunlight smile. "I'm proud of Lucy."

"I am too, which is why I'm making her team captain."

"Of the Posse?" Lucy said. "Gabe's gonna have a hissy fit."

"No—of the eight-person soccer team I'm training. Nine if Januarie passes whatever test you decide on."

"Me?"

"You're the captain."

He turned to Dad again, but Lucy didn't hear what he said. There was too much going on in her own head. Could this actually be happening? Could her dream be coming true? Her mom's dream?

"What are the chances of the city putting up some money for cleats and shin guards?" Mr. Auggy was asking.

"Slim to none," Dad said, "but it's worth a try. The next council meeting's Tuesday the eighteenth."

"Are you on it?"

Dad made a hard sound. "No—I've volunteered, but so far the mayor hasn't taken me up on it."

"He doesn't even know anything," Lucy said.

Dad put up his hand. "But I'll go to the meeting with you, Sam, and we'll see what we can stir up."

"I've got your back, Ted," Mr. Auggy said. He grinned at Lucy. "Your dad rocks, Miss Lucy."

But Lucy didn't answer. They were calling each other Sam and Ted now? She didn't know if that was a good thing or not. She didn't have much time to think about it, because the next strange thing happened.

"Luce," Dad said, "a big envelope came yesterday, and it smells like Aunt Karen. See what it is, would you?"

He pawed in the basket beside the couch and handed her a fat brown envelope. Not only did it reek of Aunt Karen's perfume, but it had Lucy's full name on it—Lucy Elizabeth Rooney. Lucy's head hurt again. Only Dad got to call her that, but there was Aunt Karen, as usual, poking herself into a place she didn't belong.

"So?" Dad said.

"It's from her—for me."

She started to stick it under the couch cushion, but Dad said, "It's probably that soccer program information. Mr. Auggy might like to see that."

He could have it. Lucy kept herself from throwing it toward him.

While Mr. Auggy looked over a three-inch stack of brochures and papers, Lucy closed her eyes. When she opened them, the room was shadowy and Mr. Auggy was gone and only Dad sat on the couch with her, as if he hadn't moved all day.

"Was I asleep that whole time?" Lucy said.

"You needed it," Dad said. His voice sounded thick. That knot thing again. "You didn't take care of what I love, champ."

Lucy felt her own knot forming. "I'm sorry."

"Don't ever do that again."

"I won't."

"I have to ask you—what did you trip over?"

"I think it was a rock," Lucy said.

"I thought you and J.J. cleaned up the field."

"We did." Lucy rubbed her eyes and sat up. "And I know that rock wasn't there when we started playing yesterday."

"What are you thinking?"

The first thing she thought was that Mr. Auggy wouldn't want her making accusations without proof. The other thing she was thinking she didn't say out loud.

"I want you to play soccer, Lucy," Dad said. "I want you to have everything you deserve. I want you to have a great childhood. But please, please be careful."

Lucy whispered, "Okay."

Then Mudge yowled from the kitchen door for his dinner and Artemis Hamm crouched down to stalk him from behind the Napping Couch and Lollipop made a beeline for Lucy's bedroom. From somewhere, Marmalade meowed sleepily, and Dad got up to feed them all and make macaroni and cheese like they always had on Sunday nights.

But something had changed. Something silent that Lucy didn't understand—except to know it was something she couldn't make the same again.

15

Dad wasn't kidding when he said Inez was coming early. She had a breakfast concoction on a tray in front of Lucy before she could even get off the couch to go to the bathroom.

"Eat this now," she said. "I will make the caldo de res for lunch."

"What's that?" Lucy said.

"Stew. Very healing."

"What's this?" She drew in a breath of steam from the plate in her lap. It smelled amazing. Dad would say Inez had stolen it from heaven.

"Machaca," Inez said.

Lucy stared into the bowl whose contents shone with grease. "Do I want to know what's in it?"

"Brisket, scrambled eggs, beans, hash browns."

"Does Mora like it?"

Inez straightened up from peering under the couch at Artemis Hamm. Lucy thought she saw a smile somewhere on her face. "No," she said. "She says she will die if she eats it."

"Then I'll probably like it," Lucy said. And she did.

When she was finished, she wriggled back into the pillows and said, "I guess I get to watch TV all day, huh?"

"Huh," Inez said as she produced a bright red notebook that said LUCY ROONEY, SOCCER CAPTAIN on the front of it. "Work from Senor Coach. Get busy."

"I have a concussion!"

"You will live."

And then Inez got busy, sweeping and polishing and scrubbing things Lucy never would have thought of. She herself had no choice but to do the twenty math problems Mr. Auggy had assigned, all of them with jokes attached to them, and copy over the paragraph she had managed to string together from her collage. By the time she was finished, Inez had the caldo de res ready, and although it looked like it had the hoof of some animal swimming in it, Lucy ate it and scraped the bowl with her finger.

Inez made her take a shower and climb into her bed for the nap she swore she didn't need. She turned on the radio so she could hear Dad's voice while she lay there.

When she woke up, Mora was sitting in her rocking chair, staring at her.

"What was it like?" she said.

"What was what like?" Lucy sat up and felt somehow naked with Mora in her room.

"Going unconscious—was it weird?"

"No—well, yeah. It was like being asleep, only not."

Mora arched an eyebrow. "Now, that clears it up. At least we don't have to do Bible study today because you're sick. I bet we could talk Abuela into letting us watch Oprah."

Lucy was about to ask her what the big deal was about Oprah when she heard a high-pitched whine outside the window.

Mora bolted to her feet. "Is that that cat?"

"Could be," Lucy said, though she knew it wasn't.

"I'm out of here," Mora said, and she was.

Lucy waited until she heard the TV go on before she got to her knees and looked out the window. Januarie was crouched below, face full of news.

"Dusty and that other girl are coming to your back door!" she spewed out.

"No they are not," Lucy said.

"Yuh-huh."

Sure enough, Lucy heard voices from the kitchen that didn't belong there.

162

"Okay, thanks," she whispered to Januarie. "I'll make it up to you."

She shut the window, ready to burrow under the covers, but Mora flung open the door and said, "You have company. Huh. You really do have friends."

Lucy didn't inform her that Dusty and Veronica did not qualify as friends. And what was with everybody invading her bedroom? She felt a sudden need to brush her hair. She tightened her ponytail and straightened her big Dad T-shirt and pulled it over her knees as she hugged them against her.

"Hi," Dusty said from the doorway.

"Hi," Veronica said from over her shoulder.

Dusty gazed around the room as if she were entering a foreign land. "Can we come in?"

"Sure," Mora said. She shut the lid on the toy chest and patted it. "You can sit here."

Their voices—as they chattered about Lucy's stuffed animals in the fireplace and the giant soccer ball on the bed and the totally cool rocking horse in the corner—covered the mournful mewing of Lollipop in the chest.

"Cool room," Dusty said as she sat on the end of Lucy's bed and leaned on the soccer ball.

Mora settled herself into the rocking chair and dug into her pocket. Inez must not have frisked her for techno today. Lucy herself focused nervously on Veronica, who looked like she was about to open Lucy's drawers.

"Are you better?" Dusty said.

"Uh-huh," Lucy said. She wasn't quite sure what to say to a roomful of girly girls—her room full. It didn't help that Januarie appeared in the doorway, scowling, chubby arms folded across her chest as if to say, "You let them in? How could you?"

"I was so scared when Mr. Auggy said you had a concussion," Dusty said.

"You could die from that," Veronica said.

Januarie hiked herself up beside Lucy. "Could you?"

"I didn't," Lucy said.

"Which is good, because we are going to have a for-real soccer team." Dusty smiled, lighting up her heart-face. "And you're the captain."

Lucy looked at each of them, but they were both smiling, Veronica with her lip hanging down.

"Is Gabe mad about that?" Lucy said.

Dusty shrugged. "He'll get over it."

"I comforted him," Veronica said with a giggle.

Ickety-ick.

"Is Gabe your boyfriend?" Mora said.

"I wish," Veronica said.

"I have a boyfriend." Mora stared into the thing she was holding, which didn't appear to be either her cell phone or her iPod.

Veronica wandered over to her, but Dusty parked her chin on the soccer ball and said to Lucy, "We are going to have such a good team. I wish we could have uniforms."

"Me too," Lucy said slowly. "I was thinking of red and blue—I don't know—"

"That's totally what I was thinking! We have to come up with a name for the whole team, though. You're good at soccer names."

"That is the coolest thing ever!"

They both looked at Veronica, who held Mora's small contraption in her hands as if it were a diamond ring.

"What is it?" Dusty said. She got up to join them. Even Januarie craned her head.

"It's an electronic diary." Mora took it carefully back from Veronica. "I keep all my secrets in it."

"About your boyfriend," Veronica said, voice velvet with envy.

"Oh, yeah, and other stuff. Very secret stuff."

Lucy could actually understand that. She'd been pretty nervous when Veronica was poking around near the underwear drawer. She had to find a safer place for the Book of Lists.

"That's why I use an electronic diary instead of a regular one," Mora was explaining. "You have to have a password to get into it."

"What is it?" Veronica said.

Dusty tucked her chin under. "Like she's so going to tell you."

"Oh, it's okay." Mora's eyes were big and shiny. Lucy figured she loved an audience. "It only opens if I say it exactly the way I recorded it. And it'll tell me if I've had intruders."

"Cool." Veronica seemed barely able to keep herself from dissolving into a coveting pool.

"See, you have to do it just like this." Mora put the device up to her lips and said, in a voice that sounded like somebody on TV, "Consuela."

"Who's Consuela?" Dusty said.

"It's the name I wish I had instead of Mora. See—" She flashed the diary toward Veronica. "I'm in."

It was obviously too cool for words this time, because Veronica just shook her head. Even Dusty looked impressed, and Januarie—Januarie was hanging over the edge of the bed, fascinated in spite of herself. The two seconds of being able to talk to another girl slithered out of Lucy like a snake that might never have been there in the first place.

"A gathering of mini-women!" someone said from the doorway.

Dad was there, face sunlight-smiling, eyes traveling toward the sounds.

"Hi, Dad."

Lucy started to scramble out of bed, but Dad said, "Stay where you are. You're still a patient."

"How did he know you were getting up?" Veronica whispered loudly.

"Because he isn't deaf," Lucy whispered back.

Dad chuckled. "A lot of people make that mistake. And you are?"

"Me?" Veronica said.

"This is Veronica," Lucy said.

"Ah—from church." Dad's eyes traveled some more. "Dusty, you here too?"

"Wow—yeah." Dusty looked impressed, more than she was over the electronic diary.

"Where's Januarie-February-June-or-July?"

"Here," said the Chihuahua voice. By some miracle, she hadn't said a word through the whole thing. Dad must have smelled her.

"What's up, little one?" he said.

"Nothin'."

"Inez made cookies."

Januarie was off the bed and in the kitchen almost before Dad could get out of the doorway.

"We shouldn't do that, Dad," Lucy said. "She has to lose weight if she's going to play soccer." She sneaked a glance at Veronica, who didn't even blink.

"She's not that chubby," Dusty said. "I was like that when I was her age."

"Not me," Mora said. "I've always been thin—that's why I'm such a good dancer."

"Do you take actual dance classes?" Veronica said, using her envy voice again.

While Mora went into a long explanation of how many classes she took every week and how many competitions her team in Alamogordo had won, Dad eased his way over to the bed and felt Lucy's forehead.

"I'm fine," she said.

"You seem better—but I still want you to stay home tomorrow."

"Another day?" Dusty said. "Can't she come back? We'll watch out for her."

Dad found Lucy and arched his eyebrows. She knew what he was thinking. She was a little confused herself.

"We'll see. I'll let you girls do your thing. Luce—take care of what I love."

"I will."

"That is so cool," Dusty said when he was gone.

"What?"

"You and your dad. It's like, you know each other so well."

"We take care of each other." Lucy wriggled a little.

"Wow," Dusty said. "Wow."

Wow was right. Lucy had to wonder if Dusty was just being nice to her because she had a concussion and nobody else in school had ever had one before. There had to be some reason why Dusty wasn't looking at her like her skin was the wrong color. Or, actually, why she was looking at her at all. It was almost fun—but you couldn't be too careful.

Dad didn't let her go back to school the next day. The worst part about that—besides not getting to play soccer—was missing J.J.

He didn't come by after school on Monday, and Januarie had no message from him. As Lucy lay on the Napping Couch Tuesday, sick of doing nothing, she thought about his face the last time she saw him. Was he still mad because she told that he was in the shed? What was she supposed to do? And besides, the only trouble he got into was having to go to Mr. Auggy every day after school. That was better than his dad yelling at him so bad he had to go hide in their backyard.

Thank you for my dad, she thought. And then she wondered who she was thanking. When Inez set up for Bible study right there at the coffee table that afternoon—with the TV Mora so longed to turn on just a few feet away—Lucy wondered something. Could you think about God without knowing you were? Like even if you were mad at him?

As Inez told her and Mora the next part of the story, Lucy figured if anybody had a right to be ticked off at him it was Ruth and Naomi, who even changed her name to Mara, which meant "bitter."

"Mora means bitter?" Mora said.

"Mara," Inez said.

"Doesn't matter. I'm going to change mine to Consuela when I'm old enough."

Naomi had a relative in Bethlehem named Senor Boaz, Inez told them.

"Bozo?" Mora said. "What is up with the names?"

"Boaz," Lucy and Inez said together.

Could this girl be any more annoying?

He had a field where Ruth went every day to pick up the leftovers so she and Naomi could eat.

"Is that like going through the dumpster behind a restaurant?" Mora said.

"Senor Boaz he is a good man," Inez said. "When he finds out what Senora Ruth is doing, he tells his other workers leave more for her."

Mora wiggled her eyebrows. "He thought she was hot."

"He does. But he shows her the respect. He does not think a beautiful young woman will want the old man."

"How old was he?" Mora said. "Like thirty or something?"

"Much older than she is."

"Then he must have been rich."

"Would you shut—hush up?" Lucy heard herself say. "I want to hear this."

Mora blinked her big eyes. "You do?"

"Yeah," Lucy said. "I do."

Inez ran her hand across the page in that way she had. "Senor Boaz finally has the cause to talk to Senora Ruth and he tells her to gather grain only in one special field, where nobody will bother her. Other hombres think she is 'hot' too."

Mora nodded. So did Lucy.

"When she asks him why he is nice to her, he says—" Inez nodded at her Bible. "I will read." She cleared her throat and began: " 'I have been told all about what you have done for your mother-in-law since the death of your husband—how you left your father and mother and your homeland and came to live with a people you did not know before. May the Lord repay you for what you have done. May you be richly rewarded by the Lord, the God of Israel, under whose wings you have come to take refuge.' "

She closed the Bible and her eyes. Mora rolled the ribbon that trailed from it around her finger.

"Did he do it?" Lucy said. "Did God reward Ruth?"

"Yes. Senor Boaz marries Senora Ruth and gives Senora Naomi a place to live."

"Cool," Mora said. "Happily ever after. I'm gonna go put that in my diary."

"What will you write?" Inez said.

"How if I'm good, I'll get to go out with Reese."

"No, Mora," Inez said sharply. "This is not what it means."

"Then what does it mean?" Lucy threw off the blanket that was suddenly smothering her. "See, I don't get it, because my mom was good, and she got killed. And my dad is good, and he got his sight taken away from him. I try to be good, and my Aunt Karen keeps saying I have to go live with her, which would be like, horrible —"

Lucy stopped, because she was breathing hard, and Mora was watching her with frightened eyes. Artemis, Marmalade, and Lollipop all fled from the living room. Only Inez stayed still and quiet.

"Mora," she said, "make the tea."

She did it without argument. Lucy folded her arms around herself and wished she could suck every word back in.

"Everything is not happily ever after for Senora Ruth," Inez said. "You will see in the next part. And it is not for Senora Naomi — she still does not have her hijos and her esposo."

Lucy let her chin drop to her propped-up knees. "Then what good does it do to believe in God if bad things are going to happen anyway?"

"How does Ruth get through these bad things?"

"She worked her tail off," Lucy said, although she knew that wasn't the answer Inez was looking for.

"And who gives her the chance to work?"

"Bozo — sorry — Boaz."

"And why does Senor Boaz have such rich fields and so many people looking up to him?"

Lucy shrugged.

"That is right," Inez said.

"Huh?"

"We do not know why some people have the good fortune and some have the bad. We all have some of each. But Senor Boaz knows God, and so the bad is not so bad, and the good is even better."

"How did he know him?"

Inez closed her eyes, as if the answer were inside her eyelids. "We all know him somehow different. You will find your way."

What if I don't want to? Lucy wanted to ask. And then she didn't want to ask. And that confused her.

"Enough for today," Inez said. "You want the quesadilla?"

"Can I have guacamole with it?"

"Si."

"The kind that looks like baby food and makes your nose run?"

"Yes."

"Please," Lucy said.

And it was better for the moment.

Lucy never thought she would be happy to go back to school, but when Dad said on Wednesday that she could, she was ready long before Januarie showed up at the back gate. J.J. wasn't with her, but Lucy was afraid to ask why. She rode across Second Street in silence.

"Don't you want to know where J.J. is?" Januarie said.

"Is he mad at me?" Lucy said.

"Kind of."

"Then no, I don't want to know."

It was the only dark part of the day, or any of the almost two weeks of days that followed.

Every day at recess, Mr. Auggy worked them hard, only to Lucy it was like working at play, and in a dream world. Each time she thought Mr. Auggy had taught her everything he knew, like he promised, she learned something new.

And just as he said, as long as she concentrated on the game, it didn't bug her so much that Gabe called her Lucy Goosey just to make her face turn the color of a hot chili pepper, or that Veronica yelled "Foul!" every time anybody touched her or Gabe. In fact, Lucy grinned like no other when Dusty finally said, "Veronica, is that the only word you know in soccer?" After that, Veronica didn't do it so much.

Now J.J.—he said almost nothing at all. Lucy noticed—because she watched him, begging him with her eyes—that he was getting better at soccer too. He could dribble with almost as much control as Gabe, and he blocked most of Gabe's shots before Januarie even saw them coming, although that wasn't saying all that much. She *wasn't* getting better at soccer. But J.J. didn't even answer Lucy when she told him at the water fountain that he rocked.

And he didn't smile back at her when she grinned in class because his paper that Mr. Auggy read out loud was longer than one sentence and made actual sense. He didn't even agree with her when she whispered to him in the milk line at lunch that Januarie was never going to be good enough for their big team. Not so much as a grunt came her way.

Those were the dark spots. The bright ones came on Saturdays when they could open up and play their best. It helped that Januarie wasn't playing. Mr. Auggy explained to her that she would have to improve her skills the captain's satisfaction, and that he would help her if she wanted. She said she did, but as far as Lucy could tell, she just spent her Saturdays pouting and glaring, especially when Lucy was talking to Dusty.

Januarie also had her lip stuck out every day after school when Dusty and Veronica walked Lucy home. Lucy didn't invite them; it just happened. Inez always invited them to stay for a snack before she shooed them off so Mora and Lucy could do their homework. Januarie got to stay too, but she was always so miserable-looking as Lucy and Dusty talked soccer and Mora and Veronica discussed imaginary boyfriends. Lucy didn't see how she was eating without getting indigestion.

It was still hard to believe that Dusty and Veronica really wanted to be her friends. Lucy wanted to ask Dusty why it was suddenly okay that she didn't know a hijo from a hija and had a last name like Rooney. But it was so different, talking to a kid her age who spoke in long sentences and didn't grunt. She actually hated to see them leave in the afternoons, except on Mondays.

She read the whole book of Ruth on her own one Sunday afternoon, but she didn't tell Inez because she liked hearing the story from her. She didn't tell her that, either, because every time she decided maybe she liked Inez after all, Inez would take over one more thing in the house. She bought the groceries and stacked them neatly in the pantry. She scrubbed the kitchen floor until it became its original creamy white; Lucy had always thought it was supposed to be brown. She folded the towels so they had creases in them, and she even bleached out Marmalade's litter box. On Saturday, Lucy couldn't put any stickers on the chart, because all the chores were done.

"When is all that happening?" Lucy asked Dad as she stood with a sheet of puffy red hearts in her hand with no place to put them.

"During the day." Dad chuckled. "You've been so busy you haven't noticed she comes in the morning now."

"Since when?"

"Since you hurt yourself and she did such a good job with everything."

Lucy poked at the hearts with her finger. "We did a good job together."

"We did fine. But you're a kid, Lucy. You shouldn't have to be taking care of—well, spending all your time working."

If he hadn't added that he was proud of her, and that Mom would have been proud of her too, she might have argued with him.

Besides, she wasn't quite sure when she would do the chores anyway. Mr. Auggy was giving more homework, though it was getting easier to finish. And he wanted them at the soccer field almost at dawn on Saturday mornings. And sometimes in the evenings, Dusty called to talk about strategy—and other stuff, like little sisters, since Januarie was almost like a younger sibling to Lucy, and Dusty had two of them who sounded even more whiney and pouty. And how Dusty wished she got along with her dad as well as Lucy did with hers. Lucy even told her about Aunt Karen, and Dusty agreed that it would be worse than the worst thing they could think of to have to go live with her.

"It would be horrible," Dusty said one night when they were on the phone.

"Horrific."

"Gross."

"Grotesque."

"Hyper-noxious."

"You made that up," Lucy said.

"I don't know as many big words as you." There was a pause. "Can I ask you something, and promise you won't get mad?"

"Promise," Lucy said, although she was sure she'd never made that promise to anyone before. It wasn't something she could usually guarantee.

"You're way smart, so how come you're in the, um, support class?"

"I think it's because I hate school," Lucy said. She flipped over on her stomach, feet kicking behind her. "But thanks for saying I'm smart."

"You totally are. But I don't see why you don't like school. If I had Mr. Auggy all day, I would LOVE going."

Lucy had to admit later, when she was trying to make a list of all the reasons she still hated school, that Dusty had a point.

— It's too much sitting — but Mr. Auggy makes us move around all the time.

— I hate to read — except the stuff he gives us is pretty interesting.

— I can't spell — only Mr. Auggy doesn't even care about that on our sloppy copies.

— I'm always in the dumb class because I don't do my work — only Mr. Auggy wouldn't think I'm a better than average girl if I didn't, and besides, Inez makes me.

She chewed on the end of her pen and wondered what would happen if she just told Inez no, she wasn't doing homework anymore. But she didn't wonder for long. It wasn't worth it, and somebody tapped on the door.

"Come in, Dad," she said.

"It isn't Dad," a tiny voice said.

Januarie poked her very round face in.

"What are you doing here?" Lucy said. "It's like past your bedtime."

"People are yelling at my house," she said. "And Mr. Auggy told me that when they yell me and J.J. are supposed to come over here."

Lucy sat up straight. "Where's J.J.?"

"He's waiting on your front steps for Mr. Auggy to come. He called him."

Januarie looked as if her face were about to crumple. Lucy patted the bed next to her, and Januarie bounded to the spot like a Saint Bernard puppy. She snuggled under Lucy's arm and gave a long sigh. They stayed that way for a minute, until Lucy realized Januarie was turning the pages of the Book of Lists.

"Don't!" Lucy said, and snatched it from her.

"What is that?" Januarie said. Her voice began to wind up.

"My personal stuff," Lucy said.

"Like Mora's secrets in that thing she's got?"

"No—more important." Lucy stuck the book under her shirt. "You're too little to understand."

The lip came out like a fold-out couch. "Why don't you like me anymore?"

"What?"

"You used to always walk with me after school and take me to Pasco's and get food and let me spy for you guys—and now you don't."

Lucy felt a flutter of guilt. "I can't go to Pasco's after school now," she said, although she knew that wasn't going to help.

Januarie twisted the pillowcase in her fingers. "Do you like Dusty more than you like me?"

"I like her different than I like you," Lucy said. Whew. She didn't know where that came from, but she was glad it did.

"If you still liked me, you would let me play soccer with you guys."

"For Pete's sake, Januarie—would you give it up?" Lucy squirmed away from her, still clutching her book. "You have to work for it, and even then it doesn't always turn out all happily ever after. Can't you just be happy with what you get to do?"

Januarie's dark eyes filled with tears until they looked like tiny cups of chocolate pudding.

"Don't cry," Lucy said.

"I will if I want." And then she sobbed into Lucy's pillow until she fell asleep there. Only then did Lollipop peek out of the toy chest.

"Coast is clear," Lucy said. But she wondered if it ever really would be.

She put the Book of Lists back in the underwear drawer and got up on her knees to look out the window. J.J. sat on the front steps with

Mr. Auggy, their heads bent together as if the conversation was very important. Lucy suddenly felt so sad she couldn't hold her head up. Was it ever going to be the same with her and J.J.?

She knew one thing: until it was, she couldn't even be close to happily ever after. Maybe if she asked him—God—she might have a better chance. Only she hadn't found her way yet, like Inez said she would. So she snuggled in next to Januarie and just hoped.

16

J.J. and Januarie showed up at their house at night two more times. J.J. always waited on the steps for Mr. Auggy, and Januarie always came inside and crawled into bed with Lucy, taking all the covers and sometimes even snoring. Lucy didn't see how Januarie could think she didn't like her. Who would put up with that if she didn't?

One night, though, Lucy had different overnight guests. On Tuesday, February 18th, Dad and Mr. Auggy went to the town council meeting, and Dad asked Inez to spend the night since the meeting could run late. Inez staying meant Mora was going to stay too.

"Cool," Dusty said when Lucy told her before school that day. "It'll be like a sleepover." She looked down at her Uggs. "I wish it was me instead."

"Me too," Januarie piped up.

Lucy hoped she wouldn't stir up something at home just so she could come over. She'd actually never had a sleepover, but she said, "Januarie, sleepovers for eleven year olds only have eleven year olds."

"Right," Dusty said. "You could have one at your house for eight year olds."

Lucy had another guilt-flutter. She couldn't imagine Januarie ever inviting other little girls to her house. Lucy herself had only been in it a few times. It smelled like wet dog and always made her want to go home where it felt safe.

"You want me to work with you on your dribbling, Januarie?" Lucy said.

"No," she said and stomped herself off to the second- and third-grade wing. The look she sent over her shoulder was meant to wither both of them, Lucy was sure.

Mora arrived that day with two tote bags, one pink and one green, both stuffed so full they wouldn't zip. All through their homework period, she brought up the fact that she was missing dance class so many times that Inez finally told her if she said it again she was going to take her electronic diary away from her. That hushed her up. It was one of those moments when Lucy liked Inez.

The four of them ate supper together, and Lucy noticed that Mora stared at Dad the entire time, especially when Lucy gave him his plate coordinates.

"So, it's like a clock," she said.

"Well, ye-ah," Lucy said, although she wanted to say, "Duh!"

"It must be so weird not to be able to see your food."

"Mora!" Inez said sharply, and added something in Spanish that couldn't have been good. Lucy was ready to add something in English, but Dad just smiled sunshine across the table at Mora.

"It gets weirder," he said. "Sometimes I come out with some interesting outfits and Lucy tells me to go change my clothes or she won't be seen with me."

"Nuh-uh!" Lucy said. She turned to Mora. "Everything's in the closet by colors, and as long as we don't change it, we're fine."

Mora put her fork down. "So—how do you, like, shave?"

"Mora," Inez said again.

But Dad shook his head. "It's all right. I like to educate people on the art of being blind."

For the rest of dinner, he told Mora how he brushed his teeth and walked to the corner where he got his ride to work and paid the bills by phone. He didn't reveal how he always knew when Lucy had gotten herself into trouble. She was waiting for that.

"So," Mora said over their dessert of flan with caramel sauce, "you can totally take care of your own self."

"Pretty much," Dad said.

Pretty much? What about how Lucy read the Sunday paper to him and how she told him what was on the menu when Aunt Karen took them to a strange restaurant and how she protected him from people who acted like he was retarded instead of just blind?

Or was Inez going to start doing all that too, until Dad didn't really need her anymore?

"Luce?" Dad said.

"Huh?"

"I said, you'll make sure Inez and Mora have everything they need while I'm at the meeting?"

"Oh," Lucy said. "Sure."

Mr. Auggy came by for Dad and assured her they would do all they could to get some equipment for the soccer team. When they left, Mora said, "That's your teacher?"

"Yeah."

Mora giggled. "He's cute."

Oh, ickety-*ick*.

When Inez told them it was time to get ready for bed—like Lucy didn't know that—Mora spent twenty minutes in the bathroom and emerged decked out in pink pajamas with straps like pieces of spaghetti and ruffles around the bottom. She smelled like a bowl of strawberries and had a large metal thing attached to her teeth that went all the way around her head. She looked like an extraterrestrial to Lucy.

"Don't say a word," Mora said. Whatever the thing was, it didn't keep her from talking.

She looked around Lucy's room. "Where do your friends usually sleep when they come over?"

"Um—"

Mora put her hands on her hips. "You've had a sleepover before, haven't you?"

"No."

"Hello! Where have you been? Okay—do you have a sleeping bag? Extra blankets—"

Lucy produced everything Mora named, and within minutes, they had two pallets on the floor side by side. Mora parked on one of them, crossed her ankles, and said, "What do you want to talk about?"

Lucy had no idea. Soccer? Mora would so not want to discuss passing strategy.

"So—do you think they'll give you money for your program?"

Lucy blinked.

"That's what the meeting's about, right?" Mora nodded as if she were very wise. "Grown-ups always say there's no money for stuff, but if you pitch enough of a fit, they find it. You should have seen what we had to go through to get our warm-up suits so we'd all match at competition." She reached for the pink bag and pulled out a photo album that she flipped open and displayed as if she were a first-grade teacher ready to read a picture book to the class. Lucy couldn't help looking at the photograph of Mora in a red tank top, a white, sparkly-striped jacket with her name embroidered on it, and bright blue pants with sparkles up the sides. It was a little too glittery for soccer, but it was definitely cool.

"They cost a lot because the inside is lined in fleece," Mora said. "But we have to stay warm or our muscles will cramp up. Once it's all about safety, grown-ups will buy anything."

"We need cleats and shin guards," Lucy said.

"That sounds like it's ugly."

"Yeah, but it'll keep us from sliding and getting bruised and stuff."

"True," Mora said, as if she actually knew what Lucy was talking about. "You want to see my awards?"

Before Lucy could answer, Mora was back in the pink bag again, pulling out wooden plaques with brass plates announcing FIRST PLACE and pictures of her team. They even wore their hair all the same.

"It is SO much work," Mora said, rolling her enormous eyes. "But we like to win."

And then, as if Lucy had asked her to, she launched into an explanation of the techniques she had to learn, complete with demonstrations across Lucy's floor, which drove Lollipop past the toy chest and completely out of the room. Lucy had to admit it was pretty interesting, although she wasn't sure why anyone would spend that kind of time going for a perfect toe touch.

When Inez said it was time to turn out the light—like Lucy didn't know that either—Mora pulled out a blanket with NEW MEXICO DANCE CHAMPIONSHIP embroidered on it and a stuffed dog wearing a replica of her uniform. She snuggled into her pallet and was asleep before Lucy could even lie down. When she did, her eyes wouldn't close.

Everything was so strange. Why didn't she want to go get Marmalade and put her next to Mora so she'd freak out if she woke up? Why could she hardly wait to get to school tomorrow to tell Dusty how all into dance Mora was? And why, actually, didn't that whole dance thing seem weird to her? She herself ate, slept, and breathed soccer. What was the difference?

Dance was girly. That was the difference. There were so many differences between her and other girls that it was hard to know if she even was one. Lucy churned on her pallet for a few minutes and then got up and soundlessly opened her underwear drawer and pulled out the Book of Lists. She peeked out into the hall, but everything was quiet. Inez was probably in the guest room. Lucy wondered as she padded down the hall whether Inez's hair even got messed up when she was in bed.

Marmalade and a sleepy Artemis joined Lucy on the Napping Couch where she wrapped up in the Navajo blanket and opened the book. There was only one list to make right now.

Ways I'm Totally Different from Other Girls
— They all like pink. I don't.
— They think boys are cute. I SO don't. Even J.J. —

She skipped past that. It hurt too much to think about J.J. right now.

— They giggle. I hardly ever do.
— They get all jazzed about iPods and electronic diaries and cell phones. I don't need any of that stuff. I just need a soccer ball and some cleats and some shin guards, because Mr. Auggy says he doesn't want us getting hurt by sliding around or being accidentally kicked. I don't want to get hurt anymore. I hated not playing soccer for three whole days. Dad said I was in

withdrawal, which, I don't know what that is, but if it, like, drives you nuts, I was in it.

Lucy stopped and rested her hand. Wow. She'd written a whole paragraph. And she hated to write. But there was more.

—They have sleepovers and I don't. Except tonight, which doesn't really count because I didn't invite Mora and she probably wouldn't have come if I had. I wonder if I could invite Dusty, and maybe Veronica. Only how do I know they really like me? They're girly-girls. I'm not.

"You are up late."

Lucy jumped and slapped the Book of Lists closed and stuck it under her thigh.

Artemis crouched as if she were stalking Inez. Lucy felt like Inez was stalking *her*, gliding without a sound to the other end of the Napping Couch.

"The Sleep escapes you?" Inez said.

Lucy had a picture of dreams scampering away, and she nodded.

"It escapes me too." Inez nodded toward Lucy's lap. "It does not escape the dangerous one."

Lucy ran her hand over Marmalade's back. "She's not really dangerous. I guess you figured that out."

"But Mora is. It is best to be careful."

Lucy swallowed guiltily.

"You are writing."

The guilt disappeared, and Lucy went stiff. She didn't care what Inez said, she wasn't showing her the book—

"I often write my troubles when they are tangled," Inez said. "Show God the knots, and he will untangle them."

"I wasn't writing to God." Lucy felt the corner of the book poking at her backside cheek. "I was just—making a list. Of stuff."

"Lists are good."

It was quiet, except for Marmalade's purring and something bubbling on the stove.

"Warm milk," Inez said. "We will drink it with nutmeg."

"Oh," Lucy said. The book was really boring into her now. She inched it out and propped it beside her.

Inez folded her hands neatly. "I write in a book. It is — hmm — it last a long time."

"Yeah," Lucy said with surprise. "I'm going to keep this forever."

"Good."

It didn't seem right not to say something back.

"Sometimes I write about what I don't like."

"God wants to hear about that, yes."

"God?" Lucy said.

"My book is sometimes how I talk to God."

Lucy put the book on top of Marmalade, who didn't budge, and fingered the gold leaves. "I didn't know I was talking to God."

"You tell the truth when you write?"

Lucy pulled the book to her chest. Inez almost smiled.

"I see that you are. We must protect our secrets."

At the moment, Lucy wished only a password would open the Book of Lists. And yet, it didn't feel like Inez was going to grab it from her.

"If you write honest thoughts, you talk to God. Your thoughts they have been answered?"

"Huh?"

"Look. Think."

Inez glided off to the kitchen, and Lucy flipped through the pages. Aunt Karen hadn't moved to Australia yet. Lucy still missed her mom. Although she had to admit she couldn't make flan or machaca or make the Bible better than Disney, she could get along without Inez just like she did before. Right?

But she no longer wanted to flush the soccer team down the toilet. She didn't really have an attitude anymore. And most of her reasons for hating school weren't that true now.

That was because of God? Even though she'd never thought of him while she was making her lists except to blame him for all the rotten stuff?

"He thinks of you," Inez said.

Lucy looked up with a start. Inez put a cup of something that smelled amazing into her hand.

"When you think of him also, that is even better."

Lucy looked down at the last thing she'd written.

They're girly-girls. I'm not.

"God can tell me what kind of girl to be?" Lucy said.

"He has already."

Lucy leaned in, ready to ask, ready to listen. But the back door opened, and Lucy heard Dad's cane tapping on the floor. Inez said, "We are here, Senor Rooney."

Dad appeared with his coat still on and his face drawn into straight lines.

"Luce, you still up?"

"Sleep escaped me," Lucy said.

Dad smiled, but there was no sunlight. He sank into his chair, and Lucy joined him on the arm, leaving Marmalade and the Book of Lists on the Napping Couch.

"They won't pay for our equipment, right?" she said.

"It's worse than that, I'm afraid, champ."

How could it be? She wasn't sure she wanted to hear.

"A big corporation has offered to buy the property where the old soccer field is and put a gas station there."

"We already have a gas station."

"This is going to be the gas station to end all gas stations, evidently. There will be a grocery store, a Pizza Hut—"

"We don't need that! We have Pasco's and Mr. Benitez's!"

"This'll be for travelers passing through," Dad said. "They plan to open up a major road from the highway. It's a big deal."

Lucy stood up. "They can't take our soccer field, Dad."

"They can if the town of Los Suenos sells it to them. The council says we need the money to fix our roads, improve our schools." He sounded like he was reading something from a paper. It wasn't Dad being convinced, and Lucy's heart plummeted all the way to her belly.

"Nothing is going to happen yet—the council hasn't decided. But needless to say, they weren't eager to put up the money for soccer equipment if there isn't going to be a field to play on."

"That's not fair!"

"You are absolutely right." Dad felt for Lucy's hand and then dropped his to the arm of the chair. "But whoever promised us fair?"

So that was it. Her dream was gone before it ever emerged from the mist of her mind. Lucy felt so heavy all she wanted to do was lie down. She picked up her book and headed down the hall. Soft footsteps followed her.

"Make the list for God about this," Inez said. And then she disappeared down the yellow rug.

What was God going to do about it?

Lucy headed into her room and tripped over Mora's bag stuffed with dance equipment. It irritated Lucy right up the back of her neck.

Mora lived in a big town. She got to do what she wanted because people cared about kids there. How was Lucy supposed to get people like Mr. Benitez to vote for cleats?

But she wanted that more than anything. And if nobody else was going to do anything about it, how could it hurt to ask God? He'd done a few things lately, maybe—

She took a flashlight out of the toy chest and sat up on her bed. With the light clamped between her propped-up knees, she wrote:

Why I Hope You, God, Give the Soccer Team to Us
— The Hispanic kids don't hate us like they used to because of soccer.
— Me and J.J. and Oscar and Emanuel and Carla Rosa are doing better in school because of soccer.
— J.J. and Januarie don't have to get yelled at by their dad because of Mr. Auggy — and soccer.
— Soccer makes me like my mom was, and that's the only kind of girl I know how to be.

Lucy licked at the tears that trailed over her lips. And then she wrapped her arms around her book and fell asleep with the lists—and maybe God—up close to her heart.

Mora hogged the bathroom the next morning, and Lucy barely had time to brush her teeth, so she was not in a good mood when she slammed out the back gate. When Januarie said, "I have to tell you something," Lucy said, "You know what? I have important things on my mind."

Januarie whimpered and ran off. If she'd had a tail, it would have been between her legs. Lucy barely had time for a guilty pang before Carla Rosa and the boys, minus J.J., were on her at the bicycle rack.

"Tell them I'm not lying," Carla Rosa said. "'Cause, guess what, my father's the mayor."

Lucy hitched at her backpack. "Did she tell you her dad said some big company wants to buy our soccer field?"

"Aw, man—then it is true." Oscar pounded his fist on the bike rack and then winced.

"Way to go, lame-o," Emanuel said.

Lucy stared at them. She hadn't heard them talk like that in weeks. Because of Mr. Auggy. Because of soccer.

"Buzzzz," she said.

"Who cares now?" Oscar said. "If we ain't got no field—"

"Why is everybody being all gloomy?" Lucy said.

Carla Rosa jiggled the big sequins on her hat. "Guess what? YOU look gloomy."

"I'm not gloomy. I'm mad."

She stomped toward the portable with the rest of them behind her.

"What's the difference?" Oscar said.

"Gloomy means you're giving up. Mad means you're going to do something about it."

"So what are we gonna do?" Emanuel said.

It no longer surprised Lucy when he talked. That was because of soccer too. Which was why she stopped at the bottom of the portable steps and looked at them all with her jaw set.

"I don't know yet, but we're not giving up."

"Guess what?" Carla Rosa whispered.

She pointed up at the door. Mr. Auggy and J.J. stood there. It was the first time J.J. had looked at her in weeks. A knot tied up in Lucy's throat. God, Inez had said, would untangle your knots.

"You're not giving up, are you?" Lucy said.

"No way," Mr. Auggy said. "J.J. and I were just talking about that."

He looked at J.J., who shrugged and shifted his eyes to the steps. But at least he didn't curl his lip at Lucy and move away from her like she had head lice.

"We'll talk about it at recess," Mr. Auggy said. "I want the whole team there." He nodded at Lucy. "That okay with you, captain?"

She wanted to know what he was thinking right NOW, but she agreed—and then practically held her breath until lunch. Dusty and Veronica met her at the cafeteria door.

"You didn't come to the cubbies this morning," Dusty said.

"Hello—we needed to talk to you," Veronica said.

"Oh," Lucy said. She didn't know that was supposed to be a regular thing.

Dusty looped her arms around Lucy's elbow and put her lips close to her ear. "I think something bad is going to go down at recess."

"You mean, what Mr. Auggy is going to tell us?" Lucy said.

"Huh? No. I mean Gabe."

Veronica crowded to her other side. "He said he is going to kick J.J.'s tail because he's getting too good on the team."

"Gabe wants to be the best," Dusty said into her right ear.

Veronica tugged her left arm. "I don't even like him as a boyfriend anymore."

"When's it going to happen?" Lucy said. She was already craning her neck to look for J.J., although he hadn't come into the cafeteria for over a week.

"While we're practicing." Dusty shook her head. "That's hideous."

Lucy broke away from them. "We have to tell Mr. Auggy."

"You mean like tattle?" Veronica's lower lip took a plunge. "I am so not doing that."

"Mr. Auggy won't do anything," Dusty said. "Nobody ever does anything to Gabe. He's the sheriff's kid—"

"Who cares?" Lucy turned to the door. "I'm finding Mr. Auggy."

"You didn't hear it from us," Veronica said.

"Lucy—" Dusty said.

But Lucy didn't turn back. This was why she didn't trust them—because when it came right down to it, they would always be loyal to their own.

And so would she.

Lucy tossed her sandwich in the garbage on the way out and tore for the field, hoping Mr. Auggy would be there, setting things up. But she didn't find him. There was only J.J.

And Gabe.

They stood facing each other in the middle of the tiny soccer field. Even as she got closer, neither one of them seemed aware that she was there. She could see their nostrils flaring like trumpets, but nothing else about them seemed small. They weren't little boys anymore.

"Why don't you just leave it?" J.J. said.

"Can't."

J.J. didn't ask him why. He just took a step forward.

A step forward. J.J. never went toward Gabe. He always backed away.

Lucy was about to take a step herself, when Gabe said, "Don't start something you can't finish."

Please, J.J. Listen to him.

"I want to finish this," J.J. said. "I'm done with you dissing me. I'm as good as you."

"Not at soccer."

"At everything."

Lucy watched as Gabe turned into a statue—stiff and hard as if he were made of cement. But his eyes were all too alive, and they glittered like flint in the sun. His face went a paler shade, and Lucy noticed for the first time that Gabe had tiny coarse hairs growing on his chin. He took a jerky step toward J.J., and Lucy waited for J.J. to lower his chin that half inch that said, "I know you're stronger than me. I know I got nothing."

But J.J. didn't lower his chin—that chin that was hairless as a peach and not nearly so tough-looking as Gabe's. She wanted to yell for him to run, duck, do something to get away from the heavy body that hurled itself at him and flattened him to the ground.

At first, all she could see were Gabe's boxer shorts sticking out of the top of his sweats as his shirt came up. Lucy had the urge to laugh, as if it couldn't possibly be happening. It must not be a real fight if she wanted to laugh. They even growled like Mudge.

But as they rolled over once, then twice, so that Gabe was still on top, the laughter strangled in her throat. Gabe pulled his fist back behind his head, which was a vicious red all the way down to his scalp. He was going to jam it right into J.J.'s face, and J.J. wouldn't fight back. She knew it.

And then Gabe bucked as if he was on a bronco, and suddenly he was on his back with J.J. sitting astride him. J.J.'s Adam's apple pumped up and down, up and down, and he breathed so loud Lucy could hear the air heaving in his chest. He was on top of Gabe—and Gabe wasn't moving. Even Gabe's face was frozen in an open-eyed startle.

J.J. cocked his fist back, face muscles working hard as he breathed. Gabe's eyes finally awakened, and he turned his head.

Bust him, J.J. Get him back for making you feel like dirt—

Don't do it, J.J. They'll never let you off like they will him—

Lucy felt like she was one big knot. Still, J.J. sat on Gabe with his arm tense as steel, threatening with his eyes. Where was God with his big untying fingers?

Gabe struggled. J.J. pinned him with his legs, with one arm. His muscles stood out, shiny and hard, like they belonged to someone else, not the boy across the street she had to protect from bullies. With the knot growing in her throat, she put her hand over her mouth. She couldn't stop it this time.

But there was somebody who could. Lucy whipped around and ran into that very person. Mr. Auggy put his finger to his lips and turned his eyes back to the boys. Other kids gathered, but nobody said a word—not with Mr. Auggy there watching too.

What was he thinking?

Lucy felt a tug at her sleeve. "Make him stop," Januarie said. "J.J.'s gonna get killed!"

Lucy looked back at J.J. He didn't look like he was in any danger from Gabe at all. He still had his fist cocked back, but as she pleaded with him silently, *J.J., don't, don't*, he opened his fingers and pressed his flat hand on Gabe's shoulder.

"It's over," J.J., said into Gabe's stricken face. "I'm as good as you, and I'm done provin' it."

He didn't even wait to see if Gabe would answer. He just stood up and wiped his mouth with the back of his hand and took a step back. And then he reached his hand down.

Gabe shook his head at it, but Mr. Auggy said quietly, "Take it, Gabe. We're done."

And so Gabe did, and J.J. helped him up. They didn't look at each other. Gabe stomped toward the building, and Veronica started after him. But Mr. Auggy said, "Leave it, Miss Veronica."

She did.

J.J. still stood at the scene of the fight. Nobody else seemed to know what to do. But Lucy suddenly knew she did.

"Ding-ding-ding, J.J.," she said.

"Oh, yeah." Mr. Auggy grinned bigger than Lucy ever thought his small mouth would go. "That deserves a ding-ding-ding if anything ever did. That's integrity, Mr. J.J."

Other, non-soccer kids mumbled to each other and drifted away as if they were disappointed. Mr. Auggy didn't seem to notice them. He put out his arms to gather the team.

"You're ready," he said when they were all around him — except Gabe.

"For what?" Carla Rosa said.

Oscar and Emanuel were too busy staring — in awe — at J.J. to even respond, until Mr. Auggy said, "You're ready to play another team."

"You lie," Dusty said and then clapped her hand over her mouth.

Mr. Auggy's eyes twinkled. "No, it's the truth. I think we have all our differences settled, and we can act like a team now. You've had the skills. Now you have the heart."

"What about Gabe?" Veronica said. "J.J. almost kicked his tail — he's not gonna give up until he gets back at him."

Mr. Auggy shook his head, along with all the other boys. "You have a lot to learn about guys, Miss Veronica. We're not like girls. When it's done—it's done."

Why, Lucy wondered, couldn't girls be like that? Boys she understood. Girls she still didn't get. Maybe she just never would.

But they were a team—boys, girls, Hispanic, white—it didn't matter.

"Who are we going to play?" she said.

Mr. Auggy rubbed the back of his head. "That I don't know yet. I'll find another team, though. Let's just be ready for them."

"We'll dominate them!" Oscar said.

"Oh, heck yeah!" Dusty said.

She snatched the ball from Lucy and ran, looking over her shoulder. Lucy ran after her, and when she caught up, Dusty put her ear close to Lucy's and said, "You were right about Mr. Auggy. Someday, I hope I'm as smart as you are about stuff."

Then she was off with the ball again. Tonight, Lucy decided, she was going to make a list: Things I Probably Don't Even Know about My Own Self.

"Let's play soccer!" Mr. Auggy called out.

And so she did.

17

Mr. Auggy was right about boys being completely different from girls.

Lucy and Mora were finishing up their homework late that afternoon when Lucy heard a car pull up at the side curb. Mora flew to the window like she was expecting Hannah Montana. She hiked herself up to the sink and flattened her nose to the glass.

"It's that cute teacher," she reported.

"Mora, down," Inez said.

"And your dad."

"Mora—"

"And a boy—cute one—if you like the bad-boy type."

"Does he have a ponytail?" Lucy said as Inez pried Mora away from the sink.

"Yeah. Skinny. He's not Hispanic—more like—"

"Apache," Lucy said. She had a stab of fear. "Is Januarie with them?"

"Why would she be? Who is he?"

"Mora," Inez said, "go watch *Oprah*."

Mora's eyes rounded. "You're not serious." And then, as if she were afraid Inez was going to change her mind, she scooted out of the kitchen, but not before she took one more gape out the window in the back door.

"Definitely cute," she said.

Lucy didn't care if J.J. was cute. She only cared that he didn't give her the slit eyes or, worse, pretend she wasn't there. It was hard not to run to her room so she didn't have to find out.

The back door opened, and Dad caned his way in. He didn't look like he'd been arguing with anybody, and Mr. Auggy was wearing the smile when he came in behind him. J.J. didn't follow, though, and Lucy's heart took a nosedive. Oh well. Inez said everything didn't always turn out happily ever after.

"Hey, Miss Lucy," Mr. Auggy said. "J.J.'s out here. He wants to talk to you."

Lucy couldn't get up. "He wants to?" she said. "Or you're making him?"

"Tone, Luce," Dad said.

"He's on his own." Mr. Auggy's voice got soft. "I think there might be a ding-ding-ding in it."

That peeled her from the chair, got her crossing the room. Still, she stopped at the door and peeked out. J.J. sat on the steps, cracking his knuckles. She'd only seen him do that once — when he got sent to Mrs. Nunez's office for skipping school because he didn't have any clean clothes and he knew Gabe would tell him he stunk.

At least he wouldn't be avoiding Gabe anymore.

"Show God the knots," somebody said.

Dad and Mr. Auggy were sitting at the table now, leaning into cups of coffee, talking in low voices. Inez stood at the stove stirring black bean soup and looking at Lucy with her wise eyes.

Show God the knots.

Okay.

Here they are: I'm afraid to go out there. I'm afraid J.J. doesn't want to be my friend anymore.

And I need him to be my friend.

Those were the knots. Nothing felt untangled, but she opened the door and went out into the cold afternoon and sat down beside J.J. without looking at him. She didn't want to see if his lip was curled up.

"Hi," he said.

"Hi," she said back. She picked at some paint peeling on the steps.

"I was stupid."

"Yeah?"

"Wanna practice fakes?" His voice went up into the stratosphere.

Lucy finally looked at the side of his face. His Adam's apple was going up and down for the second time that day. When had that started?

"Only if you're not mad at me anymore," she said.

"I'm not."

"Okay."

J.J. nodded and stood and picked up a soccer ball.

"Where'd you get that?" she said.

"Mr. Auggy."

She didn't ask why. She didn't ask what he and Mr. Auggy talked about every day before school and after school and sometimes on her front steps. She didn't ask anything. She could ask Dusty stuff like that—and Mora would tell her more than she ever wanted to know whether Lucy asked or not. But boys were different kinds of friends than girls.

She smiled. She could know that now. She sort of had girlfriends.

Lucy and J.J. practiced their fakes until it was so dark they couldn't see shadows and they needed the jackets they'd thrown onto the back steps. Mora mouthed things to Lucy as she and Inez crossed the backyard to go home—things Lucy couldn't understand, though she could guess. Something about J.J. being cute and was he her boyfriend.

No. This was better.

Dad and Mr. Auggy were still talking when she and J.J. went inside. There was a bubbling pan of enchiladas on the table for the four of them, and as they ate, the talk was all about a plan. Lucy felt her eyes getting bigger and bigger as they laid it out. Even J.J.'s icy-blues grew round.

As soon as Mr. Auggy found a team for them to play, he and Dad were going to get things rolling. Dad would talk it up on the radio and try to get community support. The stand at the field would have to be cleaned out—and, of course, the bleachers needed to be shored up for safety. As for shin guards and cleats—Mr. Auggy had found a place in Alamogordo where they could rent them. Parents might be able to afford that.

"Now all I have to do is find a team for us to—well, slaughter,"

Mr. Auggy said, eyes shining. "I'm not promising anything, but this could be a way to keep the town council from selling that property."

"What can we do?" Lucy said. "Us—the team?"

"Become the best team you can," Mr. Auggy said.

"What about Gabe?"

"Parent-teacher conferences are Friday." Mr. Auggy twitched his eyebrows. "I think the sheriff and I can figure something out for Gabe."

Lucy shook her head. "He won't do anything."

"I wouldn't be so sure about that," Dad said. "Did you ever think you wouldn't be chewing your fingernails because parent-teacher conferences were coming up?" He chuckled. "Mr. Auggy makes me want to believe in miracles myself."

It really was the first time since third grade that Lucy's stomach didn't have cocoons hanging in it, ready to transform into butterflies at the thought of her teacher filling Dad in on her "failure to live up to her potential." Wouldn't Aunt Karen have to eat a whole plateful of her words?

"Hey," she said suddenly. "That means we're out of school Friday." She got up on one knee. "We could practice on the field the whole day."

"Not without supervision," Dad said. "Remember?"

"Oh."

"Let me work on it." Mr. Auggy gave the small secret smile, and Lucy believed he really could make anything happen.

She was happily brushing her teeth that night, sharing the mirror with Artemis who was gazing at her own whiskers, when she heard the phone ring.

"Hi," Dad said, in his it's-Aunt-Karen voice.

Lucy spit in the sink and listened.

There was the usual adult stuff, and then the silence, and then Dad saying, as usual, "She's doing great."

More silence. When Dad answered it, Lucy got very still with her toothbrush poised in midair. His voice had an edge around it.

"She *is* doing great.... Yes, I know what's going on in my daughter's life.... All right, I have a conference with her teacher Friday. Why don't you come up here and sit in on it?"

What? Lucy let the toothbrush drop. Artemis crouched on the edge of the sink, ready to attack it.

Okay—wait—it was okay. Aunt Karen would never leave work to come up here on a weekday—

"Noon," Dad said. "I'll meet you at the school."

This was an outrage. While Artemis pounced on the toothbrush and batted it around the sink, Lucy made for the door, ready to tell Dad there was no way she wanted Aunt Karen at that conference.

And then she stopped, hand on the doorknob. Wasn't this what she wanted—for Aunt Karen to have to say she was sorry for ever even thinking Lucy needed to be with her to do good in school and have a soccer team and have girls for friends?

She went back to the sink and rescued her toothbrush from Artemis and counted her freckles in the mirror. There were still sixteen. She was her mother's daughter, not Aunt Karen's, and her aunt was going to see that once and for all.

Lucy was actually excited about Friday, especially since Mr. Auggy announced on Thursday that they might be able to practice on the big field for two hours Friday afternoon if he could get the adult he had in mind to supervise. He would notify Captain Lucy at 11:00 a.m.

"I'll call everybody," she said.

But at 10:45, Gabe, Veronica, Dusty, Oscar, Emanuel, Carla Rosa, J.J., and Januarie were all at Lucy's back gate.

"Tell them come in," Inez said.

They were all sitting at Lucy's table drooling over her sopapillas when the phone rang.

Mr. Auggy's voice was like Christmas morning. "You can head over there right now."

"Who's there?"

"You'll see." Mr. Auggy gave a chuckle that sounded like Dad's. They were spending way too much time together.

But the fact that they were made Lucy feel important—like she belonged to something special. She straightened her shoulders as she turned to the expectant faces and said, "Let's go, team. We've got a grown-up."

"Guess what?" Carla Rosa said as they climbed onto their bikes. "It's not my dad."

"Mine either," Dusty said. Veronica shook her head.

"I ain't got no dad right now," Oscar said.

J.J. and Januarie didn't say anything. They didn't have to.

The sizzle of mystery made them pedal furiously. But when they rounded the bend and saw the sheriff's cruiser parked under the sign, they groaned like one person. Lucy went into knots immediately. How was God going to untie this one?

"You're the captain, Lucy," Carla Rosa said. "You go talk to him."

"I ain't talkin' to him," Oscar said.

Dusty curled her hand into Lucy's. "I'll go with you."

"So what are you waitin' for, an invitation?"

Lucy jerked around. Gabe stood a few feet away, next to his beefy father, a bigger, grumpier version of Gabe himself. He wasn't in his uniform. He wore gray sweats that bulged with his muscles.

"Are we playing or what?" Gabe said. "My dad said he'd watch us."

Nobody said anything. Lucy, the captain, felt a tug inside her, like a knot was untying. She took a step forward.

"Are you going to play by the rules—I mean, Mr. Auggy's rules?" she said.

"Yes, he is." The sheriff poked his kid in the back. Gabe seemed to grow smaller. "Aren't cha?"

"Yeah." Gabe shifted his eyes to J.J. "Sorry, man."

J.J. shrugged and mumbled, "It's okay."

"I love that!" Veronica said.

Lucy had a feeling Gabe was boyfriend material again.

"All right then," Lucy said. "Let's play soccer."

It was the best practice ever. Nobody fell down. Nobody called "foul." Nobody curled a lip or muttered under their breath. Gabe called her Lucy Goosey once, but Lucy ignored him. Veronica seemed to appreciate that.

They were taking their required water break—drinking the Gatorade the sheriff handed out in bottles—when Lucy felt the familiar tug at her sleeve.

"Lucy," Januarie said, "I want to try out for the team again."

J.J. grunted, but only faintly. Lucy looked at the rest of the team, but they were just watching her. Waiting. Everything was so perfect. Why did something always have to happen to wrinkle it up?

"You said if I was ever good enough I could be on the team." The Chihuahua was emerging. "I bet I'm good enough now."

"Okay," Lucy said. "Same as before. If you can get the ball away from me and another player before we get down the field—"

"I want Carla Rosa to be the other player," she said.

"Aw man," Gabe said.

His father growled at him, and he hushed up. If Lucy had known that was all it took, she'd have sicced Mudge on him a long time ago.

But she almost had to agree with Gabe this time. Januarie was sure to lose to anybody else on the team. But Carla Rosa wasn't that much better than Januarie, especially if she got the giggles or her hat fell over her eyes or she just forgot what she was supposed to do.

Chewing on her lip, Lucy glanced at Carla. She was drawing a circle in the dirt with her toe, the way kids did when they were waiting for the grown-ups to find a nice way to say no. Lucy was the grown-up right now. She couldn't help Januarie, but maybe—

With a wary eye on the sheriff, Lucy said, "All right, Carla Rosa."

J.J.'s grunt was louder this time, but the smile that spread from sequins to sequins on Carla Rosa made it worth it.

"Me?" she said.

Oscar gave a snort. "Only 'cause you're the wor—"

"Shut up," Emanuel said.

Nobody buzzed.

"Someone throw in to us," Lucy said.

"Give me that." Sheriff Navarra held out his hands for the ball.

Of course. That was only fair. Lucy tossed it to him and ran out on the field. Carla Rosa was practically chirping as she followed. Januarie was already breathing like a little locomotive.

"Ready?" Lucy said.

Carla Rosa's sequins bobbed, and Lucy used a long, lofted pass to get the ball to her over Januarie's head. Carla took a few dribbles, steady ones, and Januarie chugged toward her. "Here!" Lucy cried, and then held her breath. But it was okay, because Carla Rosa swung her leg back and passed it straight past Januarie. Lucy trapped it, and to her amazement, Carla Rosa ran around the by-now-very-confused Januarie. Lucy passed the ball back to Carla and ran. Furrowing her brow under the sequins, Carla drilled her eyes into the ball and dribbled in a straight line, until Lucy yelled, "To me!"

Carla passed the ball to her. It went a little crooked, but it didn't matter, because Januarie was far behind them, crying out, "Wait! You're going too fast!" Carla Rosa didn't seem to hear her. She snagged the pass Lucy made to her, and as Lucy ran out ahead of her, she realized they were just a few yards from the goal.

"Take your shot, Carla Rosa!" she cried out.

Carla stopped dead, the ball trapped under her foot.

"Do it!" Lucy said.

And so she did. With a hockey stick leg, Carla Rosa smacked the ball—and it sailed over the goal line, right into the net.

A cheer went up from the sideline that matched any Lucy had dreamed up. It didn't matter that there was no goalie and anybody could have shot the ball over the goal line. Until that day, Carla Rosa hadn't been "anybody."

The Gigglers ran out to squeal over Carla. Oscar gave several long whistles between his teeth. Even J.J. was clapping, and Gabe wasn't doing anything obnoxious. The only person making an unhappy noise was Januarie.

"It isn't fair!" she wailed, round cheeks red as candy apples.

"It *is* fair, Januarie," Lucy said. She pulled her away from the rest of the team. "If you can't get the ball from Carla Rosa, how do you think you're ever going to get it from another team?"

"There isn't ever gonna be another team! My dad says it's never gonna happen. He says Mr. Auggy is full of hot air. He hates Mr. Auggy—"

"He hates everybody." J.J. was suddenly there. He even tried to put his hand on Januarie's shoulder, and Lucy had never seen him touch her before.

But Januarie wrenched away and doubled her fists and looked as if she were going to pop like a red balloon. "You know what?" she said, right at Lucy. "I hate *you!*"

She tried to run, but that wasn't happening, not as hard as she was breathing. Lucy watched her march until she disappeared on the other side of the fence.

"She shouldn't cross the highway by herself," Lucy said.

"I got it." Sheriff Navarra waved his arm at them. "Time's up anyway. You all okay on your bikes?"

They all nodded, and he left in his car. Lucy was sure Januarie was going to wet her pants when he pulled up beside her. She felt herself wilt.

"It's not your fault, Lucy," Dusty said. "That was totally fair."

Carla Rosa's face pleated. "Was I supposed to let her get the ball?"

"No!" they all said together.

"This should be a celebration for Carla Rosa," Veronica said. "I brought granola bars."

"Wow," Gabe said sarcastically.

But Veronica smacked him playfully, and all was well.

Lucy felt a little better when she got home. It was a good thing to finally have it settled that Januarie wasn't ready to play with the older kids on a real team. She'd get over it. J.J. even said he would talk to her. Lucy made him promise not to lock her in the garage.

"I don't do that stuff anymore," he said.

Lucy was sure Mr. Auggy had something to do with that.

It was 1:00. She hoped Inez had lunch ready, and as she opened the back door, she started to holler—"Can we have guacamole-that-looks-like-baby-food?" But she stopped when she heard a familiar voice—a voice that was not pleased.

"Look, this is none of your business," Aunt Karen said.

"It is my business when I take care of Senor Ted's home," Inez answered her.

Lucy felt a smile twitching at the corners of her mouth. It might be fun to hide here in the kitchen and listen to Inez stand up to Aunt Karen. If anybody could—

But the next sentence bolted her right into the hall where the two women stood face-to-face.

18

"That book belonged to my sister, and I'm not going to have Lucy messing it up!"

"No!"

Both faces whipped toward Lucy. Aunt Karen immediately licked her lips like she was going to take a bite out of her.

"Where is it, Lucy?"

"You told her?" Lucy said to Inez. "You told her about my book?"

"It's not *your* book." Aunt Karen had shifted to her you're-just-a-kid voice. "It was your mother's, and it's not a toy."

"I'm not playing with it!"

"Quite frankly, I wouldn't doubt if you were using it for a soccer ball. Now tell me where it is, or I'll find it for myself."

"No," Lucy said.

"Fine."

Aunt Karen turned on her heel and headed for Lucy's bedroom. In a rush of air, Inez got between her and the doorway.

"So sorry," Inez said. "When I am in charge of Lucy, no one will touch touch what is hers."

"You are not serious," Aunt Karen said. Lucy could only see her from the back, though she could imagine her slathering up her lips but good. "Get out of the way."

"You get the permission from Senor Ted, I let you in. Simple."

Aunt Karen raked her fingers through her hair and left her hand suspended. "What do you think you're doing?"

"My job."

"Really. Well, enjoy it while you can because you aren't going to have it much longer."

She turned on her heel and narrowed her icy eyes at Lucy. "This is so not over." She brought up a finger and pointed it right into Lucy's face. "So help me, if you put one mark on that book—it belonged to my sister, and we don't have that much left of her."

"She wasn't just your sister," Lucy said through the knot in her throat. "She was my mother."

"Oh, don't I know it." Aunt Karen brought the finger down. "You're just exactly like her—and that's what I'm trying to save you from."

"No!"

Everything stopped moving. Even the air.

"Don't save me from being like my mom," Lucy said into that stillness. "Save me from ever being like you."

Aunt Karen didn't take her eyes from Lucy's as she slowly shook her head. "You have no idea who your mother was. No idea at all."

She stalked past Lucy, heels clicking angrily across the floor to the front door, which she slammed. Lucy turned to go after her, to make her take that back, but she felt warm arms come around her from behind.

"Let God untie these knots," Inez said. "You cannot."

The knot in Lucy's throat dissolved into hot tears. "You didn't tell her about my book, did you?"

"No."

"Then who did?"

"I do not know. But I hope you have hidden it well."

Lucy didn't think anyplace was safe from Aunt Karen. But, swiping at the tears with the back of her hand, Lucy went to the underwear drawer and moved the Book of Lists to the last place Aunt Karen would stick her hand—in the bottom of the toy chest where Lollipop was even now meowing forlornly.

"She's gone," Lucy told her. "But I don't think it's for long."

But when Dad came home early from the station so Inez could go to Alamogordo for Mora's conference, Aunt Karen wasn't with him. He seemed surprised that she wasn't there waiting to take them out for sushi or something.

"She didn't come find you?" Lucy said.

"No, last time I saw her, she was coming here after the conference—which went very well, by the way." Dad poured sunshine on her with his smile. "Mr. Auggy had already told me you were doing better, but I had no idea how much better. He read us some of your papers." Dad touched her face, his hand cupped under her chin. "You're a writer like your mom, who, by the way, couldn't spell either. So—did Aunt Karen go shopping or what?"

Lucy looked at Inez, but she was paying more attention to buttoning her coat than she needed to.

"We will talk later Senor Ted," Inez said.

"I'm completely confused," Dad said. "But, then, I'm surrounded by women."

Not for long. Mr. Auggy came by later with chips and a jar of salsa, apologizing that they weren't homemade like Inez's. He also brought news.

"Sheriff Navarra says he has plenty of offenders who need to do community service. He promises he'll have the bleachers and the concession stand in shape before we even need them."

"You really are a miracle worker," Dad said.

Mr. Auggy shook his head. "It wasn't me. It was Miss Lucy."

"Me?"

"The sheriff was so impressed with the way you handled the team today—especially Gabe and Carla Rosa—he said he's on board to help any way he can."

"No way," Lucy said.

"Way."

There was one knot untied. But there was another one.

"What do we do about Januarie? I never saw her mad like that."

"She comes by it honestly," Dad said.

Mr. Auggy nodded sadly. "I'm working on Miss Januarie."

But the next morning only J.J. showed up at the back gate to go to soccer practice, and Januarie didn't come to soccer at recess. Lucy guessed Mr. Auggy hadn't had a chance to work a miracle yet.

And Lucy was still worried about Aunt Karen. She wanted to tell

Dad about what happened, but it seemed like Inez wanted to handle that one. Wow. Strange. She was actually happy to let her do it. And she was sure Inez could.

Until that night when Dad answered the phone and said, "Karen! What happened to you yesterday?"

Lucy considered hiding in the toy chest with Lollipop, but Dad said, "Oh—okay—she's right here—" and handed her the phone. Where was Inez to help with *this* double square knot? She hoped God was there.

Lucy took the phone, but before she could even say hello, Aunt Karen said, "Mr. Augustalientes said you needed a team to play."

Lucy almost said, "Who?"

"Well, I have one."

"One what?"

Aunt Karen sighed. "A team. The one my company sponsors. We have two, actually, and one of them is the same age group as yours. They can play you Saturday, March seven. Mark it on your calendar."

They didn't have a calendar, but Lucy didn't say that. She could only stammer, "Okay—um—I'll tell Mr. Auggy."

"Who?" Aunt Karen said.

Lucy smiled.

"Let me talk to your dad again, and we'll make all the arrangements."

Silence. Lucy wasn't sure what she was supposed to say.

"Um, thanks," she said finally. "That's cool, it really is. We need to show our town that we need a soccer field—"

"No. You need to see what being in a real program could be like for you. By the way—do you have a good pair of cleats, some shin guards? They told me you need those."

"No," Lucy said.

"Hello! Is no one concerned about safety—never mind, I'm not going there. I'll take care of it."

"You don't have to," Lucy said.

"Who else is going to?" Lucy could almost see her pulling her fingers through her hair like a rake. "No, this is good. You're just going to see, that's all. Let me talk to your dad."

Lucy handed him the phone and listened for signs that Aunt Karen was telling him about the Book of Lists, but it all seemed to be about dates and times and phone numbers. She was evidently going to call Mr. Auggy herself. Like Dad couldn't handle it. Maybe she should make a list of reasons why Aunt Karen should move to Mars. Australia was too close.

But at least she had gotten them a team to play, and the news of that was, to Lucy's amazement, like Dad's smile: it spread sunshine all over town.

On Monday, Dad made the announcement on the radio. Lucy, Mora, and Inez listened and cheered in the kitchen and had special lavender tea to celebrate. Lucy decided her mom would have liked that. Mora put milk in hers and said it was like the Chai she'd had at Starbucks. Whatever.

When the team went to soccer practice the next Saturday, they could only stare in awe. The bleachers were sturdy and strong and had a fresh coat of blue paint. The concession stand was painted to match, with red letters above the window proclaiming REFRESHMENTS, with colorful drawings all over the walls of it. Some of those same drawings appeared on the repaired soccer field sign.

"They look like the pottery in Mr. Esparza's museum," Lucy said.

"Who do you think painted them up there?" Mr. Auggy said. "Evidently old Mr. Esparza ran up a big tab at Pasco's, and Pasco was about to have the sheriff arrest him. This is how he paid it off."

"There's gonna be real refreshments in there?" Oscar said.

"I'm still working on that," Mr. Auggy said.

So — he had his knots to untie too. Lucy decided it couldn't hurt to ask God to untie his as well as hers.

She'd never seen him work so fast.

The next day at church, Reverend Servidio preached a sermon about the upcoming game — how people needed to support the youth. He read a story from the Bible about Jesus letting the kids sit on his lap when the disciples were telling them to go away.

"He said the children were important," the reverend said, "and so they are. Let us follow the gospel!"

For once, Lucy didn't mind Jesus so much.

Even though Pasco didn't go to church, he somehow seemed to have gotten the message. When Lucy and Dad and Mr. Auggy went to the café for lunch, he pulled up a chair at their table, said the chicken nachos were on the house, and announced that he was going to provide all the refreshments to sell at the game. The money would go to support the team's future needs.

Evidently Mr. Benitez couldn't let Felix Pasco look better than him. Wednesday, he called the radio station and told Dad to announce that he was paying for uniforms for the team. And could he announce it three times a day?

"What color do you want?" Mr. Auggy asked the team Thursday.

"Anything but pink," Lucy said.

"Ya think?" Gabe said.

Veronica raised a lanky arm. "Let us girls design them."

"No way," Oscar said. "I ain't wearin' no ruffles."

"Oscar, are you new?" Lucy pointed both thumbs to her chest. "You think I'm gonna put myself in ruffles?"

"Trust us," Dusty said.

And Lucy knew just who to ask for help.

Mora was all over it. She did drawings of possibilities and pulled a 164-piece marker set out of her backpack for color samples. The red, white, and blue ensemble they came up with—complete with warm-ups—was, as Mora put it, "fabulous."

Dad and Mr. Auggy held a meeting of the team parents and all the possible sponsors at Pasco's Café, and Lucy was allowed to attend, since she was team captain. It was a lot like listening to the team argue—before they all grew up.

When Mr. Benitez started to sputter about how much the uniforms were going to cost, Gloria said she'd kick in some money if they'd put CASA BONITA on the backs of the shirts too. Lucy was relieved when Mr. Benitez said, no, he would pay whatever it cost as long as his grocery was the only name on the shirts. She didn't think the boys would want to play for a hair salon.

Gloria sniffed, until Mr. Auggy told her the team still needed cleats and shin guards. She said she'd pay for half of that amount if the parents would pay the rest. They all agreed, except for J.J.'s parents, who weren't there.

Carla Rosa's dad—Guess what? He was the mayor—declared Saturday, March 7th, as Los Suenos Pride Day and urged the business owners to spruce up their establishments for all the visitors who were coming from El Paso. Claudia said she'd provide flower arrangements for their display windows at a discount. When eyebrows raised, she said okay, she'd do it for free. The mayor mentioned banners, and Veronica and Dusty's mothers waved their hands—like Dusty and Veronica always did—and said they were graphic designers and would make that happen. No wonder the Gigglers had such neat-looking notebooks.

"Nothin' too girly," Emanuel's father said.

"Shut up," his mother said. "They know what they're doing."

Lucy half-expected Mr. Auggy to buzz them. But mostly the results of the meeting were ding-ding-ding worthy.

"You've brought this town together," Dad said when he and Lucy and Mr. Auggy were walking home amid the leafy shadows of the cottonwoods.

"Not just me," Mr. Auggy said. "And I don't think we've seen anything yet."

Dad talked about that on the radio. And about how soccer had eased racial tensions among the kids. Dusty and Veronica were at Lucy's that day, eating quesadillas before they went off to soccer practice. Mr. Auggy had them playing after school too, and Inez let Lucy go as long as she ate something first.

"Racial tensions?" Veronica said. Her lip hung. "What does that mean?"

Lucy tore off a piece of her quesadilla, but she didn't eat it. Her mouth had gone dry.

"Isn't that like white people hating black people?" Dusty said. "We don't have any black kids at our school."

Everyone seemed to be waiting for Lucy to explain it. Even Inez.

She let her chunk of quesadilla drop to the plate. "He's talking about Hispanic people not liking anybody who isn't Hispanic."

"Huh?" Dusty said. "I think it's the other way around. At least it used to be."

"We don't do that at our school," Mora piped up. "'Course, most of the kids where I go are white, but I'm pretty popular, so it doesn't affect me."

"Who does it affect?" Dusty said, but she was looking at Lucy.

"Well," Lucy said slowly, "me."

"You?" Veronica and Dusty said together.

Dusty scrunched up her nose. "What are you talking about?"

The toy chest in the bedroom was feeling pretty attractive. Lucy looked at Inez. She was nodding. There were knots to be untied. Okay, God — here we go.

Lucy picked her words out before she opened her mouth. "You guys used to act like I wasn't even there because I was white."

"This is a joke, right?" Dusty said, only she wasn't laughing. "We never talked to you because you were always a snob to us."

"You acted like you were better than us." Veronica's lip was at an all-time low.

"Nuh-uh," Lucy said.

"Yuh-huh."

"It was like nobody else knew how to play soccer. You wouldn't answer questions when we tried to be friendly —"

"She was snotty to me too, when I first came here," Mora said. "Now we're totally like sisters — we fight and everything — but it was like she thought she was it on a stick." She snapped her fingers over her head.

Lucy stared at Dusty and Veronica. "But you were out to get me when you started playing soccer with us. You kept making me fall down."

They both shook their heads.

"Gabe was hateful to J.J. though — you can't deny that."

"Gabe is hateful to everybody," Dusty said.

Veronica gaped at her. "Not me!"

"Whatever."

Lucy got up on one leg on the chair.

"Uh-oh," Mora said. "She means business now."

"What about you telling Januarie that I said she's too fat to play soccer?"

"*What?*" Dusty looked as if Lucy had slapped her. "Why would I do that?"

"Because—"

Lucy stopped. She couldn't think of a single reason. Not anymore. But she frowned. "Then who told her that?"

"One of the boys?" Veronica said.

Mora sprang her talking fingers into action. "Boys so don't say stuff like that. If they want to hurt you, they just say it to your face. They're not as smart as we are."

"Or as stupid."

They all looked at Inez. She appeared to be simply washing potatoes, but Lucy knew better.

"Women—they can be mean," she said. "They forget they need each other so much."

Lucy felt something in her throat, but it wasn't a knot. It was something thick that made her want to hug somebody.

"Okay, so, this was all like this major misunderstanding." Dusty said. She tightened her ponytail as if she were putting a period at the end of a sentence.

"Well, yeah," Lucy said. She could already see the list she was going to make tonight: Things I Didn't Used to Understand but Now I Do.

"We better get to practice," she said.

"You're leaving me?" Mora said.

She actually looked sad. Go figure.

But her mood had changed by the time Lucy got home, just before dark. She was standing in the middle of the kitchen, shrieking and waving her electronic diary around.

"I trusted you!" she said before Lucy could even ask what was going on.

"Mora," Inez said sharply.

"Abuela—" Mora's free hand came up like an exclamation point. "Not that many people know I even have this—and nobody else could have gotten into my backpack—"

"What are you talking about?" Lucy said. Mora's eyes were so big she was afraid they'd pop out of her head.

"Intruders." Mora held the device out like it was Exhibit A on *Law and Order*. "Somebody tried to get in—only they messed up the password." The pop-eyes shrunk to slits. "You know my password."

"Right," Lucy said. "So if I wanted to get in, I could have."

Mora shook her head, so hard her ponytail snapped into her eye. "You can't say it exactly like I do."

"I didn't even try!" Lucy put her hands to the sides of her face so she wouldn't yell. Mora was doing enough yelling for both of them. "Look—I didn't try to get into your diary. I know what it's like when somebody tries to put their nose in your private stuff. I just had it happen to me the other day. Ask your abuela."

Mora looked at Inez, who nodded.

"Then who was it? Veronica and what's-her-name?"

"Dusty? No way!"

"I am just so annoyed."

The fingers went crazy as Mora shoved the diary into her backpack and muttered to herself in Spanish.

Lucy felt three knots replace the ones she'd thought were untied. She wrote about them in her Book of Lists that night.

Knots I Can't Untie, so I Need You to Untangle Them
Please, God

— Januarie hates me. She's the worst pest ever, but I
  miss her.
— Mora still thinks I tried to get into her diary, I know she
  does.
— Aunt Karen hasn't told Dad about this book. I don't
  think he'll let her take it away from me, but what

212

*if he's mad at me for having it? What if he thinks
I was being sneaky not ever telling him I found it in
the storage shed at Christmas? Enough stuff has
changed between Dad and me —*

Lucy stopped writing and scratched behind Lollipop's ear with the tip of her pen.

Not having to do so many chores *did* mean she had more time for soccer and friends—confusing as they were—and even doing home-work. But it was still hard, not feeling like Dad needed her anymore. She even wondered if he talked to Mr. Auggy about things he used to talk to her about. A sadness knot tied itself around her throat again.

*I can't do anything about any of it. I guess that's
where you come in, right? Kind of like Mr. Auggy making
miracles happen? And Dad? And maybe even me? Maybe
you're really the one doing all that —*

But how was she supposed to know that for sure? She buried her face in Lollipop's fur. Maybe that was the biggest knot of all.

"Luce?"

Lollipop leaped from the bed and into the toy chest.

"It's just Dad, silly," Lucy said.

But she was careful to tuck the Book of Lists in with the kitty before she said, "What's up, Dad?"

He poked his head in. "Did you remember to feed Mudge tonight?"

"Aw man—no." Lucy scrambled for her sweatshirt. She'd been so wrapped up in her knots she'd forgotten the best cat ever. "I'll do it now," she said.

Dad chuckled. "Better now than at three in the morning when he comes to my window yowling. You know how he hates to miss a meal."

Feeling needed by Dad again, Lucy found her shoes and went to the backyard.

"Sorry, Mudge," she said into the darkness. "I'll give you some tuna—come on."

Only silence answered her.

"Mudge? Kitty-kitty? Tuna!"

Nothing. Lucy hurried across the yard to the shed, opened the door, promised tuna—still no grumbling from the big brown tabby.

She slipped out the gate and peered behind the century plant, but only its leaves threatened to bite, not Mudge.

"Kitty-kitty-kitty!"

"Luce—what's going on?" Dad called from the back step.

"I can't find him, Dad." Lucy could hear the worry in her own voice. "He always comes for tuna."

"Try taking a can out there with you. He might be playing hard to get because you're late."

With yet another knot tying itself inside her, Lucy ran to the house, got a can of StarKist and was still pulling the top off as she took the steps in one jump.

"Mudgie—come smell—tuna, big guy!"

She walked every inch of the yard, waving the can until the smell made her stomach icky.

"He must be out hunting," Dad said finally.

"No, that's Artemis's job."

"I don't know that anybody ever told him that." Dad held out his hand. "Come on in, Luce. He'll be back."

"Will you wake me up if he gets here in the middle of the night?"

"Absolutely not," Dad said as she joined him on the steps. He slid his arm around her shoulder. "Mudge can't stay away from you, champ. You're his whole reason for living."

That didn't make Lucy feel much better. She was sure she wouldn't sleep at all, though she did, and when she ran out to the century plant in her pajamas at sunrise, there was no Mudge.

Dad didn't promise her he'd be waiting for her when she got home from school. Lucy knew he couldn't. They didn't make those kinds of promises to each other. She just added that to her list of knots for God to untie and went off miserably to school.

At least soccer practice was good. Carla Rosa showed off her new skills for Mr. Auggy, and even Gabe passed the ball to her once.

"You're playing like a team," Mr. Auggy said. "You're going to show those Pachucos what time it is now."

"Pachucos?" Lucy said.

"That's slang for being from El Paso—it's their team name."

Dusty touched Lucy's shoulder and grinned at her. "*Bolillo.*"

"Did you just call me a name?"

"I called you an Anglo—you're not Hispanic and you're not Indo. You're bolillo." Dusty got her lips close to Lucy's ear. "You're my favorite bolillo."

Veronica folded her lanky arms. "I can't believe you've lived here since you were, like, four, and you never learned any Spanish."

"I know quesadilla—machaca—asada—"

"What is this, a restaurant?" Gabe said. "Could we just play soccer?"

"Yeah," J.J. said.

And then everyone looked as if the Road Runner and Wile E. Coyote had just shaken hands.

"What about this for our team name?" Mr. Auggy said. "Los Suenos."

"Lame," Gabe said. "It's just the name of our town."

"Right. The Dreams." His eyes got misty. "If this isn't a dream come true, I don't know what is."

"The Los Suenos Dreams," Lucy said.

"Then it's Spanish *and* English." Dusty said.

"Guess what?" Carla Rosa looked at Veronica. "I love that!"

"You are so cute!" Veronica squealed.

The boys all looked at each other like silliness had just reached a new level.

Nobody had to be reminded to get water when practice was over. The afternoons were warmer now that March had begun. Lucy even asked Mr. Auggy if she could put her sweatshirt in her cubby before she went back to the portable. He told her to hurry because the bell had already rung and she didn't need to run into Mrs. Nunez.

Lucy swung happily into the cubby hall, which should have been empty, and stopped. She could feel her mouth fall open so far she could have given Veronica a run for her money. Her cubby hole was once again hurling forth its contents, only this time the culprit was caught in the act.

"Januarie!" Lucy said.

Her voice echoed in the emptiness, and Januarie's chubby self startled and tripped over Lucy's backpack, which lay gaping on the floor. She sat down hard beside it.

"It was you!" Lucy said.

"I hate you!"

The Chihuahua was growling as if she would snap off any hand that came near her. Lucy went to Januarie and put hers down anyway.

"Leave me alone!"

"I won't." Lucy squatted beside her. "You're the one who did this before, aren't you?"

"No." Januarie squeezed her eyes shut.

"You can't make it go away," Lucy said. "It was you."

"Yes."

"Why? Why did you do it and then tell me it was Dusty and Veronica?"

"Because I hate you."

"I'm not so crazy about you right now either, but I don't go throwing your stuff around and—" Something dawned on Lucy. "And tell people you said things about me that you didn't say."

Januarie opened her eyes and said, "Huh?" Lucy knew she wouldn't be able to resist for long.

"You said somebody told you that I said you were too fat to play soccer. Only nobody said that, did they? You made it up."

"You were starting to like them more than me!"

Lucy stopped with her next words halfway on her lips.

"You let them play with you guys even though they were mean to you, but you wouldn't let me play and I'm always doing stuff for you!"

Lucy now knew what a Chihuahua must sound like when it was locked in a cage. She sat all the way down on the floor beside Januarie.

"I always shared my sandwich with you at Pasco's," she said. "And I let you sleep in my bed with me when you couldn't sleep at your house because your dad was yelling. And every day I rode my bike slow to school so you wouldn't be left behind."

"But you wouldn't let me play soccer with you." Januarie turned a now tear-striped face to Lucy with more knots than Lucy had room for on a page. "And you love soccer more than anything or anybody in the whole world!"

She struggled to stand up, and Lucy stood up with her.

"You're gonna tell on me now, aren't you?"

"No," Lucy said. "Not if you put all this stuff back in my cubby. And if you come home with me after school."

Januarie whimpered. "You want me to?"

"Yeah," Lucy said. Because she felt a tug inside, and she wanted to see if it was pulling her to the right place.

She filled Dusty and Veronica in before Januarie joined them for the walk home.

"That little brat," Veronica said.

"Why does she do stuff like that?" Dusty said.

Lucy had no idea, but she was sure what she'd already discovered about Januarie's dirty work wasn't even half of it.

"You guys want to help me with something?" she said.

They both nodded. Lucy just finished telling them what she had in mind when Januarie waddled up, face darkening when she saw them.

"All of us girls are getting together," Lucy told her. "You too."

At least she didn't declare her hatred for Lucy and stomp off.

Mora was there when they all arrived, and she gave Lucy a cold look as they gathered at the table. Inez put a plate of sopapillas and butter in front of them and cocked a sharp eyebrow at Mora, who didn't even flinch. That would have made Lucy confess things she hadn't even done.

"Hey, Mora," Veronica said, as planned, "do you have your electronic diary with you?"

"Yes." Mora pointed a butter-covered finger in the air. "I don't let it out of my sight anymore since somebody tried to get into it."

Veronica's lip went into gear. "Nuh-uh!"

"Hello! Like, three times—"

Lucy watched Januarie out of the corner of her eye. She squirmed on the chair like it was full of fleas.

"Don't you have to have a password to get into it?" Dusty said, also according to the script.

"Yes!" Mora was full of exclamation points today. "And the only people who know it are me—of course—and Lucy." She directed a finger at Lucy like an accusation. "And you—" The finger went to Dusty—"And you—" Veronica—"and—"

The New Mexico desert couldn't have been more silent than Lucy's kitchen was at that moment as Mora stabbed her final finger at Januarie. And Januarie couldn't have looked guiltier than if they had caught her with the electronic diary in her hand.

"What's my password?" Mora barked at her.

"Consuela!" Januarie plastered her hands over her mouth and burst into tears. "Only I didn't say it right."

Mora flattened her upper body on the table, hands slapping the top. Veronica nearly jumped into Dusty's lap.

"What were you thinking, you little—"

"Mora," Inez said.

"I want to know why she tried to get into my stuff!"

"I know why."

They all turned to Lucy. She put her face close to Januarie's crumpled one. She kept her voice quiet, the way Mr. Auggy did. "You wanted her to think I did it, right?"

"Uh-huh."

"Because you saw me getting to be friends with her too."

Januarie nodded and snuffled up what was now trailing out her nose.

"But Januarie," Lucy said, "I don't let Mora play on our soccer team."

"I don't wa—"

Lucy kicked Mora under the table. While she was protesting, Lucy got even closer to Januarie.

"Did you think that was going to make me like you more?"

"I would be your only friend again!"

Januarie flung her chubby arms on the table and let her face fall on them. Lucy was sure she had never seen anyone cry that hard.

"That's so sad," Veronica said.

"It's tragic." Mora shook her head. "If I knew she was going to get hysterical, I wouldn't have said anything."

"That is not why she cries, I think," Inez said.

Lucy rubbed her hand across Januarie's back. "Don't cry, Januarie. We're friends again."

"Not when you find out the rest!" she wailed into her arms.

"What 'rest'?"

"Something worse!"

"What could be worse than invading somebody's privacy?" Mora looked at Lucy. "By the way, I didn't totally think it was you. You don't even know how to turn on anything electronic—"

"I took Mudge!"

Lucy froze, hand still on Januarie's shoulder.

"I took him to my house so you would think he was lost and I would bring him home and you would think I was all wonderful—only now I can't find him! And you love him better than all your other cats—"

Lucy pulled Januarie up by the shoulders and twisted her to face her. "Where did you put him at your house?"

"In the garage—"

"What I want to know is how you got him there." Mora looked warily at Marmalade, who was sleeping on top of the clothes dryer. "Your cats are evil."

"I put tuna in my mom's laundry bag and left it by that plant he hides under and he crawled in and I pulled him home."

"You did that to Mudge?" Lucy said.

"It didn't hurt him. And he was mad when I got him to the garage and I ran and then when I went back to get him he was gone." The tears started again.

"Wow," Dusty said. "I've never been in J.J.'s garage—and no of-fense but—"

She didn't have to finish. With all the junk that lived at J.J.'s, inside and out, it could take days to locate Mudge, and by then—

"Senor Mudge will not starve," Inez said. "He can live from his fat for many weeks."

Januarie gave another juicy sniff. "I put some cans of tuna in the garage."

Veronica gaped at her. "You're a lot smarter than you look."

"I'm stupid!"

"You know what—hush up." Lucy got up and grabbed her jacket.

"You are going where?" Inez said.

"I'm going in to look for Mudge."

"I'll help," Dusty said.

Veronica got up too, but Januarie practically threw herself in front of the back door.

"You can't! My dad's home!"

"So?" Mora said. Even she was digging in her bag for her jacket.

"So—no one goes." Inez jerked her head toward the table. "We all sit down and we eat."

"Does J.J. know?" Lucy said to Januarie.

She shook her head. "Don't tell him. He'll lock *me* in the garage!"

Maybe he should, Lucy wanted to say. But she closed her mouth and nibbled half-heartedly at a sopapilla, and when the girls were gone, except for Mora, who was busy changing her password on the diary, Lucy sat on the front steps to watch for J.J. She tried not to think about Mudge in that garage full of tires and old refrigerators and everything else that wouldn't fit in the front and back yards. The only good thing was that if anybody did try to grab him, he would turn their arm to shreds.

"You are talking to God about Senor Mudge."

Inez stood above her, holding Lucy's ratty jacket. Lucy moved over so she could sit down. Inez put the jacket around Lucy's shoulders as if it were a fine mink stole.

"I wasn't talking to God yet. I was trying to figure it out myself."

"Still you think backwards. Ask God first. He gives you the answer. Then you know."

Lucy poked her elbows onto her knees and rested her chin in her hands. "How do you actually know that, Inez?"

"I learned from Ruth."

"In the Bible?"

"Mmm."

"I don't get it."

Inez folded her hands in her lap in that tidy way she had. "Did Senora Ruth plan each thing? Did she know Senor Boaz will provide more leftovers for her and protect her from the young hombres?"

"No."

"Did she make herself beautiful for Senor Boaz so he will fall in love with her?"

"No. She didn't even think he would notice her."

"Senora Ruth only obeyed."

"But I don't know what to obey, Inez," Lucy said.

"The heart of God."

"Huh?"

Inez nodded toward the Clucks' house. The shadows of the junk were long and crazy, like the jumbled pieces of a puzzle no one could possibly put together.

"Poor little one."

"I don't mean to be hateful," Lucy said, "but I'm not thinking Januarie's such a poor little one right now."

"The heart of God does. That is what you obey. Senora Ruth stayed with Naomi. She gave Naomi the baby."

"What baby?"

"The baby she had when she married Senor Boaz."

"She gave it to Naomi?" Lucy turned to face Inez. "Why?"

Inez tapped her forehead. "Remember? Senora Naomi had no one left to take care of her. No sons, no grandsons. Now, yes—that baby of Ruth."

"Wow." Lucy pulled at the fleece that stuck out of the rip in her jacket sleeve. "I could never be that unselfish."

"You are already. You give your childhood for your father. You try to protect the boy J.J." She looked deep into Lucy with her wise eyes. "You are an old child. You do not know, but you have the heart of God."

Lucy wasn't so sure about that, but she dug back to something Inez said before.

"So, God thinks Januarie's a poor little one, so I should too?"

"That can be, yes."

"But I just don't get how she could even think up that stuff to do to me."

Once again, Inez nodded toward the house across the street. The shadows were longer now, and a light had come on behind one of the sheets in the downstairs window. It was such a confused, sad-looking house compared to Lucy's.

"We act as we are taught," Inez said.

Who taught Januarie to be mean?

Well, du-uh, Mora would have said. Why did J.J. and Januarie have to run to her house and call Mr. Auggy when their dad yelled, unless there was something worse than yelling going on? That was the thing Dad and Mr. Auggy didn't tell her the night she hit her head.

"Is she going to grow up to be mean like her father, then?" Lucy said.

"If she will have others to love her, no." Inez unfolded her hands and stood up. "What we love—that must come from the heart of God."

Lucy sat on the steps for a while after Inez went inside. She heard Mora inside squeal, "I have this fabulous idea, Abuela—listen to this." The rest was told in whispers, which was fine. Lucy could only think about Januarie—and Mudge—and what she loved—until J.J. appeared around the corner, hurrying with his head down. She stood up and called to him.

He kept walking, backward, so she ran to him, and with her eyes darting cautiously to his house as she talked, she told him all about Januarie.

"You think Mudge is still in my garage?" J.J. said. He was still edging toward his house, and Lucy knew why.

"You better go," she said. "Januarie said your dad's home."

His eyes opened wider, as if suddenly he knew that she might know what went on in that house surrounded by a fortress of trash.

"Don't yell at Januarie," Lucy said. "She gets yelled at enough."

J.J. gave an almost invisible nod. "I'll find Mudge, I promise."

She didn't watch him go into his house. She just hurried back to her own where she would smell melted cheese and hear Mora chattering and know that her dad was coming home. She planned to hug him the minute he came in the door.

19

Mudge wasn't back under his plant the next morning. J.J. promised that he was looking every chance he got. Lucy promised God she would try to have a heart like his and be nice to Januarie.

At least there was the soccer game to think about—and it was only one day away.

The banners that hung over the highway and Granada Street were even more beautiful than Veronica and Dusty's notebooks, proclaiming Los Suenos Pride Day and announcing the match—El Paso Pachucos vs. Los Suenos Dreams.

"What does 'vs.' stand for?" Carla Rosa wanted to know.

Nobody laughed at her. J.J. explained it like she wasn't a moron who should know that by now. He got a ding-ding-ding for that.

Every shop on Granada Street and even those along the highway had flowers in the windows and game tickets for sale inside. Mr. Benitez and Pasco were having a competition for who could sell the most. In Lucy's mind, Mr. Benitez was a total winner because the uniforms were, as Mora had predicted, fabulous. When the team was all lined up in them on Friday afternoon after their final practice, modeling them for Mr. Auggy, right down to the cleats and shin guards they had been practicing with all week, he grinned way past the small smile, all the way to his earlobes.

"This is my sueno," he said.

"Come on, Mr. Auggy," Oscar said. "You been all over the world. This ain't your dream."

"You have no idea," Mr. Auggy said.

But Lucy thought she did. They had uniforms and a name and they felt like a team and maybe they could even beat Aunt Karen's team tomorrow. It really was part of a dream, and she hoped she didn't wake up before it all happened.

Just when she didn't think it could get any better, it did. Mora greeted her at the back door when she got home, fingers going all over the place.

"I have the most fabulous surprise for you!" she said.

For a second, Lucy was afraid she was going to volunteer to do all the girl players' hair the same way for the game. Mr. Auggy already said ponytails were fine —

"You're gonna have cheerleaders for your team!"

Lucy stared as Mora pulled out her cell phone, pushed a button, and displayed a picture on the tiny screen. Lucy recognized Mora's dance team, only they were all in short navy blue skirts and white T-shirts that said, LOS SUENOS DREAMS in sparkly red letters. Each girl had her hair in French braids so the soccer ball earrings hanging from their ears could be seen.

"We're totally going to be your cheerleaders," Mora said — well, shrieked. "I bet those lame Pachucos don't have cheerleaders."

"Mora," Inez said. But her voice hid a laugh beneath it, Lucy could tell.

"This is so cool," Lucy said. "I mean it, Mora — it's just — "

"I know!" Mora cried, and flung herself at Lucy in a fingers-flying hug.

As Dusty would have said, *Wow. Just wow.*

Lucy was awake with the sun the next morning, even though the game wasn't until 10:00. She checked to see if Mudge was back first, and when the place under the century plant was still vacant, she closed her eyes and said out loud, "God — please take care of him. Untie his knots." Because if he was still in J.J.'s garage, there would be no end to the knots he had to deal with.

Dad made pancakes, though Lucy could only eat half her usual stack. Dad teased her about liking Inez's cooking more than his, but she was just too excited—nervous—everything. He even said the chores could wait—this was game day.

Lucy loved the sound of that. Game Day. Maybe—if the town council didn't sell the field and people thought the Los Suenos Dreams were fabulous—maybe there would be lots of Game Days ahead.

At 8:30, Lucy told Dad the biggest van she'd ever seen had just pulled up in front of their house. Aunt Karen parked behind it in her car and hopped out, wearing a bright turquoise jacket with gold embroidered letters that spelled out Pachucos. It didn't look quite right on her—like she had borrowed it from some guy because she was cold.

Lucy and Dad met her on the front porch, and Aunt Karen stopped short at the bottom of the steps and lowered her sunglasses.

"Where did you get a uniform?" she said.

"You thought I'd be in an old ratty T-shirt, huh?" Lucy said.

Dad squeezed her arm. "Incredible community support. So—you have your team with you?"

"And our coach," Aunt Karen said. "A few of the parents are driving up too."

"Why didn't everybody's parents come?" Lucy said. "ALL our team's parents will be there."

Aunt Karen put her sunglasses back on. "They're busy people. It's not like this is the game of the century."

Lucy felt like Aunt Karen had just stuck her with a pin and all the air was going out.

"So where's this field?" Aunt Karen said.

She said "this field" the same way she said "this house." Lucy sucked her air back in. Aunt Karen was going to see today—she was just going to see—and then "this thing" about Lucy needing to live with her was going to be over for good.

Lucy couldn't wait any longer to ride to the field with J.J. Mr. Auggy said he'd pick her up, but she wanted to go on bikes like always. She didn't want to mess up her game by doing anything different.

She waited by the back gate for what seemed like forever, glancing at her watch every few seconds. When Mr. Auggy arrived to get Dad, she was still standing there and J.J. still hadn't appeared.

"You've got your game face on, captain!" Mr. Auggy said before he went into the house.

Lucy didn't tell him it wasn't a game face. It was a scared face. What if J.J. didn't show up?

And then he was there, without his bike, face stiff as a shin guard.

"Let's go," he said.

"Where's your bike?" Lucy's heart was pounding. "J.J., what's wrong?"

"Run," he said.

And Lucy would have, if someone hadn't screamed from the corner in a voice that rooted her right to the sidewalk. There were words in the scream, bad ones, but all Lucy heard was the anger. And all she saw was Mr. Cluck coming at them, his teeth gritted like the front grill of a truck. J.J. flattened himself to the fence.

When he got to them, J.J.'s father stabbed his hand toward J.J., and then he stopped and stared at Lucy as if he'd just discovered she was there. He was so close to her she could smell him, and it made her want to throw up.

The hand drew back. "Where do you think you're goin'?" Mr. Cluck growled at J.J.

J.J. didn't answer. Lucy was sure he was so scared he couldn't. And so it was somebody else who said, "We have a soccer game today."

Only when J.J.'s father turned his glistening eyes on her was Lucy really sure she was the one who had said it.

"He ain't goin' nowhere."

"But he's on the team. We've been practicing for weeks—"

"Lucy."

It was Dad, talking before the gate was even open. Mr. Auggy stepped out with him, his hand outstretched as if he were going to shake the hand of this awful man with the stinky breath.

"Mr. Cluck," he said.

J.J.'s father sneered at his outstretched hand.

Mr. Auggy dropped it to his side. "Is there a problem?"

"No kiddin' there's a problem. You were gonna 'help' him stay

outta trouble. It's not workin'. He's got a worse attitude than ever."
With a jerk, Mr. Cluck curled his fingers around the back of J.J.'s neck
so hard Lucy could feel it herself. "Guess you're gonna have to play
your little football game without him."

"Soccer," Lucy whispered.

No one seemed to hear her as Mr. Cluck half-dragged J.J. down
the street and Mr. Auggy called after him and Dad found his way to
Lucy's side.

"You okay, champ?" he said.

"No! He can't do that, can he?"

Dad gave a huge sigh. "Yes, I'm afraid he can."

"Can't you do something, Mr. Auggy?"

Mr. Auggy took off his ball cap and smoothed his hair with an
unhappy hand and jammed the hat back on. "I'm sorry, Lucy. He's the
parent. He has the right—"

"No he doesn't. He doesn't have any right to be horrible to J.J. It's
not fair!"

"Nobody ever promised us fair, Luce," Dad said. But he sounded
like he found it just as hideous as she did.

Lucy sagged against the fence. She didn't know which knot to turn
to first. It was going to be so messed up, playing without J.J. He was
their midfielder.

And he had worked so hard—harder than anybody because he had
to deal with Gabe all the time.

"Come on, Luce, ride with us," Dad said. "It's too late to go on
your bike."

With her heart in the pit of her stomach, Lucy climbed into the
backseat of Mr. Auggy's Jeep and sat down hard. Why wouldn't his
dad let him go? Did he find out Mudge was in the garage? No, that
was stupid. Was it because he hated Mr. Auggy? Januarie had told her
that, and she'd just seen it with her own eyes.

Or was it what she'd figured out that night with Inez ... that J.J.
lived with a very mean man who did more than just yell at him.

"He's gonna hit J.J. when they get inside the house," she said.

They had just pulled up to the soccer field behind the enormous van. Mr. Auggy pressed the brakes, hard, and looked at her in the rearview mirror.

"Why do you say that, Miss Lucy?"

"Because he almost did it before you got out there, only he noticed me. But I think he's done it before, and that's why J.J.'s so mad all the time."

Dad tilted his head, and Mr. Auggy looked at him as if he could see. They seemed to have a whole conversation without saying a word.

"That's right, isn't it?" Lucy said.

"You saw him start to hit J.J.?" Mr. Auggy said.

Lucy nodded.

"You've done a lot, Sam," Dad said, "but I think it's time."

Lucy felt like one big knot. Had she just gotten J.J. into more trouble?

Mr. Auggy twisted to look at her. "I want you to put this out of your mind right now," he said.

"How can I?"

"Because you're the captain, and whatever you tell your team, they'll do."

"So, I need to tell them J.J. can't play but we'll be fine?"

"We will be. How do you think we can move people around?"

Lucy tried to get her thoughts out of J.J.'s house. "Okay," she said slowly. "We'll just go back to being forwards and backs. It'll be less confusing for Carla Rosa anyway."

"Excellent." Mr. Auggy put up his hand for her to grip. "You're a good leader, and you have a strong team. You can do this."

Lucy thought she could. She grabbed her bag and got out of the car with confidence. And then it all drained away as she watched the van in front of her empty. Aunt Karen's team climbed off one by one. Tall. Looking older than eleven. She lost count at fifteen.

Mr. Auggy was already shaking their coach's hand.

"Dad?" Lucy said.

"Yeah, champ? What's wrong?"

She stood on her tiptoes to reach his ear. "Their whole team is boys. All of them."

Dad's brow wrinkled, and then he chuckled—that sound she loved so much, that sound that made everything okay.

"Why is that a problem, champ?" he said. "I've never known you to play with anything but boys until recently."

That was true.

"Are they big?"

"Huge," Lucy said.

"Good—they won't be able to run as fast."

"You think?"

"It's all about heart, champ," Dad said. "That's what your mom used to say. She was all heart—and so are you."

Lucy straightened her shoulders and mentally counted her freckles. Okay. *God—no knots. Please untangle us and let us go.*

The team was behind the concession stand, which already smelled like funnel cakes and nachos. Carla Rosa was on her before Lucy could open her mouth.

"Guess what—"

"I know—it's all boys—so what?"

"Hello!" Veronica said. She had lost all control of her bottom lip. "I'm scared."

"They'll trample us!" Dusty said.

Carla Rosa whimpered.

And then Lucy heard something else. High-pitched girls' voices were yelling, "What about—what about—what about our Suenos?"

A roar answered them—or at least it seemed like a roar to Lucy. The team ran to the side of the concession stand and peeked around. The bleachers were full of people, familiar people—the ones who cut their hair and sold them their candy bars and yelled at them for picking their roses. And their kids. And some folks Lucy didn't even know who appeared to be as excited as they were. In front of them was Mora's dance team, swinging hips they didn't have and shouting, "What about—what about—what about our Suenos?"

"Where did we get cheerleaders?" Gabe said.

Oscar nudged him. "What about—the whole town is here!"

It was true, and they looked like a happy town, waving the red, white, and blue pom-poms Inez was handing out.

Inez?

In one corner of the bleachers, a group of grown-ups dressed in clothes like the ones in the windows in Ruidosa sat watching the rest like they were witnessing a play put on by a kindergarten class. Some of them had turquoise jackets in their laps, as if they were holding them for someone and they better hurry up and come back and get them. Lucy didn't even have to look for Pachuco cheerleaders.

"Oh, they're dead," Gabe said. "Come on, we can take them."

"Yes, we can," Lucy said.

"We at least have to try. I mean, look at that." Dusty tightened her ponytail. "I'm in."

"Heck, yeah," Gabe said.

He nudged Emanuel, who nodded and punched Oscar, who looked around for someone to poke. Lucy caught her breath.

"Um, you guys," Lucy said, "J.J.'s dad won't let him play today."

This time there were no whimpers—only angry shouts of "What?" and "That's messed up." Lucy quieted them with one hand up and explained what they were going to do.

"Okay, now I'm really smoked," Gabe said. "We gotta win this for J.J."

"I love that," Veronica said.

Lucy could only think that she really was having a dream.

Mr. Auggy led them out onto the field for warm-up. The crowd in the bleachers went wild, and Lucy felt as if she were in the Olympics. Energy surged all the way out to her fingers, and she was ready. She could tell the rest of her team was too. Dusty and Veronica flipped their ponytails like young horses, and she was pretty sure Gabe was snorting smoke from his nostrils as they all stretched. She felt a pang of hurt for J.J., but then Mr. Auggy said it was time. It wasn't a dream with pieces missing. It was real.

There was one referee on the field: Reverend Servidio in long pants and sneakers and a black sweater. He looked like Mr. Rogers at a funeral.

"He's our ref?" Gabe whispered—sort of loudly—to Lucy.

"He's the only one they could get who wasn't related to somebody on the team and used to play soccer and could still run." She didn't say that Dad had added, "Without having a heart attack."

She wondered if he had talked to God about this game. It couldn't hurt. Especially since one of the linesmen, the one provided by the El Paso team, looked all official in black shorts and shirt and knee socks that covered his shin guards.

Things became dreamlike again. Lucy and the captain of the Pachucos went to the center of the field. He was a head taller than Lucy and had more hair on his chin than Gabe. They flipped a coin—Lucy won the toss—and the crowd went wild as if she'd scored a goal. When the Dreams got into formation for the kickoff, they shook their pom-poms and stomped their feet until Lucy hoped the sheriff's workers had done an extra-good job or the bleachers were going to fall down. And the game hadn't even started yet.

When it did, there was a lot to cheer about. The Pachucos were fast and fancy, but Mr. Auggy had warned them about that. Lucy coached her team: "Steady, Oscar." "Take your time, Dusty." And they settled down.

There were a couple of offsides calls, but Mr. Auggy kept saying that was okay. And there were no fouls on their team. Clean play, Mr. Auggy always said. They moved the ball down the field, passing to each other, evading the presence of their opponents just as they'd practiced with each other. When one stocky Pachuco tripped Carla Rosa, his own ref blew the whistle and Carla got a direct free kick. It was way too far from their goal for even Gabe to have gotten it in, but it charged the Dreams up. The ball came so close to the goal on their next drive that Lucy could feel every nerve in her body standing up cheering. It just needed a nudge, the slider shot J.J. was so good at. Emanuel wasn't as good at it. The goalie picked up the ball, and Lucy's team was at the ready. He looked around, his teammates yelling "To me!" The whistle blew.

"You only have six seconds to do something with that ball, son," Reverend Servidio said.

"That wasn't six seconds!" the goalie said.

"Indirect kick for the Dreams."

Lucy glanced behind her. Veronica was hanging back, but she looked alert.

"To Veronica!" Lucy called.

Emanuel passed the ball right to her, and they were in control again.

That didn't last long.

The Pachucos began to chatter to each other in Spanish and closed in on every Dream who got the ball. Lucy yelled for them to shield!—turn! She herself used the fakes she and J.J. had practiced—but when she saw an opening and passed the ball to Carla Rosa, it was swept away. The Dreams were suddenly like clowns on the field, running this way and that to find the ball, which was being dribbled straight for the goal. Oscar came to life—the crowd screamed—and the ball shot right between his legs. Only a spattering of clapping could be heard over the moan from the bleachers.

"It's okay, Oscar!" Lucy called to him. "Spread the defense!"

Nobody seemed to move.

"Hello! Spread out!"

"Let's go!" Gabe cried.

Lucy focused on the ball, which Mr. Chin Hair was dribbling lazily. He was leaning and lunging like he had fancy moves, but he wasn't doing anything with his feet. Lucy kept her eyes on the ball. She didn't want to make a move until she was sure she could get it.

And then her chance came. Mr. Chin Hair let the ball get a little too far away from him, and Lucy pounced. She was off toward her goal—with another hulking couldn't-possibly-be-eleven-year-old boy on her, arms out wide, trying to block her vision.

"To me!" she heard Dusty cry.

Lucy turned and passed the ball to her, and she took off. Mr. Chin Hair flew toward her and contained her. Another Pachuco got the ball, but suddenly Gabe had it.

Back and forth it went until a whistle blew. Lucy shielded her eyes with her hand and said, "What? Did somebody foul?"

"That's the half," the other ref said. "Take a rest, girl."

The team ran to the back of the concession stand where Mr. Auggy waited with water.

"Way to go, team!" he said.

"They're ahead of us," Gabe said. And then he downed an entire bottle of water.

"They should have scored six goals by now with the training they've had. You have them on the run."

"We do, don't we?" Lucy said.

"That's what I'm talkin' about," Oscar said, and poured his bottle over his head.

"Drink, all of you," Mr. Auggy said. "The second half is going to be harder. You'll get tired—"

And we don't have J.J. He never seemed to get tired. And he could fake like no other. And he had that great slider. Lucy blinked away surprising tears. He was probably ripping his sheet curtains to shreds by now.

"Hey, Mr. Auggy."

Lucy looked at Gabe, who was peering around the side of the concession stand. People were lined up for Pasco's funnel cakes, and Gabe was weaving his head around trying to see between them. "You seen my dad?"

"He was here," Mr. Auggy said. "He had to go take care of something. He'll be back."

"Who's breakin' the law today?" Oscar said. "Everybody's here."

Everybody except J.J. and his family. Lucy forced herself not to think about it. God was going to have to untie that knot.

The whistle blew, and Mr. Auggy gathered the team for one more pep talk. Everyone nodded and grinned.

"We're gonna score," Gabe said.

They gave a Dream cheer and headed for the field. They were all in formation for the kickoff when the whistle blew again.

"What's wrong?" Lucy said.

The officials ran over to Mr. Auggy and the other coach and bent their heads together.

"Hey—you."

Lucy glanced over at Mr. Chin Hair. "Me?"

"Yeah, Bossy Chick."

He edged closer. Lucy stayed where she was and counted the fuzzy whiskers.

"Just a little heads-up," he said.

"What?"

"We're done cuttin' you slack. We're gonna wipe this field up with you guys this half."

Behind her, Gabe growled, but Lucy waved him off.

"So?" Chin Hair said.

"So—nothin'. We're just here to play soccer."

The whistle blew again, and the refs ran back onto the field, with two players. One was just a shorter version of all the other Pachucos. The other—was J.J.

"I love that!" Veronica cried.

Mr. Chin Hair sent his voice up into a mocking soprano. "I love that!"

But Lucy didn't care. She grinned at J.J. and said, "We're just forward and back—play your specialty."

J.J. nodded, the whistle blew, and they were off again.

Having J.J. with them seemed to give everyone fresh energy. Although the Pachucos played harder and faster than they had in the first half, the Dreams kept the ball as much as they did. Nobody scored a goal, on either team, but the Dreams came so close twice that Lucy could feel the whole town holding its breath.

And then the mistakes started happening. Emanuel kicked the ball out of bounds. Carla Rosa got offsides twice, and Lucy could tell she was getting confused. J.J. had a perfect slider, but he got his foot on the defender instead of the ball and was called for tripping.

"Stay cool!" Lucy told them.

But hair was standing up in spikes and faces were flushed beyond chili pepper color and Carla Rosa's eyes looked as glazed as Mr. Esparza's pottery. But it was Mr. Esparza—and Mr. Benitez—and Gloria—and all the rest of them chanting Mora's cheers that kept Lucy encouraging her team, telling them they could do it. And so they kept playing.

The Pachucos scored another goal, even though Oscar did everything but throw himself in front of a train to stop it. It wasn't his fault. The other seven of them hadn't stopped it either. The Dreams looked deflated. Lucy herself was close to tears.

And then she heard something. At first, her beyond-tired mind thought it was Mom—telling her, "Come on, champ, you can do it!"

But in reality, it sounded more like a Chihuahua yelping.

"I'm tired, Lucy," Carla Rosa said as they scattered for a throw-in.

"Guess what?" Lucy said. "So am I—but we're not gonna quit until it's over because the Dreams don't die."

"Yeah!" someone else said.

It was J.J. And then it was Oscar and Emanuel and Dusty and Veronica. And even Gabe.

"The Dreams don't die!" they chanted. "The Dreams don't die!"

Suddenly more people were saying it. The people in the stands. Mr. Auggy on the sideline. The Dreams don't die!

Lucy felt knots untying inside her, one after another, until she was one long string that moved silkily toward the ball that some Pachuco tossed carelessly onto the field from the sideline. It was hers, and she dribbled it straight at the goal.

J.J. appeared like a gift, and she passed it to him. His pass back was a little high, but she took it with her head. The crowd turned itself inside out. J.J. got it to Dusty, and Lucy ran toward the line her team brothers had formed ahead of her. The wide-shouldered goalie yelled at his teammates, and they shifted to the left where Dusty was headed. She passed the ball to Gabe, who lunged right. The wall went with him—and Lucy had the perfect shot. All she needed was the ball.

But Gabe wouldn't give it up. She knew that. Sure, they had their agreement. But this was a real game. He would want the glory.

"Lucy Goosey!"

Gabe gave the ball a smack and sent it straight to her. She had to get it with her left foot—but Mr. Auggy really had taught her everything. Without waiting for it to get any more perfect, Lucy took her shot. The goalie dove—his body seemed to hang in midair—and then he was down. The ball nestled itself safely into the corner.

Lucy was sure the crowd didn't cheer that loud at the World Cup. She only faintly heard the whistle blow, only vaguely knew the game was over, only partly understood that they had lost by one point.

She could only hear her Dad yelling "Champ!" and Januarie yelping like an entire pound and Mora leading the crowd in "The Dreams don't die! The Dreams don't die!"

"But, guess what, we lost," Carla Rosa said.

"I know," Lucy said, "but we played."

"And they loved us," Veronica said. "I love that!"

And as Lucy wiped at the happy tears, she did too.

20

Pasco announced a party for everyone at the café. It was lunchtime, and he said the grilled cheese and chicken nachos were on the house. Lucy's mouth watered—she even hoped there were pickles—but she was still too excited to eat.

To her surprise, the Pachucos sat down with the Dreams, which brought Mora to no end of squealing. She took pictures of all of them with her camera phone. Veronica, of course, said she loved it. Januarie hung on Mr. Auggy's arm until Lucy invited her to sit with them. She jumped on some Pachuco's lap before Lucy even had the words out. Fortunately, he acted like he might have little sisters and was used to it.

Mr. Chin Hair nudged Lucy's arm and said, "Hey, no offense. I was just tryin' to throw you off."

"It's okay," Lucy said.

"I didn't, though. You play good—for a girl."

"She plays good for anybody." Gabe poked Oscar. "Right?"

"She'll kick your tail around the block," Oscar said.

Dusty leaned her head on Lucy's arm. "And look cute doing it."

"But she hates pink," Veronica said. "I love pink—"

Lucy was put out of that misery by the squeal of the microphone Reverend Servidio was trying to adjust. Mr. Benitez stepped up to it and cleared his throat like he had the biggest hairball yet.

"I bet he's gonna yell at us for losing," J.J. whispered to Lucy.

But people didn't usually yell after they said, "I have never been prouder in my life than I was today."

People whistled and clapped until Mr. Benitez put up his hand.

"I was so proud to see my team, representing my store, give the El Paso Pachucos a run for their money."

"What do you mean 'your team,' Benitez?" Pasco said. "It's our team — our town's team!"

The room burst into clapping and cheering again.

"You'd think they were the ones out there playing," Gabe said behind his hand.

"They kind of were," Lucy said.

"So — " Mr. Benitez waved down the whistling again. "I for one am going to vote at town council to turn down the offer of a big corporation to buy our soccer field!"

There was more cheering, and Lucy thought she would burst. The noise kept on until Mr. Auggy took the microphone. Then Gabe stood up and told everybody to listen.

"I share your pride, Mr. Benitez," he said. "I have played soccer all over the world but this — this is my Dream Team."

"He really is attractive."

Lucy jumped at the voice in her ear. Aunt Karen was crouched down behind her chair, running her hand down Lucy's arm. "I was proud of you today — I really was."

"Thanks," Lucy said. She swallowed down a rising knot. With Aunt Karen, there was always a knot. "Thanks for bringing the team."

"They're nice, aren't they? I told them to go easy — that I just wanted the coach to see you play."

Lucy looked back at the table, but the team all seemed focused on cheering for Mr. Auggy. "You told them to go easy on us?" she said to Aunt Karen in a low voice.

Aunt Karen licked her lips. "I'm not some kind of ogre, Lucy. I know that's what you think, but I didn't want you made a fool of — I just wanted you to see — "

"I don't want to talk about this now." Lucy said. And she turned back to her team. When she looked again, Aunt Karen was gone. But the sting was still there. At least the other team members hadn't heard that. And she was never going to tell them.

In fact, it was 2:00 before the El Paso coach stood up and said his team needed to head for Texas. The Dreams walked the Pachucos out to their van, complete with cheerleaders, and Lucy was sure she saw Mora exchanging cell phone numbers with one kid. Inez was too busy talking about roses with Mrs. Benitez to see her.

When they pulled away and Lucy's team was still on the sidewalk, Aunt Karen planted herself in front of them.

Oh, nuh-*uh*.

"You have a good little team," she said, as if she knew anything about soccer.

Lucy heard J.J. grunt.

"Is Lucy a good captain?"

"She's the best," Dusty said.

"I'm sure. She's always been bossy!" Aunt Karen laughed. Nobody else did. Not even Carla Rosa.

"I hope you won't be too mad at me when we take her away from you next year." She put her arm around Lucy's shoulders and gave her a squeeze. "Our coach wants her for his girls' select team. I'm sure you don't know what that is, but it's a huge honor. I don't see how she can pass it up." She smiled into Lucy's face. "It's what her mom would want her to do."

She gave Lucy's shoulder one more squeeze, smiled at the team, and clicked over to Dad and Mr. Auggy. She was in high heels now, and the turquoise jacket was gone. Lucy had never wanted Aunt Karen to move to Australia or Mars or anywhere more than she did at that moment.

"Are you really moving to El Paso?" Dusty said.

"Why didn't you tell us?" Oscar poked Emanuel. "That's messed up."

Every face in front of her was fixed in an I-don't-believe-it stare.

"I didn't know," Lucy said.

"But are you going?" Veronica looked at Dusty. "She's leaving us?"

"No!" Lucy said. "I don't know—"

"We just got our team and our field—"

"Yeah, but if her mom would want her to—"

"Guess what—she loved her mom—"

"Stop!" Lucy said.

Five minutes ago, she would have told Aunt Karen right there on the sidewalk that she was never moving to El Paso with her and she might as well give it up forever—

And then she'd said those words: "It's what her mom would want her to do."

Would she?

The biggest knot ever tied itself around Lucy's heart. Because she didn't know. Up until the moment Aunt Karen had said those words, Lucy had felt like she knew what her mom wanted her to do: be like her. And that was what she wanted too. But this Lucy didn't know. It wasn't in any of the stories Dad told or in the smells she left behind or in the furniture she'd painted for Lucy's room. That was all she had of Mom, and that didn't tell her what to do next.

And she was never going to know.

"You okay, Miss Lucy?"

Mr. Auggy was at her elbow, and the team was gone. Dad stood on the other side, cane ready.

"No," Lucy said.

"We'll be okay from here," Dad said.

He nudged her arm, and Lucy let him hold on to it. They walked down the block to their house in the still-warm March day without talking, until they got there and he said, "Let's sit on the steps a while."

When Lucy got them situated, Dad said, "I heard."

"You mean Aunt Karen?"

"I heard what she said, about your mom."

Lucy was suddenly afraid—afraid Dad would know something that would mean she had to do what she didn't want to do.

"That was a dirty trick—her using that." His voice was sharp. "I told her so too."

"But—Dad—was it true?"

"Only your mother could really tell you that."

"Then I'll never know."

"Fortunately, your mother was like you." Dad chuckled. "She always made her wishes known—always."

Lucy shook her head. "I don't get it."

"There was a piece of paper that—got lost with your mom—but I know what she wrote on it."

"Dad—"

"'Things I want to teach Lucy'—that's what she wrote down. She shared it with me when we were flying to Iraq. 'Number one: How to play soccer like Mia Hamm, or at least like me, which isn't all that bad.'" Dad's face flooded with sunshine. "'Number two: How to love with everything she has, because that is the only way to love.' And 'Number three,' which is my favorite part, 'How to be a woman, as soon as I find out myself.'"

Lucy was afraid to speak, afraid her voice would make her mother's beautiful words disappear.

"She was going to write that in a book she bought before we left," Dad said. "But she was afraid she'd mess it up, so she left it behind, though I have no idea what happened to it." He chuckled. "She had the worst handwriting. She wanted to collect all her lists for you on pieces of paper and then copy them into the book when we got home."

"I have the book, Dad." Lucy squeezed her shoulders in. "And I've been writing in it. I should have asked you, but—"

"You found it?" Dad searched the sky with his unseeing eyes, as if he were looking for Mom herself. "Where was it? Never mind, Luce, you keep it. It should be yours—and your mother would love that you're writing in it." He felt for her hand and held it, hard.

"Aunt Karen doesn't think so. She found out that I have it—I don't know how, but—" Lucy's eyes went to Januarie's house. "Well, I think I do now, but anyway—"

"That book doesn't belong to Aunt Karen," Dad said.

"And neither do I," Lucy said.

He cocked his head. "You've made your decision then?"

Before she could answer, a yowl arose—a familiar yowl that came not from the back gate but from across the street.

"That's Mudge," Dad said.

Lucy was down the steps and out the front gate before Dad could even get his cane unfolded. J.J.'s front door opened, and Januarie stepped out, holding a bag that wiggled and bulged and howled as if there were three cats inside—instead of just hers.

"I found him," Januarie said. "Could you take him before he bites me through this thing?"

Lucy didn't have to be asked twice. Januarie met her on the sidewalk, and Lucy pulled open the mouth of the cloth bag. Mudge was in her arms, telling her in no uncertain terms how upset he was over the treatment he'd received. Lucy was sure there was something in there about expecting tuna every day for the rest of his life.

"Where was he?" Lucy said, face half buried in his fur.

Januarie looked down at her shoes.

"He was in a cage out in the back." J.J. hiked over an old bathtub and joined them. "My dad put him back there."

"Why?" Lucy said.

"Doesn't matter," Dad said from behind her. "We have him back now—thanks kids."

"But will he—will your dad—"

"Gone," J.J. said.

"Where?"

"Jail."

"Why?"

"Sheriff took him—'cause he just did."

That was all Lucy needed to know anyway.

"Sorry," she said.

"It's better now."

"So—Januarie-February-June-or-July," Dad said, very quickly, Lucy thought. "You and your brother want to come over for pizza? I'm buying."

"Of course, you're buying," Januarie said, "You're the grown-up!"

As J.J. and Lucy followed Dad and Januarie across the street, J.J. grunted.

"What?" Lucy said.

"You going to El Paso?"

"No. Never."

"Better tell Dusty and them. They're cryin'."

"Over me?"

"Yeah. It's girly."

"Yeah," Lucy said, "It is."

"I don't get it."

But Lucy decided maybe she did.

That night, after eating pizza and giving Januarie the pink jacket she was never, ever going to wear and checking to make sure Mudge was safely back under his plant, Lucy curled up with Lollipop to make another list.

Things That Still Don't Make That Much Sense but Maybe You, God, Will Help Me Figure Out

—The two months are over, but I still want to keep Inez.

—Aunt Karen said she wanted to protect me from being like my mom.

—J.J.'s dad is supposed to love him like my dad loves me, only he's so mean to him that the sheriff had to take him away.

—You're God, but things don't always turn out happily every after.

—I will still never, ever wear pink. Is that okay?

She started to nestle the Book of Lists in with Lollipop, but she stopped. Instead, she set it on the dresser, next to her soccer ball.

She was sure her mother would want it that way.

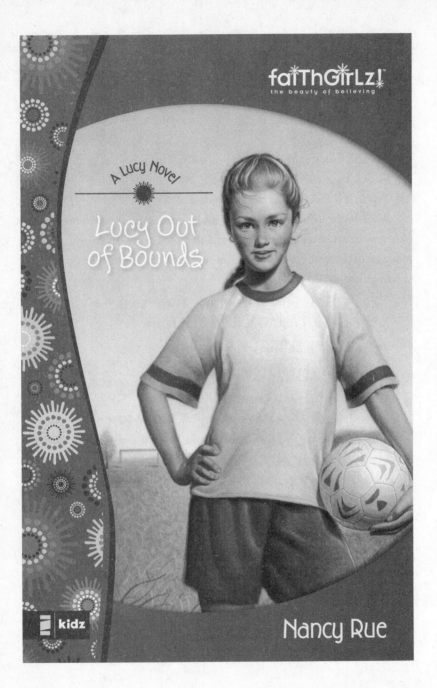

faiThGiRLz!™
the beauty of believing

A Lucy Novel

Lucy Out
of Bounds

Nancy Rue

kidz

1

Why J.J. Is My Best Friend Even Though He's a Boy and Boys Are Mostly Absurd Little Creeps

Lucy stuck her pen through the rubber band in her ponytail and looked at her cat Marmalade, curled up in the rocking chair. He blinked back out of his orange face as if he'd heard what she wrote and was very much offended.

"I'm not talking about you, silly," she said to him. "You're a Cat-Boy. That's different from a Human-Boy." She grunted. "If you can call most boys human."

Untangling her pen from its blonde perching place — and wondering how it got into a snarl just sitting there for seven seconds — she went back to the J.J. list.

- He lives across the street so we can send signals to each other if one of us is grounded. Usually it's him. Only, today it's me.
- He doesn't think it's lame to ride bikes.
- He loves soccer as much as I do, and he doesn't care that I'm better than him. We both want to be professionals someday.

Marmalade yawned — loud — and licked his cat-lips.

"Okay, okay," Lucy said. "I'm getting to the important stuff."

- He doesn't feel my back to see if I'm wearing a bra and think it's funny — like SOME boys do. Ickety-ick.

She scowled. The last time Aunt Karen visited from El Paso, she kept talking about how it was time for Lucy to get a bra. Had Mom worn one when *she* was only eleven years old? That probably wasn't something Lucy could ask Dad without dying of embarrassment. She squeezed her pen and went back to the page.

- If I'm kicking stones and J.J. asks me what's wrong and I say I don't want to talk about it, he says okay and we go kick a soccer ball instead.
- He never looks at me like I'm from Planet Weird. Which some people do. Like Mora when I say I'm never wearing a bra. Ever.
- When J.J. gets me in trouble, he always tells my dad it was his fault. Except for this last time. Because I wouldn't let him, because J.J. would have gotten in way more trouble than me, so I took the blame, which is why I'm grounded for a whole day.

Lucy dropped the pen and shook her hand, letting her fingers flap against each other. That was a lot of writing. Inez, her weekday nanny, always said Lucy's lists were her way of praying, so even though she might be hand-crippled for life, she did feel better.

Marmalade obviously did too, because he was now curled in a ball like a tangerine, breathing his very plump self up and down in the middle. Sleep-wheezing sounds were also coming from the half-open toy chest, where Lollipop, Lucy's round, black kitty was snoozing.

It must be incredibly boring being cats. Feeling better seemed to make them want to lick their hairy paws and go to sleep. It made Lucy want to bounce out the door and get a soccer game going, or ride her bike in the desert with J.J., or at the very least go check out whatever her dad was clanging around in the kitchen.

But you couldn't do any of those things when you were grounded. At least the March wind had stopped beating against the house and the long shadows were making stripes on her blue walls. That meant the day of groundation was almost over, and tomorrow she could start fresh.

Lucy carefully nestled the Book of Lists on her pillow and got to her knees on the bed, propping her chin against the tile windowsill to gaze out at Granada Street. It was a sleepy Saturday, except for the sound of the hammers a block over on Tularosa Street where workers were turning the old, falling-apart hotel into a restaurant.

The cottonwood trees that lined her street were letting loose a swirl of white fibers, and between those and the new spring leaves, she couldn't see J.J.'s house as well as she could in winter. It was impossible to tell if he was sending her any shadow signals with a flashlight from behind the sheet covering his upstairs window. J.J. making a bunny with his fingers meant, "I'm hopping on over." Devil's horns meant, "Januarie"—that was his sister—"is driving me nuts."

Dad's clanging in the kitchen stopped in a too-fast way. Marmalade uncurled like a popping spring and stood on the seat of the rocker with every orange hair standing up on end. Marmalade never moved that quickly unless there was food involved.

Lucy scrambled across the bed and got to her door, yelling, "Dad?"—at the very same moment her father said, "Luce?"

She sailed across the wide hallway—not bothering to ride the yellow Navajo rug on the tile the way she usually did—and almost collided with Dad in the kitchen doorway. His hands were spread out to either side in their "Now, Lucy, calm down" sign. But his face looked about as calm as a cat in a kitty-carrier. His triangle nose and squared-off chin formed white, frightened angles that made Lucy's mouth go dry.

"What's going on, Dad?"

"I'm not sure. I need your eyes."

He tilted his salt-and-pepper-crew-cut head toward the back door. "I heard something I didn't like in the yard. I don't want you to go out there."

"Why?"

"Because I think it's some kind of wild cat."

"In our *yard?*"

Dad rubbed his palm up and down her arm. "I'm probably over-reacting, but let's check it out."

Lucy lunged for the door.

"Window, Luce," Dad said.

She dragged a chair to the sink and climbed up on it. Her father had been blind for four years, and she still couldn't figure out how he knew absolutely everything she was doing—or was going to do—before she even did it. J.J. couldn't either. He thought she could get away with a whole lot more than she ever did.

Leaning across the sink, Lucy slid the Christmas cactus aside on the windowsill so she could support herself with her hands. The backyard was already a puzzle of shadows, and at first, she didn't see anything unusual except—

"Uh-oh," she said.

"What?"

"Looks like Artemis got into the garbage again. That bag that had that disgusting Thai food Aunt Karen brought is all over the place." She started to pull away from the window. "I'll go out and pick it up."

"Keep looking," Dad said. "I closed the cans with those big bungee cords. Artemis couldn't have gotten them undone."

Lucy didn't remind Dad that Artemis, their hunter cat, was practically Terminator Kitty when really nasty trash was involved. She got one knee up on the sink and peered past the red-checked curtains again.

"The bungee is still on the lid," she reported. "She ripped into the side of the trash can."

"*She* didn't."

"Well, there's a big ol' hole there."

"Do you see claw marks?"

Lucy pressed her forehead on the glass, and a chill wormed its way up her back. Right where the gray plastic had been ripped away, thick gashes scrawled down the can as if someone had made them with a big nail.

"Yeah," she said. "And they aren't Artemis's. Or Marmalade's—or Lolli's—or Mudge's—"

"It's a good thing we only have four cats," Dad said, "or we could be here for days." The dry, Dad-calm was back in his voice. "You keep watching. I'm calling Sheriff Navarra."

Lucy pulled her other knee up and settled into the sink. It was a good thing she'd done all the dishes and wiped everything dry in an attempt to get out of groundation, although that never worked on Dad.

From this position, Lucy could survey the whole yard, which fanned out from the big Mexican elder tree in the middle to the fence surrounding the house like a row of straight gray teeth. The umbrella was still down on the table on the patio, and the chairs leaned with their faces against the house, waiting for enough spring in the air so she and Dad could come out and sit in them. The gate on the side sagged as always beneath its fringe of cautious wisteria vine just coming into bloom—the same kind of plant that covered the toolshed and had started to creep up the dead tree by the back fence.

"Whatever it was, it's gone now," Lucy said.

Dad closed his cell phone against his chest and dropped it into his pocket. Two fierce lines formed between his eyebrows. "That's a definite bummer."

"How come?"

"The sheriff's on his way. He's going to think we're imagining things. Okay—be like the kitties. Look for movement. Up high—not on the ground."

Lucy pulled her eyes to the top of the fence, the roof of the toolshed, the rickety arch over the gate. Nothing moved. Not until she went back to the dead tree, where a shadow was passing over it.

"What?" Dad said.

"I think I saw something—"

"Shhh!"

Lucy froze and let Dad tilt his head and listen. People said a blind man didn't really have a better sense of hearing than anyone else, but Dad could practically hear a cobweb fluttering in a corner.

"Do you see Artemis?" he said.

Lucy searched the top of the fence again, where Artemis Hamm normally inched, tightrope-walker style, when she was stalking a mouse or a quail who was just trying to keep her kids in tow. No sign of Artemis.

And then Lucy heard what Dad must have heard: the low growl of their huntress feline, the kind she made when some other cat was trying to horn in on the prey she'd done all the work to catch.

"Under the dead tree." Dad put both hands on her shoulders. "Is Artemis down there?"

Lucy saw her cat's mottled coat, the one that looked like God couldn't make up his mind on what kind of cat he wanted Artemis Hamm to be. She crouched at the bottom of the dead tree, staring up as if it had come to life.

Because it had. Lucy gasped as she watched one paw and then another, each the size of Artemis's head, creep its way down the spongy bark, smothering its woodpecker holes, until pointed, tufted, devilish ears came into view.

"It's a bobcat!" Lucy said. "Dad—he's going after Artemis!"

Dad let go of Lucy's shoulders, and she scrambled down from the sink—but not before he got his hand up.

"You stay in this house, and I mean it," he said.

"He'll get Artemis!"

"He'll get you too. I'm calling Sheriff Navarra again—"

The rest of whatever he was going to say was lost in a screech so horrible even Dad looked bolted to the floor. Lucy hoisted herself back up onto the sink and flattened her face against the window. The big cat was almost to the ground, but there was no helpless Artemis flailing in his mouth.

There was only J.J., facing the animal with a shovel in his hand and a smear of sheer horror across his face.

A Lucy Novel
Written by Nancy Rue

New from Faithgirlz! By bestselling author Nancy Rue.

Lucy Rooney is a feisty, precocious tomboy who questions everything—even God. It's not hard to see why: a horrible accident killed her mother and blinded her father, turning her life upside down. It will take a strong but gentle housekeeper—who insists on Bible study and homework when all Lucy wants to do is play soccer—to show Lucy that there are many ways to become the woman God intends her to be.

Book 1: Lucy Doesn't Wear Pink
ISBN 978-0-310-71450-7

Book 3: Lucy's Perfect Summer
ISBN 978-0-310-71452-1

Book 2: Lucy Out of Bounds
ISBN 978-0-310-71451-4

Book 4: Lucy Finds Her Way
ISBN 978-0-310-71453-8

Available now at your local bookstore!
Visit www.faithgirlz.com, it's the place for girls ages 9-12.

Sophie Series
Written by Nancy Rue

Meet Sophie LaCroix, a creative soul who's destined to become a great film director someday. But many times, her overactive imagination gets her in trouble!

Book 1: Sophie's World
IBSN: 978-0-310-70756-1

Book 2: Sophie's Secret
ISBN: 978-0-310-70757-8

Book 3: Sophie Under Pressure
ISBN: 978-0-310-71840-6

Book 4: Sophie Steps Up
ISBN: 978-0-310-71841-3

Book 5: Sophie's First Dance
ISBN: 978-0-310-70760-8

Book 6: Sophie's Stormy Summer
ISBN: 978-0-310-70761-5

Book 7: Sophie's Friendship Fiasco
ISBN: 978-0-310-71842-0

Book 8: Sophie and the New Girl
ISBN: 978-0-310-71843-7

Book 9: Sophie Flakes Out
ISBN: 978-0-310-71024-0

Book 10: Sophie Loves Jimmy
ISBN: 978-0-310-71025-7

Book 11: Sophie's Drama
ISBN: 978-0-310-71844-4

Book 12: Sophie Gets Real
ISBN: 978-0-310-71845-1

Available now at your local bookstore!
Visit www.faithgirlz.com, it's the place for girls ages 9-12.

Introduce your mom to Nancy Rue!

Today's mom is raising her 8-to-12-year-old daughter in a society that compels her little girl to grow up too fast. *Moms' Ultimate Guide to the Tween Girl World* gives mothers practical advice and spiritual inspiration to guide their mini-women into adolescence as strong, confident, authentic, and God-centered young women; even in a morally challenged society and without losing their childhoods before they're ready.

Nancy Rue has written over 100 books for girls, is the editor of the Faithgirlz Bible, and is a popular speaker and radio guest with her expertise in tween and teen issues. She and husband Jim have raised a daughter of their own and now live in Tennessee.

Visit Nancy at NancyRue.com

Available wherever books are sold.

ZONDERVAN®
.com

We want to hear from you. Please send your comments about this book to us in care of zreview@zondervan.com. Thank you.

ZONDERVAN.com/
AUTHORTRACKER
follow your favorite authors